A *LESS THAN ZERO* ROCKSTAR ROMANCE
ENDLESS
ENCORE
KAYLENE WINTER

I0782462

A *LESS THAN ZERO* ROCKSTAR ROMANCE

ENDLESS

ENCORE

KAYLENE WINTER

Sensitivity Statement

Prologue - Present Day

HOW DID I GET here?

I'm all alone. Away from my wife. My band. For who knows how long. Not that it matters. I'm not certain if any of them will ever speak to me again after I blew my life to smithereens. I know I wouldn't. After all of the love and trust my band brothers showed me over the years, how did I repay them?

I lied to them.

Treated them like shit.

Blamed them for things that weren't their fault.

Selfishly made them put up with my bullshit.

Worse? I sold Zoey a package of goods I couldn't deliver. I sucked her back into my life for my own selfish purposes. Hiding my truth. A truth that has bitten me in the ass, just as I knew it would. A truth that has changed the very fabric of my life and that of the people around me.

God.

Zoey is the only woman I'll ever love, and after what I did? Things will never be the same. For that, I take full responsibility. Doesn't make it easier to bear. I'm a realist. There's no way she could possibly honor the commitments we made to each other now. There's no way she could possibly still love me.

Let alone stay married to me.

I'm in agony. Every part of me aches. My heart. My body. *My soul.*

It's completely my fault. All of this could have been avoided. Years of therapy gave me all the tools. Stubbornly, I ignored the warning signals when they were blaring everywhere around me. Instead, I rushed Zoey into getting married before she knew what she was really signing up for. Begged her to get pregnant before confessing a past that would permeate every part of our future. All in some desperate attempt to hold on to her.

To hold on to us.

Sure, I'd convinced myself I was fine. Healed. Hell, I thought I knew better. I really, really did. I was lying to myself, though. And lying to everyone who matters to me. I've destroyed my life. Irreparably so. My past few months have been a master class in reckless, impulsive behavior. Now, I'll pay the price forever.

With everything that I've lost, there's one important reason I'm here. A singular motivation. I *want* to get well. *Need* to get well. If only to be part of my son's life. To have a chance to be the father I know I can be. I'm going to do anything and everything I can to make it up to him, even if he hasn't been born yet.

I may have burned my bridges with everyone closest to me, but I'll never do that to him.

Ever.

I set Zoey free last night. Just like she did for me all those years ago. I get why she did it now. When you truly love someone, you want them to have everything good in the world. Even if it's without you.

Especially if it's without you.

We're tied together forever. Having a baby is what I—we both—wanted. If I'm lucky, I'll have a new start. A new life. Zoey and I will raise our son together, even if we're apart. He'll be here soon.

Which is why I find myself at this treatment center. It's my chance to find a way to live with myself. Hopefully, to reestablish healthy relationships with the people who are most important to me. Maybe even put the past behind me, without forgetting that it will always be a part of me.

Lying on the double bed in my sparse room, I take in my surroundings. A small window looks out into the desert. Adobe tile lines one wall. The built-in wardrobe and desk are all constructed out of warm, brown wood. The bathroom is large, finished in caramel tile. It's a lot nicer than I thought it would be. Very upscale South-western.

Appropriate, I guess. The treatment facility is in the middle of Arizona. Where it's quiet. Where I'll have absolutely no distractions.

For the first time in my life, it's just me. Facing myself. Figuring out who I am and who I want to be.

I'm scared absolutely shitless.

Someone knocks on the door. "Tyson, I'm here to take you to your first appointment."

Immediately, the emotions take over.

I don't want this to be happening.

But it is. *It fucking is.*

"I'll be right there," I manage to choke out. Tears spill down my cheeks. I open the door.

"Are you ready to begin the rest of your life?" The middle-aged nurse with horn-rimmed glasses smiles encouragingly at me.

I nod, unable to speak.

I hope so. I really fucking hope so.

Chapter One

Eight Months Prior

I GAZE UP AT my gorgeous fiancé, Tyson Rainier. After a whirlwind few months of travel, we're in bed in our house in West Seattle. I'm tucked under his arm, my cheek rests on his chest. His other arm is flung over his head. Chocolate waves of his long mane cascade over the pillow. A smattering of stubble spreads across his square jaw. Little puffs of air dissipate from his full lips in a steady rhythm.

Ty's band, Less Than Zero or LTZ, is nearing the end of its year-long hiatus to reset and recharge. His bandmates are busy working on their own passion projects. Ty started a foundation and appointed me CEO. We've done a lot of work with the leadership team, but mostly Ty and I have spent the entire year goofing off. Traveling. Laughing. Talking. Dreaming. Eating.

Living life. Together.

Building our life. Together.

Just...being. Together.

On our terms. Finally.

Before he was famous and I was only eighteen, we were forced apart. It took eight years, a series of misunderstandings and a few speed bumps, but we managed to reunite. Get to know each other again. Now, we're engaged and, hopefully, soon we'll get married. I wouldn't trade the past few months for anything. I've never laughed so hard. Loved so deeply. Felt so connected to one human being. We've been making up for lost time, and if I had any doubts before, I definitely don't now.

Ty and I are meant to be.

With the band's hiatus coming to an end soon, we're slowly transitioning out of vacation mode into a routine. Our new normal. Neither of us are sure exactly how it's going to work, but so long as we're together again? Nothing can come between us.

Because we don't take anything about our relationship for granted. Not after too many missed years, months, days, hours, minutes, and seconds.

I treasure every single moment we have. Ty is a very complicated man, but also the most honest, kindhearted, generous person I know. My eyes mist a bit as I think about how far he's come from the young man he was when we first met. Unlike me, he grew up with nothing except an addict mother who's so far gone, she tried to sell fake stories to the tabloids last year for a big payday. I admire my fiancé so much. He's never been defined by his past. Instead, he single-handedly pulled himself out of the gutter and made something of himself. Despite the odds.

God, I love him. *Really* and truly love him. Every single part of him.

"Are you watching me sleep?" Ty's eyes slowly blink open. He yawns and rolls to his side so he's facing me. "Who's my creepy girl?"

For some strange reason, we both love to watch each other sleep. We're self-aware enough to know it's kind of psycho, so we've made it into one of our many inside jokes. I smooth his hair away from his forehead, laughing. "That's me. Don't worry, I haven't been creeping on you for long."

His brow furrows. Ty doesn't even realize how well he's perfected his angsty-concerned expression. It's adorable. "How are you feeling?"

A couple of months ago, I developed my first aura migraine. I thought it was a one-off, but no. I've had a few, each one has been worse than the last. Two weeks ago, an episode took me out for nearly forty-eight hours. Dark room. Complete quiet. Agony. My appetite is only just returning now. Even though Ty has the best physicians on call, nothing has worked. After the last episode, I had a ton of different tests done. Now we know a bit more about why it's happening. Estrogen from my birth control pills. I have no choice. In order to stop the debilitating headaches and decrease my risk of stroke, I can't take them anymore.

Which presents us with a bit of a problem. Ty and I have a lot of sex. Making up for eight years of lost time does *not* suck. Actually, sometimes it does.

If you know what I mean.

"Stop worrying. I'm fine." I kiss the crinkles on his forehead away. "I'm feeling so much better, I've come up with a solution to our problem. I think an IUD might be our best option."

Ty gently massages the base of my neck. He shakes his head, "Well, I've been thinking too. In my opinion, we should just ditch birth control altogether."

"What?" I'm blown away. "Are you serious?"

Ty rests his head on his forearm and blinks up at me. He's delectable. Vulnerable. "Of course I am, Z. I want babies. I don't see why we can't start now."

"It just surprises me." I stroke his soft tresses. "I figured we'd wait a bit. Get married first."

Ty cocks an eyebrow, but his eyes are bright with excitement. "C'mon. I've been telling you all year how much I want you barefoot and pregnant. Maybe these migraines are the universe's way of telling us it's time."

"Ty..." My body tenses. The hesitation and slight panic in my expression dims the light in his.

Just for a second. He curves his lips into a slight smile to cover up his disappointment. "Oh. Okay. Never mind. We can wait until you feel more ready."

I trail my fingertips down his bicep and clasp his fingers with mine and squeeze. "It's not that I don't feel ready. We've actually never really talked about it seriously. Like how many do we want? Do we want to home school or send them to public school? What are our holiday traditions? How will we discipline them? Stuff like that."

"We need to talk about discipline?" Ty's eyes widen. There's something behind his expression. Could it be...fear?

I shrug. "Sure. My point is we've never talked about the logistics of you and me as parents. What happens with the foundation? What about when you go on the road again with LTZ? There's so many things to discuss. Don't you think we need to do that first?"

"Uh, I'm not sure why we can't figure all that stuff out as we go along."

"Okay, even if that's true. We're not ready *yet*, are we?" I'm not usually a wing-it kind of girl. He knows this. This conversation has me stressed at the idea of throwing caution to the wind. Children are too important not to have some sort of plan.

I see another flash of hurt in his eyes, which he once again covers up immediately with concern. "Shit, Z. I didn't mean to pressure you. At the end of the day, I only want you to be healthy. Free from the migraines. That's what's most important to me."

His words are exactly what I expected. Ty moves mountains to make sure my needs are met. He makes me feel treasured. He always says if I'm happy, then he's happy.

Which is sweet. But...there are two of us in this relationship. I want to make sure his needs are met too. It's important for us to work through our differences if we're not on the same page. Make decisions *together*. "You're not pressuring me, babe. I'm just surprised you're so passionate about wanting a baby right *now*."

"Yeah, I do want kids." Ty's entire face is dreamy. As if he's picturing himself holding a tiny human. He reaches over and traces my shoulder blade. "But only when you do too."

"Ty, my ovaries are firing on all cylinders hearing you talk this way. But, remember when we were having dinner with Zane and Fiona last month? You said you're terrified of becoming a father." His off-the-cuff comment seemed insignificant at the time. Since then, I've found myself thinking about his words. A lot.

Ty folds his arms under his head and stares at the ceiling. "Uh, it was just a general statement. I mean, I *am* terrified. A bit. Aren't you? Parenting is scary. You can *really* fuck up your kids if you're not careful."

His eyebrows knit and he grows quiet.

"What do you mean?" It's all I can do to suppress a shudder. His choice of words pierces my soul for some reason.

"Z. Stop. There's no need to psychoanalyze it. You're either ready for the next phase of our lives together or you're not. I'm patient. We're in this for the long haul."

I don't press him because I love this man with every ounce of my being. I also don't want to crush his dreams. I could be ready. We just need to talk about it. Without hurting his feelings. I'm trying to figure out how to articulate my views when Ty's deep voice snaps me out of my thoughts. "Are you okay? You have a weird look on your face. It's not another headache, is it?"

"God. No. I just got lost in my own thoughts. Picturing us with a son who is as handsome as you is a great visual."

His entire face lights up with such utter reverence, I melt. "I love you, Zoey Pearson."

"I love you too, Tyson Rainier. I don't want you to think I'm not ready to start the next part of our life together. I am. Why don't we first set our wedding date? It's high time you made me your wife."

Ty's smile nearly jumps off his face. "Fuck, yeah it is!"

"My parents will be stoked." I throw my arms around his neck and plant a big kiss on his lips. "It's not like I haven't been thinking about it, you know. In my mind our ceremony is something small and private. A catered dinner after. The guys. The girls. My folks. Oh, and Carter. I really don't want a big circus. Nothing we're going to need extra security for. Just our inner circle."

Ty is swept up by my enthusiasm. "Absolutely. Should we do it here at the house? Everyone's still in town for a few weeks. I don't think it takes long to get a marriage license."

"Three days." I nod.

"You already checked?"

"Of course. Months ago. What do you take me for?" I clap my hands like a kid. "A girl's got to be prepared when her man finally gives her the green light."

"Z..." Ty grabs my hand mid-clap and holds it up. My ten-carat engagement ring sparkles in the sunlight. "You're telling me this isn't the biggest green light known to man?"

I splay my fingers and twist my wrist so the diamond glitters brightly. "Nope, it's more blinding white."

When I look back into his deep-blue eyes, it's only a millisecond before Ty's lips crush mine. I clasp his face and thread my fingers through his hair. We cling to each other. Get lost in our kisses.

Things heat up quickly, as they always do.

Of course his phone picks that time to blare that obnoxious *Baby Shark* song, which is Zane's ringtone.

"Ignoring it." Ty cups my breast as he peppers kisses on my neck behind my ear.

"Good." I hook my leg over his hip. "Let's celebrate."

His phone goes silent. Only for a nanosecond.

Baby Shark doo doo da doo... immediately starts up again. Mood killed. I roll back over and motion for him to pick up. Groaning, Ty stretches his arm backward to grab the phone off the charger.

Ty sighs before he accepts the call and mutters, "I'm sorry. He won't stop until I pick up."

"Don't I know it."

Zane Rocks is LTZ's guitarist, Ty's best friend and current interrupter of sex. He called a band meeting today. The other guys, Jace Deveraux and Connor McLoughlin, are coming over later this morning to discuss LTZ's plans to come out of their hiatus.

"Yeah?" Ty answers the phone, swinging his legs over the side of the bed so his back is toward me. I can hear Zane talking a mile a minute but I can't make out what he's saying.

I shut my eyes and the intermittent "uh-huhs" and "yeahs" Ty emits lull me into a second wave of drowsiness. I begin picturing our wedding. How we'll decorate. What we'll wear. What food we will serve. The flowers. Ty looking yummy in a suit. Before I know it, he's gently shaking me awake.

"Z. We had to move the meeting up. Connor has family business." Ty kisses my temple. "They'll be here in less than an hour. Can we pick up where we left off once they're gone?"

I stroke the stubble on his cheek. "That sounds like heaven."

His gaze stays on mine for a moment longer before he gives me a quick kiss. "I need to take a shower. Go back to sleep, butterfly."

I watch his fine ass disappear down the short hallway in our master suite to the bathroom. I contemplate whether to join him. Decide against it. The sooner he's done with band business, the sooner we can be back in our own little love bubble.

That's when the realization hits me. Like a lightning bolt.

For all of my hemming and hawing, I don't want to go back on birth control. Who knows how long it will take us to conceive? Why am I always such a worry-wart? I. Want. A. Baby. There. I've said it. Well, thought it. Yes. A baby. Our baby. Soon. Having a family with Ty is what I've dreamed about since I was eighteen.

The only problem? The one thing that is niggling at me? Will Ty's past have any effect on his parenting capabilities? I'm not really worried, per se. Other than briefly meeting his therapist last year, I just don't have a lot of information. It's not a topic that's comfortable for him. He assures me he's dealt with his past in therapy. That it's all behind him. And it shows. It really does. He's the most confident and well-adjusted person I know.

Except...it's just... Call it a premonition.

No, a gut feeling.

Is there some reason he won't ever talk about his childhood?

I don't want to be one of those jerks who looks for trouble when none exists. Not when things are so perfect.

Maybe I should get out of the house for a bit while Ty meets with his bandmates.

Yeah, a little perspective. That's just what I need.

Chapter Two

I'M THE HAPPIEST I'VE ever been in my life. *Blissfully* happy. Content. Peaceful, even. Zoey Pearson is the love of my life. My greatest joy. Waking up next to her every day is all I've dreamed about for nearly a decade. She's my best friend. I'm her destiny and she's mine. She's in my blood. My air. My heart. *My soul.*

There is no doubt in my mind about any of this.

Yet, as I stand here zoning out in the shower thinking about our conversation of a few minutes ago, I'm a bit shell-shocked. Holy fucking hell. We're getting married.

Full steam ahead. On top of that, I actually suggested we needed to ditch birth control. I mean, I really want kids but with how often we fuck? She'll be pregnant before the week's over.

Talking about it is one thing. An actual baby is another.

I'm spinning. I know I am. My impulsive tendencies emerge when I'm struggling with my self-worth. Despite how happy I am, I've been having a hard time. My anxiety is in overdrive lately. I'm having moments of wondering if I can actually go through with all of this. Who the hell do I think I am? Zoey comes from a great family with two parents who love her and are still married. I'm...well, the opposite. What do I know about being a good husband? A good father?

What if I'm not worthy of her? Of our future children?

What if I drag them down?

Fuck.

No, really. *Fuck.*

I thought I was past all this shit. I've done so much hard work. I've had extensive therapy. I felt completely at ease with myself for a long time. Now? I haven't felt this anxious in years. My blood pressure must be through the roof.

It's *not* fucking cool.

Before I can stop myself, my fist smashes against the shower wall. I squeeze my eyes shut. Take a deep breath. Let the water sluice over my body. Center myself.

When negative, destructive thoughts creep into my head, I *know* its because of my life sentence.

CPTSD.

Complex post-traumatic stress disorder.

A diagnosis no one on earth but me and my therapist, Lisa Kinkaid, knows about. She's also the only one who knows the true extent of the abuse and trauma I suffered growing up. I'd been doing so well in dealing with it, but I had help. Anxiety medication. Therapy with Lisa. A meticulous routine. Which I'd been religious about for years.

By the time Zoey and I got engaged, I begged Lisa for help weaning myself off the meds. Mainly, because I was ashamed about needing them. I was relentless. She reluctantly agreed, as long as I continued to follow my strict regimen. No drugs or alcohol. Daily meditation. Lots of exercise. Clean diet. And, I had to tell Zoey I was in therapy. Which I did. Not because of Lisa. I'd made a vow never to keep anything from her.

Somehow, I convinced myself that my half truth ticked the "honesty box".

But it didn't. Not by a long shot.

Jesus. What's even worse? I promised Lisa I'd double up on our therapy sessions so she could monitor my state of mind as the meds wore off. But that didn't happen. Instead, I stopped counseling altogether.

Not *exactly* deliberately. Zoey and I have been traveling. Having the best time together. Every day has been an adventure. But the year is nearly over and we're now settling back into our real life. She's going to be full-time at the foundation. LTZ's hiatus is about to come to an end, which means recording more songs. Touring, probably. Being away for long stretches of time. Performing. Publicity. Leading my band into a new era.

In other words, the vacation's over.

I'm fucking good at my job. I even *love* my job. It's just, with the renewed anxiety I'm feeling? I'm not quite ready to go back. For many years, I had a hard time adjusting to being the lead singer in the world's most popular band. But, I settled in. Stepped it up. *I had to.* It was the only way for me to make something of myself. It always took a lot out of me. Especially when we first got popular, because I was still consumed with grief at losing Zoey. To manage my stress, I went off the deep end with my party-boy antics for a few years.

It got so bad, Zane and Carter introduced me to Lisa, because they thought I needed rehab. Everybody thought so, including myself. I was convinced I was heading down the same addictive path as my mother.

Back then, Lisa and I had months of intense therapy sessions where I unloaded a lot of horrific shit. This led to my diagnosis of CPTSD and my treatment plan. Ironically, sex, drugs and alcohol are what I used to cope, not the other way around. Also ironic? It's been surprisingly easy to keep my CPTSD diagnosis secret. Thank fuck. Everyone thinks I'm a recovering addict. I'm congratulated all the time for my "recovery."

In actuality, you don't ever recover from CPTSD.

You only learn to live with it.

When I first learned I had a mental illness, I was crushed. I knew—without a shadow of a doubt—I'd never tell a soul. Ever. Not the band. Not Zoey. No one.

Sure, it's not a stigma anymore. There's a lot of awareness and support. There's absolutely nothing to be ashamed of. It's not my fault. Blah. Blah. Blah. It's just that...it's easy to say when it's not you. I've always fig-ured, why tell people you're mentally ill when you can just claim you're an addict? I mean, the treatment is basically the same in my case. It makes perfect sense to keep up the ruse.

Alcohol. Cannabis. Coke—which was my drug of choice. Even if I could technically dabble, they don't interact well with my anti-anxiety meds. Besides, I've found that I don't really have a desire to drink or get high anymore. Exercise, diet, and breathing regimens have changed my life. Now I have Zoey back. All natural highs. Better highs.

I suppose it could be cool to have a glass of wine with dinner or a beer with the guys now and then. But why bother? It would raise red flags with the people closest to me. I'll happily abstain for the rest of my life. It's no big deal.

On the other hand, it fucking pisses me off that no matter how much money, success, love, or support I have in my life now, my past shit sticks with me. Like gum on my goddamn shoe. Even after all these years. I'm utterly terrified to admit my truth to anyone.

Maybe even to myself.

Don't get me wrong, I *know* I should tell Zoey the full story. Especially after the promises we've made. She deserves the truth. Trust me when I say I've nearly blurted the words so many times. It's just that every time I start to tell her, I just...

Can't.

Fuck me. If we're getting married and talking about having kids, it's so fucking wrong to keep a secret this big from her. It makes me a horrible human being. It's not right for her to commit her life to me and not know about my diagnosis.

Or is it?

Fuck. No. It's not. Every minute I wait makes it get harder and harder. Even now, I can't bear to deal with the can of worms I'll open if I tell her. Especially when she has no idea how much loving her has saved me. How, even when we were apart, my love for Zoey kept me alive. She can never know how close I came to...

Fuck. Don't go there.

Fuck.

Fuckity-fuck-fuck-fuck.

Nope. I can't talk about some of that stuff. Ever. Again. Lisa is the only one who will ever know, and I'm keeping it that way. Confessing my truth once is all I can ever bear. It's too fucking painful to let the words slip out of my mouth again.

So, no. Final decision. I can't tell Zoey. I won't let my stupid CPTSD diagnosis fuck up my second chance with her. Not when we've fought so hard to be together. My mental illness will *not* be something else we have to survive. Zoey and I are getting married. We're having beautiful babies. I'm going to pamper and take care of her and my kids forever. Make love to her until my dick falls off. Teach my children how to be kind and productive humans.

I'm breaking the fucking cycle. I'm keeping the past in the past.

Because even if *I'm* broken, I'm not weak. I'm going to be the strong, capable man Zoey deserves. She's my everything.

Everything.

The way she looks at me with her big hazel eyes? Like there's no one else on earth? It sends tingles up my spine. The good kind.

The *very* best kind.

I'll learn how to live with the guilt of my lie-by-omission. Of breaking my promise to be completely truthful with her. Of deceiving her every minute I withhold this information. It's not right.

I know it.

It's just...

As if she's sensing the tornado in my brain, Zoey appears wearing only a tiny LTZ t-shirt. It barely skims the tops of her thighs and I can see she doesn't have panties on. She leans against the tile wall next to our walk-in shower. "You've been in here forever, babe. Aren't the guys supposed to be here soon?"

"Shit. Yeah. You know how much I love a long rinse." I quickly wash the shampoo out of my hair and the soap off my body. When I step out of our charcoal-tiled walk-in shower, Zoey hands me a towel. I quickly wrap it around my waist.

"You were so deep in thought, you didn't notice me for a long time." Zoey reaches up and strokes the nearly invisible scars buried in my eyebrow. "Are you okay? What's going on?"

I steel myself for the lie. "Nothing. Just thinking about band stuff."

She hoists herself on the long counter in between our sinks and watches me dry off. "You know, it wouldn't hurt my feelings if we didn't rush the wedding. I hope talking about getting married in such a whirlwind didn't freak you out."

"Are you kidding me? I'd marry you right this second. I'm dreading this meeting because I'm not really ready to go back to the band grind and I'm not sure how to tell them." I paste on the fake smile I use when I'm forced to schmooze at VIP parties. "Who knows, the guys have a lot going on. Maybe they'll feel the same way."

"Make sure you take your time today to talk it through. You haven't all been together in a while." Zoey bites her lip. "I'll give you some space. I think I'm going to grab lunch with my mom."

I shake out my long hair and pull it back into a knot at the base of my neck so it doesn't drip all over me. "Oh yeah? You gonna fill her in about our wedding plans?"

"Yep." She giggles and gestures for me to come closer, parting her thighs to reveal that, indeed, she does not have on any panties. My dick fills immediately.

Happily, I step in between her legs. Our lips press together. My thumbs lazily stroke her temples. Our kisses become more urgent. Zoey's little breathy moans nearly do me in. I need to be inside her. Get lost in her. Chase all the bad things out of my head and replace them with the good things.

Things like: Zoey is perfect.

Making love to her is perfect.

My life is perfect.

Her hands skim down my sides and unfasten the towel, which drops in a puddle at my feet. She strokes my cock with a firm grip, just how I like it. I lift her t-shirt over her head. Her nipples are tight, pink bullets, begging to be tasted. So I do. Lave them with my tongue and give each of them little nibbles.

"Do we have time?" Zoey moans when I insert two fingers into her soaking pussy. Find that little spongy place inside her that makes her quiver. "Please say we have time."

My thumb slips through her folds and wiggles against her clit. "*Always.* I will *always* have time for this."

Zoey's head lolls back at my dual attack on her pleasure spots. She releases my cock to steady herself by gripping the counter on either side of my hips. Her legs fall even farther open, giving me the most erotic view of my fingers plunging in and out of her wetness.

I can't help but smile when her eyes glaze over. Within seconds she's trembling and arching her back, nearly smacking her head against the mirror when she gushes her release.

Immediately I crouch down between her legs. Spread her open to lap up her tangy juices. Zoey's thighs clamp against my ears, holding me in place. She grips my head too. I alternate flicking my tongue and sucking on her sensitive bud. In moments, she detonates again.

"Ohmyfucking God. Yes. Ty. Yes," Zoey keens, thrusting her hips against my lips.

When her spasms wane, I kiss my way up her pubis, stomach, and breasts to capture her mouth. Our eyes meet. The utter depth of her love for me permeates my entire being, sending tingles down my spine.

Without a word, I grip my cock and we both watch me feed my long, thick length inside her.

Sweet mother of Jesus. Her pink, velvet pussy is my slice of heaven. I press her legs as wide as they can go with my palms to savor the view of my cock gliding in and out of her puffy lips. It's mesmerizing to witness how aroused she gets when we fuck. Every single time.

Her moans are the most beautiful music I've ever created.

Every so often, I bend to suck her nipples, my favorite candy. It's my turn to groan when she reaches around with both hands to grab my ass and yank me toward her, causing me to plunge even deeper into her wet heat. Her head falls forward and nestles against my neck. I wrap my arms around her lower back.

The slaps of our bodies and feral grunts of our pleasure fill the bathroom. It's so good. It's *always* so good.

She's the only woman I'll ever want.

Forever.

My balls draw up. I know I'm going to come so hard it's going to ruin me. Zoey clamps around my cock with yet another orgasm. I can't hold back and empty inside her. Groaning with cach spurt.

All of a sudden, a realization permeates my brain like a thunderbolt. *She's just gone off the pill.* What the fuck have I done? I can't control my reaction. My heart races. I can't catch my breath. Trying to keep my cool, I step back to pull out. Oblivious to my distress, Zoey clings to my ass to keep us locked together so she can ride out her aftershocks.

Just like we've done hundreds of times.

Except, I freak the fuck out, lurching backward to break our connection. My release streams out of her. Lightheaded, I tumble to the floor, bracing myself against the wall. I gulp air like a madman because my wet dick reminds me of what just happened.

"Holy shit, Ty?" Zoey jumps down off the counter, kneels next to me and presses her palm to my forehead. "Are you okay? Talk to me!"

I can't answer. I also can't look at her so I keep my eyes closed. Breathe in on four counts. Hold it for seven counts. Breath out on eight counts. Repeat. Repeat. Repeat.

Breathing exercises. One of my most-used coping techniques.

After a few minutes, it works.

My heart finally stops racing. Slowly, I open my eyes. Zoey is clearly spooked. She's gripping my hand like a vise. I know how she feels firsthand. It's beyond scary to see the person you love most in the world suffer right in front of you.

"I'm okay. I'm sorry." I push the hair off her face with my finger. "Come here."

She nods. Sinks against me and snakes her arm around my side. Kisses my clavicle. I pull her onto my lap, wrap my arms around her and squeeze.

"Don't worry, butterfly. I just came so hard it made me lightheaded," I whisper against her temple. "I'm okay now."

Another lie. Maybe if I say it enough it will be true.

It's got to be true.

I won't let it not be true.

In fact, I'm making my own vow to myself right now: it *is* fucking true. From this point forward, my past is staying where it belongs.

Behind me.

Even if it fucking kills me.

Chapter Three

TRAFFIC SUCKED GETTING OUT of West Seattle. I didn't mind, though. It gave me a bit more time to think. As excited as I am to move up our wedding, after the bathroom incident, a niggling feeling I've not been wanting to deal with is back in full force. Something seems to be off with Ty. I've felt it for a couple of months, at least since I started having the crazy migraines. Maybe even before.

His freak-out after we had sex this morning was scary. Something like that has never happened before. He was so apologetic and loving, I let it go. Still, I can't help but wonder, despite all our talk of weddings and babies, are we taking things too fast? I hope not. He came inside me, there's a small chance I'm already pregnant. Although I'm here to talk to my mom about our wedding plans, I might need her advice about this, I think.

"Zoey? What are you having?" My mom, Olivia Pearson, taps the top of my menu. She's adorable in her athleisurewear. A black-and-white Chanel tracksuit. A gift from Ty for her birthday.

I look up to see a perky brunette in a tight black sweater staring at me, tapping her pen against her lip. Quickly, I glance down to skim the salads, hoping she doesn't recognize me. Usually, I'm safe enough if I'm not with Ty. "Sorry, I'll have the cobb. Side of fries and tartar."

"It's such a nice surprise to get some time with you. How long will Ty be in his meeting?" Mom says before taking a long swig of her iced tea.

"I dunno. A while. He'll text me." I can't help but fidget in my seat. "Things with the band are still up in the air right now."

Mom glances out the window. I follow her gaze. We're at a pub across the street from Greenlake. It's an unseasonably gorgeous sunny but cold day. Hundreds of people are out and about. Kids play soccer. Joggers and bikers loop around the lake. There are a million dogs of every breed on walks with their owners. I love this neighborhood. It's so vibrant.

"Are you going to tell me what's going on?" Mom reaches for my hand. Her pink-red nails are nearly the same shade as mine. "Is everything okay?"

"Well...we've made a decision about the wedding. We're getting married at the house."

My mom bursts out of her chair and pulls me out of mine into a ginormous hug. "Oh, sweetheart! That's wonderful."

"Shhh," I scold and shoo Mom back to her seat. "I don't want to attract too much attention. If someone recognizes me, we'll probably need to leave."

My love story with Ty has been a press sensation for many years now. To LTZ fans - before we got back together - I was the anonymous bitch who broke his heart. Ever since we reunited, we mostly have supporters who follow our every move. But, we also have some detractors who aren't very nice. His fame—and now mine by association—means we have full-time security and follow a very deliberate protocol to keep some semblance of privacy.

For me, being low-key is number one on the list.

Probably because I'm not a big fan of being a public figure. My husband-to-be always will be though, so I've come to terms with it. As the CEO of Ty's foundation, I have to maintain a professional and public profile. His fans are still far more fascinated by the woman he wrote LTZ's most famous album about—me. So, I never deliberately draw attention to myself.

But, I'm not stupid. After too many fugly pictures of me on social media, I always dress as though I'll be photographed when I'm in public. Just in case. Today, I'm wearing black jeans, a white sweater, and a long, silver puffer coat. My hair is pulled back into a ponytail. Minimal makeup. Simple. Again, it's important to blend in but look good. Thank God for my BFF, Alex, a former famous influencer, who has this shit locked down pat. Her guidance has been essential.

"I'm sorry. It's hard for me to remember sometimes." Mom sighs as she sits down.

I reach over and squeeze her hand. "No, I'm sorry. Getting married to a crazy-famous person is complicated."

"I think the crisis has been averted." Mom looks around the pub. No one seems to be paying any attention to us.

"Yeah." A gorgeous little girl with dark hair and blue eyes outside the window catches my attention. She's probably two or three years old and looks so much like Ty, I can feel my eyes begin to mist up. God, I want him to have a daughter. She'd be the luckiest little girl in the world. My thoughts are interrupted when the server sets our food in front of us. I absently chew on a fry. Yum. Fresh cut. Ty's ruined me, I can't do frozen anymore.

Mom steals a crispy potato and asks, "So, have you set a date?"

I chuckle. "Don't freak out."

Mom cocks an eyebrow. "Oh-kay. Officially freaking out."

"Probably in the next couple of weeks. I'm hoping you and Dad can come over one night this week so we can work out the details?"

"You're pregnant," Mom says matter-of-factly.

I roll my eyes. "Um...no."

"Why the rush then? Don't you want to have more time to plan? I always pictured you two having some sort of big Hollywood wedding."

Out of the corner of my eye I see a couple of women sitting at the bar. Nonchalantly aiming their phones at us. I catch my mom's eye and subtly tilt my head in their direction. "Let's table this conversation for now. Do you have time for a walk around the lake after we're done?"

"Absolutely. We need to take advantage of this weather."

We finish our meals. Mom pays the bill. Across the street at the park, we find an empty bench and admire the various trees and bushes that surround the lake. It's that time of year when the autumn leaves are a million shades of orange, red, and yellow. Breathtaking.

Mom puts her arm around me. I lean into her and rest my head on her shoulder. Surprisingly, I start to cry. Mom squeezes my arm. "Oh, Zoey. What's going on?"

"You weren't too far off about being pregnant. It's official. I have to go off the pill." I sit up and wipe the tears from my eyes with my thumbs. "Ty said he wants to ditch birth control altogether. God, I want that so much. I want to start our family..."

"But…" Mom reaches up to smooth the hair out of my face.

"I'm worried he's not ready."

"Why?"

I rest my head on my arm, which is draped over the back of the bench. "We've never talked about what kind of parents we want to be. He always changes the subject. Like it makes him uncomfortable. With his mother being… I'm just not sure he's had a lot of good parental role models."

"But you both have me and your dad, the best role models in the world. Stop worrying, you'll figure all that stuff out. I say, give me some grandbabies. ASAP." Mom throws back her head and laughs.

"I want to. I just…" Tears leak out of my eyes again.

"Oh, no!" Mom tugs me against her. "I didn't mean to make light. It's going to be okay. I promise."

"I hope so. I'm really excited to get married, don't get me wrong. It's just that I can't shake the feeling he's struggling with something. It's probably the band and getting back to work. I just don't know. He claims he's fine."

"I wouldn't worry too much about it, Zoey. You've had a year being on endless vacation. Now that you're coming down to earth, both of you have a bit of an adjustment. Don't make a mountain out of a molehill." Mom grips my hand. "Unless... Are you having second thoughts about marrying him? Because if you are, I'm team Zoey all the way."

I shake my head vigorously. "No! No second thoughts at all. I *love* him. I just want to be there for him. He always takes care of me. It's just if he is going through something, I wish he'd talk to me about it. I don't want to slip into bad patterns."

"He will, baby. Sometimes men need a little space."

I close my eyes for a second to think. "I don't think that's it. It's more like he gives me mixed messages. He's passionate about wanting kids one day but is terrified of being a good dad the next. This morning he told me to stop using any birth control. When I tried to talk with him about it? He turned it around on me. Like I was the one who wasn't ready, when I am. I really am. I want kids so bad, Mom. Am I wrong to be just a little concerned?"

"Huh. Well, it's a little strange."

"I can't help but wonder..." I swallow a lump in my throat. "I can't help but wonder if there's more to his story."

Mom squints and cocks her head. "Like what?"

"I wonder what happened to him as a kid."

"Ah, sweetheart." Mom squeezes my arm. "Why?"

"Ty never, ever talks about his childhood. At all. I mean, I know some basics. Things he told me when we first started dating. Stuff he said in the interview he gave last year after his mother tried to blackmail him. Other than that? He'll listen to me blather on about me and Alex when we were little, but he never contributes his own memories to the conversation. Even when I ask direct questions, like 'do you have school pictures?' he finds a way not to answer directly."

"I don't know, honey. He's so well-adjusted. I don't know much about this stuff, but it seems to me he's done remarkably well dealing with a mother who's an addict." Mom bites her lip and squints off into the distance. "What exactly are you worried about?"

"I'm not sure. But let's just say the thought of someone deliberately hurting Ty makes me want to commit murder. I really wonder if there's more to what he's told me."

We look at each other in silence. Our eyes lock. Mom takes a deep breath and lets it out. "Shit."

"Yeah. Shit."

"Let's walk around the lake. Clear our heads. Talk about wedding dresses for a bit." She stands and pulls me up with her. "I want to absorb for a second."

I'm so grateful for my mother. We're so much alike. When either of us have something complicated on our minds, we have to analyze it to death before taking any action. It makes her a great salesperson. It's why I became a lawyer. Needless to say, getting a little exercise does make me feel better.

We complete the three-mile loop, and I quickly shoot Ty a text so he doesn't worry that I'm not home yet. When I look up from my phone, my mom grips my shoulders. "Okay. I'm not sure if this is what you want to hear, but if you can't talk to Ty directly about this, I think you should get some couple's counseling."

My nose wrinkles almost uncontrollably. I've never been one to talk about my inner feelings. Even when I went through a long depression after I left Ty. Somehow, I've been able to muddle through. I look down at the sidewalk. Kick a crack with my toe.

"You're not a fan." Mom wraps her arms around me. Reluctantly, I hug her back.

"He has a therapist, Mom. A woman he's been seeing for years. It's how he turned his life around."

"Zoey. No. Couple's counseling is different. It gives you tools to communicate."

I pull away. "I really don't think we need it. I tell him everything. He can tell me anything. I think we're good."

She raises an eyebrow.

Point taken.

Mom sighs. "I love Ty. He's part of our family. But, if you're going to make this relationship work. If you're going to build a life with him. If you're going to marry him and have babies with him. You and I shouldn't be having this conversation. You're the one falling into old patterns, my darling daughter. Put your big-girl panties on and talk to your fiancé."

I squeeze my eyes shut. She's right, it's déjà vu. Instead of talking to Ty, I'm seeking other people's opinions about our business. "God. You are soooo right."

We walk toward the parking lot. Before I get into the car, Mom touches my sleeve. "Don't discount couple's counseling. Lots of priests require it before they'll agree to perform a wedding ceremony."

"Yeah, I don't see us using a priest." I giggle. "Carter will probably get ordained online or something."

"Still."

"I get it. I'll talk to Ty. If that doesn't work, I'll look into couple's counseling." Even though I don't think I will. He's already in therapy. This is my issue, most likely. I'm making too much of nothing.

We say our goodbyes and within minutes I'm cruising toward home in my new black Mercedes AMG GT Roadster. When I call Ty, he answers right away.

"Hey, how's Olivia?" His voice sounds bright. Cheerful.

Good, the meeting must be going well. "She's great. Excited for us."

"I knew she would be. That's cool."

"Are you alone?" I pull onto I-5 and head south toward our neighborhood.

"Connor went home, he had some family business to take care of. Zane and Jace are still here. Should I tell them to get lost?" I hear Zane protest in the background.

I can't help but smile. I adore Ty's bandmates. "No, make them stay, I want to give them both hugs."

"Okay, I love you, Z."

"Love you, too."

Just like that, I feel better. Talking with my mom always grounds me. Ty seems fine, I've been worrying about—

That's when a lightbulb really goes off.

I've figured it all out.

We. Had. Sex. Without. Protection.

Holy shit. I'm such an idiot. I know exactly why he was brooding in the shower. Based on the conversation we'd had earlier, he thought I wasn't ready for kids with him. He freaked out because he didn't want me to think he deliberately tried to get me pregnant. God, I love him. There's no one on this earth who cares about my feelings more than Ty.

You know what? I care about his feelings too. I'm going to give Ty the respect of believing what he tells me. Why would he suggest going off birth control if he wasn't ready to have kids?

He wouldn't.

I can't wait to get home. I'm going to apologize to my fiancé and tell him that we're ditching birth control for good. I'm more than ready to have babies with him.

He's going to be so happy.

No, *we're* going to be so happy.

Chapter Four

BY THE TIME ZOEY left to meet her mom, I barely had time to catch my breath before Jace showed up. Zane and Connor followed minutes later. Even though I've seen my bandmates individually from time to time over the past few months, the four of us haven't all been together in a while.

It feels good for us to all be in one place. I'm also glad to have a diversion from obsessing over how badly I freaked out this morning. In the middle of fucking my fiancée. I'm not ready to unpack that just yet.

We convene in my recently updated home studio in the basement. I really hope the guys are on the same page as me. It's not time for us to go back to work. Not quite yet. "My dudes, I hate to admit it but I feckin' missed you." Connor plops down in one of the six giant, overstuffed chairs in the main control room. His smile is so big it nearly lights up the room.

Zane, the ball of energy that he is, jumps into his lap and plants a big smooch on his cheek. "You're never allowed to fuck off to Ireland again. I don't care if you own ten homes there."

"You're a lunatic!" Connor shoves Zane and holds him off with one muscular arm when he attempts to climb back on top of him. "For the record, it's just *one* house in Ireland. We're getting our new place ready in LA. Looks like it will be home base for a while, so it will. Ronni's pitching producing and potentially starring in a new series."

Jace leans against the wall, taking it all in. All quiet, cool confidence. His long, blond hair flows around his shoulders. He smirks at Connor's and Zane's antics.

After they settle down, I show the guys around the studio and the state-of-the art upgrades. A new WS 948

Delta SSL Console. A ton of the latest outboard units. Brand-new backline. Not to mention custom acoustic paneling. Best of all, in addition to the seating area, I installed a small but functional chef's kitchen, complete with Wolfe appliances and a SubZero refrigerator. There are two small bathrooms and a huge guest bedroom with a master bath.

Ordinarily, when I'm recording, I get in a zone. Before I know it, hours—or even days—have passed. That's why it's imperative to have everything I need on hand. A lot of the upgrades were in motion before Zoey moved in last year. She encouraged me to finish it up while we were traveling so it would be ready when we got home.

It's one of the many things I love about her. Unwavering support. Rather than chastise me for holing up down here, she'll probably come down and quietly read in one of the comfortable chairs. Not to bother me, just to be near me.

God, how I love her.

"The studio turned out awesome. Maybe we should just record the next stuff here." Jace runs his hand along the mixing board. "You have enough guest rooms, we could all just stay with you."

Zane throws an arm around me. "You look like you're going to faint, Ty. Don't worry, he's just kidding."

"All of you are welcome to stay here any time. For however long you want." I pretend-choke Zane. "Except you. I see you too much as it is."

Zane, Fiona, and Mia live in a brand-new house a few blocks away. Whenever Zoey and I are in town, we're generally at each other's houses at least once or twice a week.

Jace shakes his head. "Just so you know, Ty, Poppy sent me with a grave warning that if you and Zoey don't come out to stay at the ranch soon, she'll come here and drive you over herself."

"Zoey's coordinating something. I overheard her on the phone with Alex." I turn my attention to our drummer. "You and I need to do better about making it possible for our girls to hang out."

"True that." Jace nods, then looks off into the distance. He's clearly thinking about something that has nothing to do with LTZ.

"My dudes, please. Let's get down to business. Da's going in for his procedure tomorrow, so I gotta get back home." Connor gestures for all of us to sit down.

I begin the meeting. "My brothers, I'm just going to keep it simple. I need more time. I hope you understand."

"Thank God." Zane surprises me. "Fee is buried with everything that needs to get done for the restaurant opening. We need a few months to dial it all in."

"I'm cool with that." Jace beats a distracted rhythm on the arms of the chair with his palms.

Connor sighs heavily. "Aye. That's grand. The thought of going back out on the road right now? Feck no. But I do miss writing and recording. And playing, if I'm honest. I want to come up with a plan so the kids can be with us. One that lets us take a lot of long breaks. I don't ever want to be gone for years at a time again."

Everyone mumbles their agreement.

"Ty, do you want to start writing? I have a few ideas." Zane fidgets a bit. "No pressure, just fun?"

"Sure, I have a ton of stuff to demo." I nod. "Let's start in the new year, though. I want to finish our hiatus. To finish clearing my head."

"Is that what they're calling it now?" Jace raises an eyebrow.

"He's clearing something." Connor laughs.

I can't help but laugh along with them. I love these guys. "Well, it brings up something I need to tell you. Zoey and I are getting married sometime in the next couple of weeks. We just decided this morning, so I don't have the exact date. It won't be a big wedding. Just her family. Carter. All of us. The girls. The kids. I think that's it."

"Fucking awesome!" Zane pops up and launches himself at me. I catch him and we hug it out. He sits on the edge of my chair.

"Before we set the date, I wanted to check in with all of you to figure out what's most convenient for everyone." I smile at the thought of our wedding. Being around the guys today has been medicinal. Right now, I have no anxiety whatsoever. All I feel is excited to marry Zoey and to hang out with my band again.

"Dude, whatever day you pick, we'll be there. Text me when and where." Connor stands and makes his way toward the door. "Seriously. Congratulations. I'm sorry but I gotta jet. Duty calls."

Connor's fierce love for his family is admirable. He has a million brothers. His dad has been ill for years, and he's always been the backup father-figure to his siblings.

I'm so glad he found love with Ronni, my former fake girlfriend. They're perfect together. Our formerly gruff, scary bassist is so happy these days, and it looks good on him.

After Connor leaves, Jace, Zane, and I head upstairs. They convince me to make a snack, so I make buttered crab rolls for the three of us. "Be warned, Fiona's threatening to recruit you. She's having a hell of a time staffing up," Zane says through a mouthful of buttery crustacean.

Jace licks sauce off his fingers. "You could just wear a wig. No one will recognize you."

"Ha ha." I roll my eyes. I notice Zoey's calling to check in. We chat briefly. "FYI. You guys aren't allowed to leave, Zoey wants to see you both."

"Shit." Zane's eyes go wide. "What did I do?"

"What didn't you do? The list is so long." Jace takes his plate to the sink and rinses it off.

We head to the living room and slip back into our back-and-forth banter. I'm so comfortable with these guys. I guess that's what happens when you're together 24/7 for nearly nine solid years. We've been through so much. They really are my family. My only family.

Well, aside from Zoey, now.

God, I've got to apologize to her about this morning. I feel so stupid. I never want her to feel bad when we're having sex, and I could tell she was hurt by my freakout. As if on cue, I hear her come in through the front door. I look up to see my butterfly in all her glory. Long, blonde hair, wild and nearly to her waist. Black-rimmed glasses. My sexy little schoolgirl. I can't help but lurch off my seat, swoop her up and give her a kiss.

"Jesus." Jace rolls his eyes good-naturedly. "You two never stop."

"Are you being serious right now? Last time I was over at your house I literally caught you going down on my best friend in the horse barn. I'll never unsee that." Zoey shakes her finger at our drummer.

He just grins. Arches an eyebrow.

Zane comes up behind her and wraps his arms around her. "Fee wanted me to tell you hello and that she's sorry things are so crazy right now."

"It's fine, I get it." Zoey hugs him back. "We can't wait to be there when the restaurant opens."

Jace's phone buzzes. "Poppy, I'm still at Ty and Zoey's, you're on speaker. Say hello."

"Hey, everyone." Alex's voice permeates the room. "Send my man home, will you? I need his help for our expanding family. Oh, and Zoey? We're making a date for you to come over. No excuses."

"Yes, ma'am," Zoey answers in a singsong voice.

I'm dumbfounded. "Holy shit! Is Alex pregnant?"

"*Fuck* no." Jace curls his lip and then bursts into laughter. "We just added two new horses to the ranch. Do you ever listen to anything I say?"

I feel Zane's palm on my shoulder. "Don't sweat it. You zoned out earlier when he told us the story."

From the day and hour Zane befriended me in high school, he's looked out for me. Even when I try to push him away. He brought me into his family. Shared his father with me. It was Zane who helped me through my breakup with Zoey. He and Carter pointed me in the right direction with Lisa. It's always been Zane in the background. Never interfering, just quietly having my back. Even covering for me when I zone out.

I'm not sure if he knows how much I appreciate him. How much it's meant to me all these years. At some point, I really need to tell him.

"Welp, I've got to head out to catch the ferry." Jace gets up, embraces Zoey and fist-bumps me. "Dude, great day. Thanks for the crab roll. See you next weekend, Z."

Zane pulls Zoey and me into a hug. "I'm outta here too. I've gotta rescue Fee. She'll never leave the kitchen if I don't give her a good reason."

"I'm sure you'll think of something." Zoey swats him.

We walk them to the door and just like that, I'm alone with the woman who rocks my entire world. I fold her into my arms. She melts into me. We stand in our foyer for a few minutes, tightly wound together. Saying nothing. We don't need to, being together like this is bliss.

"You look happy." Zoey pulls away slightly, rests her hands on my shoulders and trains her eyes on mine.

I press my forehead to hers. "I *am* happy. I have so much to be happy for."

"I sure hope so. I felt really bad after I left." Zoey strokes my check with her thumb. "I know I hurt your feelings today when I said we weren't ready to have kids. It was insensitive of me. If you say you want babies, I believe you."

"I do. I really want us to have kids." I nod because deep down it's how I feel. Wanting and being ready for it are too different things, though. Especially with my shitty history. I push the thoughts aside. It's easy to do when I'm softly kissing her pink lips. Nuzzling her neck. Breathing in her citrusy, floral scent.

"We didn't use protection this morning, you know. Is that why you got a little weird?" Zoey smiles through our kisses.

I think about what to say that is true, even if it isn't the whole truth. "Yeah. I guess I freaked out and thought I pushed you into something you weren't ready for."

Zoey lights up. "I knew it. And for the record, I want to have a baby with you so badly. Everyone else is settling down and I want that so much. Let's do it. Throw caution to the wind. Let your little spermies fly free. You're going to be such a great daddy. "

"Yeah? You really think so?" My heart thunders in my chest.

She squeezes me tightly. "Yeah. I really *know* so."

"Um, spermies?"

"Yep. Spermies."

"Okay, I'm ready. Let's do it," I lie through my teeth.

"Ohmygod, Ty, we're going to have so much fun getting me pregnant!" Zoey holds her finger up and grabs a bag sitting on the kitchen counter. "Give me a minute, I have a surprise."

I stand there a little shell-shocked.

Holy fuck.

We're really going through with this.

Chapter Five

I SMILE WHEN I look at myself in the bathroom mirror. On my way home, I passed a darling new lingerie store in Fremont. Inspired, I snapped up a gorgeous sheer black polka-dotted ruffle thong and matching bralette. I've popped into the powder room to change before seducing my man. He loves me in lingerie. I'm going to show him just how much I'm on board with everything.

What I didn't count on were all the crisscrossing straps on this stupid bra, which makes it a bitch to put on. I've been in here far longer than planned. It should be worth it though, I look pretty hot if I do say so myself.

I also needed a minute. To process. I'm not sure why I was freaking out so badly earlier. I know my fiancé. Better than anyone on the planet. There was really no need to second-guess anything earlier and send myself into a frenzy. God, we're so into each other. There's no one else in the world for either of us. We've spent the past few months in our own world, for the most part. Blissfully planning our future together. Talking about everything from politics to pop culture. Plus, a whole lot of laughing and being silly.

It was the first time either of us were able to just live in the moment. Explore the world. Eat amazing food. Relax. Get lost in our passion for each other. We've made love under the Northern Lights. On private islands. In a cabin on the Swiss Alps. We've had hot, blow-your-socks off, transcendent sex in elevators. Staircases. Swimming pools. Alleys. Wine cellars. On private jets. Yachts.

We've also combined forces to do rewarding, life-changing work for his foundation. It cemented what we knew to be true—we're really compatible, even as business partners.

My life with Ty is amazing. Idyllic. Magical.

There is no point in looking for cracks in our relationship. There are none. We've taken such great care to learn and grow together.

"Did you drown?" I hear Ty call out from the living room.

"Sorry, babe. I'll be right out." I stride out with my best lioness prowl to find Ty waiting for me. Shirtless and yummy on our cushy couch overlooking downtown Seattle. His head rests back against the cushions, but he's slumped down so low, his hips are at the edge of the couch. Piercing blue eyes track my moves. I glide toward him, giving him a little show.

As I get closer, by the way Ty's eyebrow arches and he licks his lips, I'm pretty sure he now realizes my getup is see through. I notice the top button of his jeans is unbuttoned. His beautiful shaft is so hard, I can see it straining to break free. Ty trails his fingertips down his cut abs and lowers his zipper. Takes out his cock and pumps as I approach. Lubricates himself with the little bead of moisture at the tip.

When I'm right in front of him, I drop to my knees. Smooth my hands up his thighs. Suck the crown of his cock between my lips, giving the fingers he's gripping it with little licks. Ty moans and taps the tip of his cock on my tongue. He pushes in and watches it disappear through hooded eyes.

"You're so fucking beautiful. You have no idea how good your mouth feels, Zoey," he practically growls. Encouraged, I hollow my cheeks to take him deeper. Suck and swirl my tongue along the underside of his cock. Lick and suckle his balls before repeating the entire process. Soon, he's making deep, grunting noises. Undulating his hips to push himself deeper toward my throat.

I love giving him this pleasure, but he still rarely lets me suck him completely off. He doesn't today either. When I feel his balls tighten, Ty encloses the base of his shaft with his fingers and gently tips my chin up with his finger. Motions for me to stop.

So I do.

Still kneeling, I wait to see what he has in mind. His cock lays wet and glistening from my saliva against his belly. I lick my lips, "You know I love it when you let me blow you."

Ty's smile is almost shy when he stands, pushes his jeans down and steps out of them. He's not quite so shy when he roughly turns me and pulls my back against his chest. Runs his hands all over my body. Pushes the cups of the bralette to the sides, exposing my tits. Then slides the tiny, ruffled black thong down my legs. When I step out of it, he resumes a seated position on the couch and watches me. "I'm going to fuck you so hard," he growls.

Looking over my shoulder, I wiggle my ass and bend over so he can see how aroused I am from behind. "You always make me so wet, Ty. I need you inside me."

"Holy Jesus, Z." Ty grabs my waist and pulls me onto his lap. I position my legs over his thighs so his enormous dick rests in between my pussy lips. Ty cups my breasts from behind and rolls my nipples. Hard pinches send jolts directly to my core. I reach down to direct his cock inside me. Slowly. Until he's buried so deep it feels like we're one person.

We grind together to find our rhythm. Ty bands his arms around my waist. I wrap my arms around his and rest my head in the crevice of Ty's neck. He bounces me up and down on his cock so my tits bounce and jiggle around the bralette, which is one of his favorite things in the world. Fucking me when I still have a little bit of clothing on. Score one for the lingerie shopping spree.

"Holy Christ," he pants. Ty's finger sneaks downward and begins to rapidly circle my clit to our rhythm. My pussy spasms around his cock from all the stimulation. Undaunted, he rubs harder and thrusts upward with more force.

God, we've perfected how to get each other off. I can't help but scream his name when I come all over his cock and fingers. He backs off a bit but doesn't stop. He press-es against my pubis with his palm and massages. Creat-ing sweet friction against his cock, which is still buried inside me. Sending little aftershocks of bliss through my core.

This man plays my body even better than he plays guitar. He knows literally every single thing about how to give me pleasure.

When my spasms finally subside, I relax back against him. My face tilts up to his. Our eyes meet. We kiss. Taste. Suckle. His hands are all over me. Gentle this time. He caresses my arms. My breasts. My stomach. He worships my body all while rolling his hips upward. Slow thrusts remind me we are joined in every way.

"I love you," I murmur against his mouth. "You're perfect for me, you know."

"Mmmm." He doesn't answer, just gently repositions us, careful to keep us connected.

Now lying sideways on the couch, he reaches under my thigh and hooks it over his arm. His other arm cradles my head. My small frame is enveloped by his large one, which is comforting and sexy all at the same time. Ty picks up the pace, jackhammering into me from behind. At this angle, each motion causes the crown of his dick to rub against my G-spot. At the speed he's going, I'm gushing around him. I look down to see my clit is swollen and erect. Ty loves to watch me finger myself, so I rub my little nub using my juices as lube. Moan when his fingers join mine again.

"Come again, Z." Ty suckles my earlobe. "I want you to go over again before I blow."

My reply comes out garbled. He's ramming into me so hard and the extraordinary stimulation to both my clit and G-spot is so intense, I can't articulate a thing. Pure joy. That's all I can think when my entire body quakes with another explosive release. Ty slows down, circling his hips to allow me to settle but stays so incredibly deep inside me. I lie back against his arm. He captures my lips with his. Rubs his hands along my sides. Pulls the straps of my bralette down, freeing my arms and breasts. Cuddles me against him. He whispers, "Can we try something a little, um, unconventional?"

"Yes," I reply without any hesitation. Trying anything with Ty makes me shudder with anticipation. We love variety in our sex life.

"Okay, Z, here we go." In one fluid motion, Ty hooks his arms under my legs and twists me around, essentially positioning me so I'm nearly upside down. He sits on the back of the couch looking down at me, pulls my legs over his thighs and drags me up so my head and shoulders are on the seat cushion. Somehow, my pussy is now perfectly aligned with his cock.

Ty grins down at me. "Holy hell, this is exactly what I pictured in my mind. Your cunt is soaking wet. Your clit is swollen. Fuck, I did that to you." His look of awe as he positions his cock at my entrance and pushes inside me from above makes me moan. I can't really move, but I get an incredible visual of his dick gliding in and out of me, glistening with my juices.

I grab his ankles, which rest on either side of my head, for stability. My tits jiggle each time he pounds down into me. I can't help but keen and whimper. How could I not? He's never been so deep. It feels incredible. I start mumbling all sorts of porn-star encouragements. I can't help it. We're porn-star fucking. In a porn-star position.

One that isn't sustainable. My neck begins to ache, but I'm so into what we're doing, I ignore it. He's so in tune with me, he notices my discomfort immediately. Ty's hands skate along my waist and wrap around my lower back. "Come here, butterfly," Ty lifts me up and into his lap, still managing to remain seated on the back of the couch. God love my man with the incredible core strength.

I wrap my arms around his shoulders and bury my face in his neck. Oh Lord, how good he smells. Always grapefruit and leather. His big hands travel down to grip both of my ass cheeks. He rocks me back and forth against him so my clit rubs against his pubic bone.

"I love you so fucking much," Ty murmurs against my hair. "I hope you never doubt that."

His comment, given what we're in the middle of, takes me by surprise. "I *never* doubt it. I never doubt us."

"Promise?" Ty squeezes me tighter.

God, the way his dick is so deep inside me right now is making my brain foggy. "Ahh. Ohh. God, babe. Yes. Without question."

"Holy shit, Z. I can't hold out anymore, I'm coming, babe. Can you get there again, too?" Ty rasps and presses the small of my back so my clit gets even more stimulation against his pubic bone.

"Just keep doing what you're doing. It feels..." My head lolls back in utter bliss.

"Like molten magic," Ty finishes my sentence with more poetic words than I could ever eke out.

Our bodies grind together. Fast and furious. I feel like I'm about to be turned inside-out when my orgasm crashes through my body. Ty's hot release floods me. I slump against him. He clings to me as we slither down the back of the couch to the seat cushions. I'm a literal noodle. He feathers soft little kisses all along my cheekbone and around my face. His cock still quivers inside me. How we've managed to remain connected, I have no comprehension.

We stay like that for a long time. Eventually, coming down to earth. Reclining lengthwise, face-to-face.

"We're going to need an upholstery cleaner before we have guests over again," I muse.

"Worth it." Ty cups my face. "That was pretty fucking incredible."

"It always is. I can't wait to be your wife, Ty." I take my own turn softly kissing his entire face. "I'm looking forward to this next chapter for us. And for every other chapter we have together. We're meant for each other. Through thick and thin."

Ty closes his eyes as though my words are washing over him. "I never thought I'd have this, Zoey. I never knew..."

He shakes his head. Holds me closer. Doesn't finish his thought.

"What didn't you know?"

"I just didn't grow up with examples of the relationship we have. Sometimes, I feel out of my depth. Your parents are so cool. So in love after all these years. I want us to have that. I want to give that to you."

Ty's so earnest and open right now, I decide to take a risk. "We *already* have it. You give it to me every day. I hope I give that to you. You trust your heart and soul with me, don't you?"

"Of course." His brows knit together, almost in worry.

"Good. Because I trust my heart and soul with you. Implicitly. We're going to spend the rest of our lives learning every little thing about each other, Ty." I twirl a lock of his hair around my finger.

He gulps. Hides a wince. Nods. "Okay."

"You do know if something is bothering you, I'm here for you." I give him a butterfly kiss on the cheek and pull away to look at his handsome face. "Always."

Ty squeezes his eyes shut tightly. "I don't want to keep anything from you, butterfly. I really don't. It's just..."

"Shhh." I place my finger against his lips. "No pressure. We have our whole lives. I want you to know that nothing you could ever say to me will affect how I feel about you. Or make me look at you differently. I meant it when I said you are perfect. Because you are. Well, aside from when you let one rip under the covers. I'm not sure you should ever get that comfortable."

He laughs. "Bad habits from being on a tour bus with a bunch of heathen bandmates and crew."

I cock an eyebrow. Then laugh along with him.

"Seriously, Z. I appreciate you saying that." Ty gazes at me with what can only be described as awe. "What did I do to deserve you?"

"I could ask you the same thing, you know. I don't think it's about deserving, though. It's about choosing each other over everything else. And I do, Ty. I choose you."

"I'll choose you every fucking day of my life, butterfly." Ty kisses me so thoroughly I feel it all the way to my toes.

My entire body is warm. Satiated. Spent.

My heart is filled with unconditional love for this man. Together, I know we'll get through anything life throws at us.

No question.

Chapter Six

ONE OF MY FAVORITE benefits of being famous is having access to services on a moment's notice. It's a privilege, for sure. Considering my shitty upbringing, it's not one I take for granted.

Our wedding plans are coming together so easily. Z is most definitely not the bridezilla-type. Thank fuck. One of the zillion reasons I love her.

I'm, well, a dude. A dude who has only been to one wedding in my entire life. I truly have no idea what goes into planning my own. I'm quite happy to do what I'm told. Zoey put together a project list. We are dividing and conquering armed with iron-clad NDAs for every vendor to sign. Our plans might be simple, but we're not naive. We want our day to go off without a hitch.

Or leaks to the press.

Flowers. Food. Photography. We're ready except for one thing, and today both of us are taking care of the final detail: our clothes.

I'm with Zane inside his thousand-square-foot walk-in closet getting fitted for a bespoke black Australian Merino wool suit. Zane is getting a similar suit in charcoal gray. The tailor is with us now and will fit Connor and Jace later at their own homes.

Zoey, on the other hand, is out with her mom, Alex, Fiona, and Ronni for a wedding dress fitting. Alex is her maid of honor. Fee and Mae are her bridesmaids. Carter is officiating. It's kind of funny that all of our guests, except for her parents and Connor's twin baby boys, will be in the wedding party.

Eight more days and it can't come soon enough, as far as I'm concerned. I've done a lot of thinking about Zoey's beautiful words to me the other night. When she told me she'd choose me over everything else. It's touched me. I really believe her. I've decided to tell her about my diagnosis. I'll keep the details to a minimum, but she deserves to know.

Once we're married, though. Because then, she'll really be mine forever. I won't ever worry about her leaving again.

"Are you sure she's not preggo?" Zane teases me. "You guys are getting married in an awful hurry."

I elbow him in the ribs. "You know we'd have been married a long time ago if it was up to me. We've just had such a great time this year, who had time to plan a wedding? Neither of us wanted to wait anymore. I think it's working out perfectly. No drama. All love."

"That's beautiful, man." Zane plants a kiss on my forehead.

I playfully push him away. "The foundation has taken up a lot more time than I'd planned, but it's really rewarding. I love working with Zoey."

"Jeez. I can relate. I'm not sure what Fee was thinking opening a fine-dining restaurant on top of reopening The Mission." Zane sucks in his lips and pushes them back out. "It's seriously interfering with my master plan to knock her up. I want to see her with a belly full of my kid. We're not getting any younger."

I give him the side-eye. "You guys have plenty of time. But, I get it. Zoey just went off birth control because of her migraines. So..."

"Bro!" Zane's eyes go wide.

"I know." I smile over at him. "Can you believe it?"

"Wow. Look at us. Married men. Gorgeous wives. Now kids? We've come a long way from being reject losers in high school." Zane's smile is contagious. I'm grinning like a fool too.

Especially when I consider what he's said. Zane's being kind by lumping us together. He was popular, but I most certainly *was* a reject loser. Until he took me under his wing. Shared his dad with me. Gave me the opportunity to put together a band like LTZ.

He's right though, my life is completely different *now*. And I'm grateful. That's why it was really pissing me off when the darkness threatened to pull me under a couple weeks ago. Things are so much better now, and I'm glad I worked my way through it. Skills I learned from therapy helped, and my coping tools turned things around.

My diagnosis doesn't define me. *I won't let it.*

I don't say any of this to Zane though. "Yeah. It's a trip."

We finish with the tailor and head down to the kitchen. Zane brings out some cheese, crackers, a bowl of fresh strawberries, and a couple of Pellegrinos. We sit at the counter of his seventeen-foot white marble island to snack.

"So, my brother." Zane clinks his bottle of fizzy water against mine. "Tell me the truth. How are you? You seemed a little off at the band meeting. Is everything okay?"

"Dude, stop worrying about me all the time. I know you mean well, but everything is fine. Perfect. I've never been happier. I'm in love and finally marrying the woman of my dreams." I can feel my brow furrow with annoyance. Fuck. So much for feeling good about things. Still, my words come out a bit harsher than I intended.

"Oh, God. Ty. No. I wasn't trying to stir anything up. I'm genuinely asking. If you need anything, I'm here. I was a nervous wreck before my wedding. You helped calm me down, don't you remember?"

I press my palm to my forehead. Jesus. Overly sensitive much? One minute I'm fine. The next minute...fuck. I've got to pull my shit together. "Yeah. Shit. I remember. I'm sorry. I guess I *am* a little punchy. It's just so weird when you want something for so long and now it's a reality, you know?"

"Yeah." Zane's face is dreamy. "I get it."

Of course he does. Zane and Fiona had a million obstacles to climb before they finally were able to really be together. "We definitely have that in common."

Zane just smiles at me. Shrugs.

"So, um, I've been meaning to tell you... I guess I just want to say, um. Fuck. Dude, you kept me going all of those years, you know. I don't ever tell you how much I appreciate you. Our friendship. How much, I, um, I mean all of us in the band call each other brothers, but you really *are* my brother." I stumble over my sentences. Mainly because words can never express how much Zane means to me.

After a pause, he launches himself at me. We bro hug tightly. Pound each other's backs with our fists. Zane pulls away, grips my face in both hands and plants another big smooch on my forehead. "Of course you *are* my brother. We *are* brothers. *Real* brothers. I love you, dude. We're family. We'll *always* be family."

I'm caught off-guard. There's a lump in my throat. My chest is tight. All of a sudden, I don't know how to handle this. It's one thing for me to think this way of Zane, because I have no true family. But for him to also feel this way about me when he does? It's so. Um...

Overwhelming.

I pull Zane back into another bro hug. Try to buy a minute to pull my shit together. When I pull back, my eyes are wet anyway.

"That...um. Means so much." I choke out. "I—"

"It's okay, Ty. I *know*." Zane nods serenely.

"No, it's important to me to tell you. I...uh. It's just that." I can't stop word vomiting. "I never really had any family. I struggle a bit. I'm not sure if I'm capable—"

Zane holds his hand up to stop me from talking. "Ty, I won't hear you say a bad word about yourself. Just don't. Call Lisa. If you're struggling, there's no shame in getting help, remember that. I've never told anyone in the band this, but my mom had me in therapy from the time I was six years old."

"What?" My jaw drops.

"Dude, she moved us to Colorado after Fiona and I watched Carter overdose in a park. It sucked. I lost my dad. I lost my best friend. No one liked me in the new school. I was bullied. Even though I had my grandparents and my mom, Carter was so fucked-up, he basically abandoned me." Zane slaps the counter with his open palm. "I was a total fucking mess. Miserable."

I'm flabbergasted. "Why didn't you ever tell me?"

"I dunno." He shrugs. "You seemed to have a lot on your plate when we first met. Even though you never said anything at the time, both Carter and I suspected your mom had issues. Obviously, Carter knew the signs and suspected she was an addict. Maybe that's why I gravitated toward you. Unlike me, you didn't have someone to look out for you. You clearly had the fortitude to care of yourself. Fuck, man, I couldn't have done what you did. You're one of the strongest people I know."

Wow. Fucking. Wow.

"I never really thought..." I stutter. "You and Carter always seemed cool. Close. I know you had some tension on occasion and he's never hidden that he had demons, but..."

"Meh. It's a long time ago. We've worked through it. It's in the past."

I sit back down and chew on a strawberry. I'm not sure what to say. Issues with my mother that I tried so hard to keep secret still managed to not only dominate the band, but my friendship with Zane. I guess I wasn't so good at hiding it. "It's cool you've been able to put it behind you."

"Cheers to moving forward." Zane holds up his Pellegrino and I clink it with mine.

I gear up for my next topic of conversation. "One of the reasons I wanted us to do the fitting together is I was hoping you'll be my best man?"

"I fucking thought you'd never ask. Of *course* I'm your best man.If you didn't ask me I'd have shown up to do the job anyway." Zane's smile jumps off his face.

We both get up and the bro hugs are back in full force. And a few tears, I'm not ashamed to admit.

"Aww, boys. Are you having a special moment?" Fiona's voice startles both of us and we separate.

"Uh, *yeah*. I'm Ty's best man," Zane gloats. "I told you he was going to ask me today."

Fiona smirks. Her dark-purple hair cascades around her shoulders. "Congratulations. You're both fucking adorable."

"Well that's true." Zane preens and bounces over to his wife. "That's why you can *never* resist me."

"Oh, I *can* resist you." She bats at him.

Zane clutches his heart as though she's crushed it and falls to the floor dramatically. "Why would you though?"

I love the dynamic between Fee and Zane. You can tell they've known each other from birth. "How did the dress stuff go? I haven't checked in with Zoey for a bit."

"Ah-*may*-zing," Fee answers as she drags Zane up from the floor. He promptly puts his arm around her and kisses her temple. "You won't be able to keep your hands off her."

Instantly, I visualize Zoey in nothing but a bridal veil and white garter posing in the doorway to our bedroom. My cock twinges and I can feel my face redden. Jesus, I've got to have her. Now. I glance at my jacket draped over the back of the chair and pull out my phone from the pocket. Sure enough, I've missed a few texts from her. I quickly reply, letting her know I'll be home in a few minutes.

I can think of nothing else but getting home and stripping her naked. My sex drive when it comes to Zoey has always been off the charts, from the very first time we fooled around in the band room at Carter's house. After that, we couldn't keep our hands off each other. Although, It took me a long time to actually have sex with her, mostly due to my own, uh, hang-ups. Which didn't get better when she left me the morning after I took her virginity.

I was celibate for a couple years after we broke up. Then I went the other direction and turned into my mother. I fucked a lot of random people before deciding I'd only allow myself to get blow jobs. Sex itself felt too, I dunno, intimate.

Since we've been back together, making love to Zoey has provided me with the most validating love I've ever had. I literally can't get enough. I want to bathe in our closeness. To soak up every ounce of her love for me. The only time I ever feel completely whole and at peace is when I'm balls-deep inside her. If that makes me sound crazy, well I am. Technically. But I'm not going to feel shame for being crazy in love with the most beautiful, loving girl in the world.

I quickly say my goodbyes to Zane and Fee and jog the few blocks home. I find Zoey buried in her phone. Sitting on the sofa in the exact location of our gymnastic fuck-a-thon of a couple days ago. She's adorable in black-framed glasses. Her bare legs are tucked up under a black sweater dress.

She glances up. "Hey, how did the fitting go?"

"The suit's gonna be awesome." I plop down next to her and scoop her feet up into my lap and proceed to massage her soles with my thumbs.

Zoey moans and lies back. "Good God, that's amazing. How'd you know I had to keep my torture shoes on during the alterations?"

"Poor baby." I bring her foot up to my mouth and kiss and then suckle her pretty red-tipped toes. She squirms, but her little moans tell me she likes what I'm doing so I keep her foot captive and continue.

"Holy shit, Ty. Who knew toe sucking would make me so wet." Zoey presses her knees open so her dress rides up her soft thighs.

I place her foot on the couch and drag her panties down her legs and throw them to the ground. Her pussy is, indeed, soaking. My dick, which was already painfully straining against my jeans, immediately threatens to burst right through. Ignoring it for now, I drape her thighs over my shoulders and bury my face into her sweet pussy. My tongue drags along her slit and laps up her juices, which have a slightly metallic taste today. I spread her pussy lips open with my fingers so I can lick and suckle her clit unencumbered.

It doesn't take long before Zoey comes all over my face. When her spasms subside, I grin up at her through her spread legs. Zoey gazes down at me with dreamy eyes, but they sproing open in horror. "Oh no! I'm so sorry, Ty."

"What?" I stare at her, unsure of what's going on.

"I must have my period." Looking horrified, she sits up and thumbs something off my lip and shows it to me. A tiny smear of pink. "Ick. That's disgusting."

I pull her into my lap. "Nothing about you is disgusting, Z. You always taste amazing. I don't mind. Don't worry."

"Well, it felt...incredible." She strokes my hair and leans into me. "Apparently, my parts are very sensitive when I'm on my period."

"Well, can we *finally* put period sex on the table then?" I waggle my eyebrows at her.

"Maybe." She looks off into the distance. "Although, I guess this means I'm not pregnant. Which is actually surprising considering how many times we've..."

Part of me is a little disappointed, but I'm still so aroused I push the thought out of my mind. Instead, I reach in between her legs and push my finger inside her and wiggle. "Will you let me fuck you, babe?"

"You're sure it's not gross?"

I laugh and add another finger. "It really doesn't bother me."

Our eyes lock. Trust and love replace any misgivings she might have. Zoey nods and shifts in my lap so she can reach down and free my cock from its tortuous prison inside my jeans. She hikes her dress up, straddles me, and sinks down on top of my dick. Her arms wind around my neck. I grip her hips tightly. Our mouths fuse together and I rock her back and forth gently against me. Slowly we generate an intense friction. A rolling buildup that erupts in a gentle but explosive release for both of us.

Afterward, I carry her back to the master where we shower and clean up. We change and spend the early evening in cozy track suits. Wrapped around each other in front of the fire in our bedroom. Watching some sort of true crime series about the Night Stalker on Netflix.

I'm so content. I feel so good.

What a perfect day.

I have a perfect life.

That's what I'm thinking when a phone rings in the kitchen. *Fuck.* It's my bat phone. A special mobile device I keep solely for emergencies. Only six people in the world have the number. The guys. Katherine, our manager. Sergey, my head of security. And now Zoey.

The only other time I've ever heard it ring was over a year ago when Sergey called to let me know Zoey had been hit by a taxi in New York.

Dread fills my gut. Zoey and I sprint to the kitchen. "Hello?" I manage to answer before it goes to voice-mail.

I put it on speaker. A voice I'm not expecting fills the room. "Ty, it's Katherine. I'm afraid I have some upsetting news..."

Zoey instantly wraps her hands around my bicep and rests her head against my shoulder. Protectively. Our manager's voice sounds far, far away, almost like she's in a bubble. I listen to her speak. Try to comprehend the words.

It's startling news.

But, not all that unexpected. In many ways, I've been waiting for this call my entire life.

My mother was found a few hours ago in an alley in Pioneer Square. She's been beaten so badly she's on life support at Harborview Hospital. Odds are, she's not going to make it to the morning.

I slump onto a barstool at the counter.

Jada strikes again.

Her timing is always perfect.

Perfectly fucked.

Chapter Seven

I CLING TO TY'S hand and try to keep up with his long strides through the hospital corridor. Sergey follows close behind, although tonight his presence doesn't seem necessary.

No one seems to notice Seattle's most famous rock star is in the building, thank God. Probably because we're both still in our sweats. Ty's hair is tucked up under a black beanie. Mine is in a knot on top of my head. We look like anyone else who is at the hospital for an emergency.

We're heading toward the ICU, where Ty's mother is on life support. I'm not sure what to expect. No one close to me has ever died, and it doesn't sound like Jada is going to make it.

A doctor is waiting for us when we arrive. "Mr. Rainier? I'm Dr. Reginald Kwandu. Right this way."

"Is she going to make it?" Ty asks as we follow him past the nurses station, his voice devoid of emotion.

"You should be prepared for the worst." Dr. Kwandu hurries along the hallway and looks at us over his shoulder. "We may not have much time."

He stops in front of a room and gestures for Ty to go inside. I hold back, completely unsure of what to do. I watch him approach a bed where an emaciated woman with black-and-gray streaked hair is hooked up to about a million tubes. Her face is black and purple. One of her arms is exposed, connected to some monitors. It's bandaged from her wrist to her shoulder.

Glancing around, the entire room is filled with beeping and blaring machines. Colorful monitors surround her bed. A strange hum emanates from the overhead light. Ty moves toward the bed and stares down at her. Then looks around at all of the equipment she's hooked up to and glances back at me.

Even though he's keeping his cool, something flickers in his eyes before he shuts it down and regains a steely resolve.

I'm out of my depth. It's surreal standing here in the ICU waiting for a woman I've never met—who was a horrible mother to my fiancé—take her last breath. To say the least. Ty's energy is so hard to read, I feel myself start to panic a bit. I manage to suck it up and tamp down my feelings. Right now, he needs me and I'll be here for him. I reach down and enclose his big hand with both of mine and squeeze. He doesn't react. He just stares down at his mother lying in the bed, being kept alive by machines.

I summon the courage to look more closely at Jada, a woman I've never laid eyes on until now. It's startling. She barely looks human. That's how badly she's been beaten.

Before I can stop myself, I burst into tears.

"Don't you dare fucking cry for her, Z." Ty's cold voice startles me. "This is no surprise. She finally got what she deserves."

Shocked, I look back at Dr. Kwandu. He studies a clipboard, not paying attention to us. Or, he's politely ignoring Ty's outburst. Either way, I suppose he's seen it all as an ICU doctor. Or, at the very least, he doesn't get too invested in the myriad of family reactions he must witness every day.

"Ty, I know she's not been a good influence in your life, but she *is* your mother." I try to keep my voice quiet so I don't draw attention to us. "It's got to hurt to see her like this."

Ty drops my hand. His face devoid of emotion, but his voice is brutally angry. "Do you want me to sugarcoat it, or do you want me to be honest, Zoey?"

I try to covertly put my finger to my lips to warn him to keep his voice down. Even though I don't think anyone recognizes us yet and Sergey is close by, I'm always hypervigilant. There could be people listening and even filming us right now for all we know.

Ty ignores me and continues his rant.

"You have no idea what this woman put me though." He turns back to Jada. "Do you hear that, *Mom*? You were never a fucking mother to me. You're a worthless piece of shit. I *hope* you're suffering. You made me suffer every day of my life and all I've ever wanted was to be free of you. So I *hope* you die. Leave me in fucking peace. The world will be a better place without you in it."

Never, ever, ever have I heard Ty speak with such a cold, cruel tone in my life. Inadvertently, I shiver. Chills are not only running down my spine, but along my shoulders and up my neck. I know everyone processes shock differently, but something tells me that what Ty just said are the most honest words he's ever spoken.

"Excuse me, Mr. Rainier, I truly don't mean to interrupt, please meet Sarine Diaz, your caseworker. She'll stay with you and go over a few things." Dr. Kwandu gestures to a middle-aged woman with dark-brown hair.

She steps forward and Dr. Kwandu departs. "Pleased to meet you, Mr. Rainier."

"Look, um, Ms. Diaz?" Ty fixes her with a look I've only seen him use when he's in full rockstar mode. "For me, this is not a sad situation. I apologize if this is going to come out harshly, but the only reason I'm here is to burn this image of her in my mind. I'm not going to hold her hand. I'm not going to give her comfort. She gave birth to me, but other than that she's already dead to me."

Tears stream down my face. Not for Jada.

For Ty.

My heart is breaking. Although I've always suspected there was more to his story than what he's been willing to share. Somehow, his reaction right now brings it all to light. What horror must he have lived through if he can't muster up even an ounce of empathy for his own mother. Lying here beaten. Dying.

What did Jada do to him?

Ms. Diaz doesn't visibly react. Instead she gestures to Jada and carries on with business. "Your mother suffered blunt-force trauma to her face and skull. It appears that she has other broken bones, although we haven't done x-rays yet. Her bloodwork has been sent out for a toxicology report. We suspect she's been using."

"Big fucking surprise," Ty snarls.

Ms. Diaz continues, "Her organs are shutting down. These machines are keeping her alive."

"Why not unplug them?" Ty's face is granite.

"We have to complete protocol, Mr. Rainier. It won't be long now." Ms. Diaz's voice is compassionate, non-judgmental. "I'll leave the two of you to...uh, process. I'll be at the nurse's station if you have any questions."

When she leaves, I pull Ty into my body and wrap my arms around him. "Are you okay?"

"I've been expecting this day for thirty years," he mutters into my ear.

What do I do? *What?* "Babe...no matter what happened to you as a kid, you deserved so much more."

I cling to him. Hoping to fill him with comfort. He tightens his arms around me after a bit. We hold each other at the foot of Jada's bed. Suddenly, a flashing blue light startles us apart. An alarm blares. The monitor his mother is hooked up to flatlines. A swarm of medical staff flood the room and push past us to surround Ty's mom. Someone pulls out paddles and shocks her. Jada's body jerks. The monitor is still indicating flatline. The process repeats about a half a dozen times. Ty and I just stare. It doesn't feel real. It's more like we're extras in an episode of *Grey's Anatomy*.

In slow motion, the doctors and nurses step away from Jada's bed. I look up at Ty. He stares at his mother's lifeless body.

"Call. Time of death. 11:49," I hear someone say. Ty's handsome face is still devoid of emotion. His blue eyes are dull. All of the anger is just...gone.

Replaced with— I don't even know. Emptiness?

Soon after, we're ushered out of the room to the waiting area. We sit, side by side, silently. I reach for Ty's hand. He lets me take it, but it's flaccid. Unresponsive.

At some point, Ms. Diaz approaches us. "Mr. Rainier, I have a few things to go over. I'll bring you to your mother first, though."

I follow them back into the same room where Jada died. Now she lies free of all the tubes and monitors. A blanket covers her lower body. Her hands are folded over her stomach.. Her bruised face looks strangely at peace.

Like her soul is free.

Like her demons are gone.

I can't stop more tears from falling. Because her son is not free. He has his own demons. Somehow, I understand that now.

"Ah, babe. Don't cry." Ty's arm snakes around my shoulder. "I know this is a lot. If you want, I can get Sergey to take you home and I'll finish up here."

Leave it to Ty. His default is taking care of me when he's lost his only blood family member. "I'm just overwhelmed, not for me. For you. I just want to make it better."

He sighs heavily. Leans his head against mine. "It *is* better. I don't have to live my life waiting for this moment ever again."

"Do you want to talk?"

"Um...no. Not now, butterfly."

I lace my fingers through his hand that rests over my shoulder. He squeezes. Leans his head back and closes his eyes. His long, brown hair cascades down his shoulders. Dark stubble dusts his chiseled jawline. He's the most beautiful man on the planet, inside and out. My heart breaks for him. For the loss. Not so much the loss of his mother, but the loss of his childhood. The loss of so much...else.

He never had what I had. Support. Unconditional love. Basic needs being met. I never fully comprehended what that meant. Ty's reaction today has put things in perspective for me. I vow to be there for him, no matter what he needs. He may not have his own family, but he has me now. I'm his family and I'm never leaving him. I'll never let him feel unloved and unwanted again.

"We can leave, babe." I stretch up to kiss his cheek. "Or we can stay. Whatever you want to do, I have your back."

Ty's eyes blink open, his expression unreadable. "I think it's best if I just get this over with. I don't want this to interfere with our wedding, Z."

"Sure." The thought hadn't even crossed my mind. We have a funeral to plan now too. "If it eases any stress, we can postpone a couple of weeks, I'm fine with that. We'll need to have a service for your mom at least, right?"

Ty looks at me as if I have two heads. "Fuck no. Who would I even invite? Her drug dealer? I'll have her cremated and that will be that."

"Oh. Right." I nod. "Then you and I can do something nice to send her off."

Ty yanks his hand from mine. "Zoey, you have no idea. None. And I'm *glad* you don't. We're not doing anything for Jada. I'll figure out if I have any legal obligations. Other than that, this chapter of my life is finally fucking over. You don't have to make everything nice. Not everything *is* nice. Really. I'm fine. This day has been coming forever."

Fuck. I don't know what to say. I fold my arms across my chest and look down at the floor. I've upset him. I didn't mean to.

Ty moves in front of me and unfurls my arms. He intertwines his fingers with mine. "Oh, Z. I'm sorry. I really didn't mean to snap at you. You're doing and saying all the right things. This is just..."

"A lot," I finish.

"Yeah."

"It's okay. I love you, I'm not going anywhere." I pull him down to me and press my lips against his.

He shuts his eyes and touches his forehead to mine. "Thank God, butterfly."

We remain that way until Ms. Diaz approaches a few minutes later. "Mr. Rainier? I'm ready for you."

I sit beside Ty as he signs different documents. Makes a few decisions related to the cremation and is presented with a plastic bag full of Jada's dirty, foul-smelling clothes. As we leave the hospital, Ty chucks the bag in the trash before we get to the car. Somehow, I don't think discarding her personal items will provide him with the closure he needs.

For now, I'll just follow his lead.

And hope he doesn't fall apart.

But if he does, I'll be here to put him back together.

Chapter Eight

I'M CLIMBING THE FUCKING walls.

Zoey's been gone all day and she'll be gone most of the night. She has her final wedding dress fitting, then dinner and a girl's night out with all the other women. Sort of like her bachelorette party, I suppose.

It's fine. She deserves some fun.

Something a little more celebratory than her future mother-in-law dying of an overdose. Or a beating. Or both. Something a little more upbeat than me brooding around the house, trying to pretend things are okay.

It's not like Zoey could be a better partner to me. That would be impossible. She's handled the situation perfectly. She never pressures me to talk. She's supportive of my desire to close this chapter and move the fuck on with my life. Because that's all I want to do. Forget the past and embrace the future.

Or some shit.

Tonight, however, I sit in the house alone. Thinking. Which isn't necessarily a good thing. When I'm by myself, the anger I feel toward Jada threatens to bubble over. Which is the last thing I want before my wedding. To prevent myself from erupting, I've been a breathing-exercise, treadmill-running, weightlifting maniac. Thank God I have a state-of-the art gym in my house. It's helping. Kinda.

I really should call Lisa, but I know she's going to tell me things I don't want to hear. I'm not sure I can handle her disappointment in me on top of everything else right now.

Another day of struggling to keep my shit together.

Tomorrow, I pick up Jada's ashes. I don't really want them, but no one else does either. I'm her only relative, which makes me the lucky asshole who has no choice but to take responsibility. I mean, it's ridiculous. What the fuck am I going to do with them? There's no way they're going up on the mantel. Not that I have a mantel. My fireplace is modern. Made of rolled steel.

Jesus. I'm losing it. Who cares what my fireplace is made of?

I decide to find another productive distraction and head downstairs to the practice room. Glancing around, I spot my treasured Breedlove and decide to get blessedly lost in music. I'm down in my cave for hours making up riffs. Trying out lyrics. So, I nearly jump out of my skin when the door opens and Zane walks in. "Jesus fucking Christ, dude. I've been calling you for the past two hours. Can't you pick up the damn phone?"

"You just scared the shit outta me!" I put down my guitar. "Is something wrong?"

"Um, is there something you want to tell me?" Zane sits on an amp and crosses his arms. Fixes me with a pointed look.

I'm drawing a blank. "Uh?"

Before I know it, Zane has me crushed in a hug. "I'm so sorry about your mom. What can I do?"

I allow the hug to continue for another few seconds before disengaging and picking my guitar back up as a shield. "Let me guess, Zoey told Fee and..."

"Fucking right she did." Zane paces. "This is a big deal, Ty. You should have let me—us—know."

Shit. That means Connor and Jace are probably on their way. Part of me is relieved not to be alone with my thoughts. The other part doesn't want to deal with the people closest to me giving me sympathy.

"When are they getting here?" I strum a few chords and give Zane my most withering glare.

"We're already here, douchebag." Jace enters the room with Connor close behind. "How are you holding up?"

My bandmates line up in a row across from me. Each of them looking at me like concerned parents. Not that I'd actually fucking know what a concerned parent looks like. "I'm fine. It was inevitable. I'm mostly pissed I have to deal with it right before the wedding."

"I'm surprised you didn't postpone." Connor walks over to my laptop and hits stop on the recording. "We all would have understood, you know."

Connor and Jace know even less about my mom than Zane and Zoey do. I guess I understand why they're all worried about me. I mean, I'd feel the same way if one of their parents died. I just don't want to get into it right now.

Or ever.

"My brothers. Listen to me when I say my mother wasn't cut out to be a parent. She didn't behave like one when I was a kid. All she wanted from me as an adult was money. Her death is actually a relief. I'll never have to worry about her selling me out again."

Silence permeates the room. I'm sure my words seem harsh. But my life is what it is.

Jace nods. "Okay. Got it."

"Ty, we're sorry. I know it's a sore spot, we won't bring it up again." Zane reaches over and plucks my guitar from me. "Changing the subject. You need to go upstairs and get out of the sweats. *Stat*. The four of us are going for dinner. You may not want a bachelor party, but you can at least have a celebratory meal with your band brothers."

This sounds like a public-spectacle nightmare. "Uh, the four of us out at a restaurant? Really?"

"Fuck, dude, what do you take me for? We've got shit handled. You're getting married the day after tomorrow.

Let's go and have a low-key night together. We're not taking no for an answer." Zane shakes his head at me like I'm a naughty schoolboy.

My heart suddenly fills with warmth. I didn't know I needed this, but now that it's being offered, I gladly dash upstairs and change. We pile into Connor's Range Rover. Twenty minutes later the four of us pull up to the new Mission.

"Surprise!" Zane, who is sitting next to me in the back seat, elbows me. "Fiona and her team are cooking us a pre-wedding feast!"

I'm blown away. Zane leads the way into the new restaurant space adjacent to the club. It's far from finished, but what's done is incredible. The sleek, modern reception area has long, plush velvet sofas in rich cream and charcoal gray. Just beyond, a stunning crystal light fixture hangs above a twelve-seat, U-shaped dining table facing a high-tech open kitchen.

I can't help but gawk.

"Want a tour?" Fiona steps out from the ginormous walk-in cooler. Her hair is slicked back under a white scarf. Zane bops over to her side and smiles proudly.

"Fuck yeah." Jace looks around wide-eyed. "This is gorgeous."

Fiona leads us through all of the culinary stations. Sauce. Meat. Fish. Garnish. Vegetable. Appetizer. Dessert. The floor-to-ceiling wine room, which is a construction staging area right now. The restaurant is going to be like nothing Seattle has ever seen.

"When I was a line cook at the bistro, I worked in some bad-ass kitchens, but this is unbelievable, Fee." I give her a big hug. "If you ever need a guest chef, I'm not worthy but I'd love to cook here."

Fiona laughs. "Are you kidding, Ty? I might hold you to that. We've spent so much money on this place, I'll need to sell out two seatings for an entire year just to break even."

"Somehow, I don't think that's going to be a problem." I drag my finger on the marble countertop and smile at her.

We're interrupted by the sound of squeals and giggles. To my utter delight, Zoey, Alex, and Ronni have arrived and join us in the dining room.

Zoey, looking luscious in a low-cut black jumpsuit, launches herself into my arms. "Were you surprised?

I've tried so hard to keep this secret. Did you suspect something was up?"

"Not at all, butterfly." I wrap my arms around her. "This is awesome!"

"I'm sorry about your mom, Ty." Ronni grips my shoulder and Connor doesn't even wince. We've come a long way since I fake-dated his wife for publicity purposes and he nearly tore my head off every time I escorted her to a red-carpet event.

"Everyone, seriously. I'm fine. It was a long time coming. If you don't mind, I'd rather focus on the most important thing in my life. I'm finally marrying the most amazing woman in the world." I bend down and kiss Zoey. Not just any kiss, a scorcher.

When we come up for air, Alex, Fee, and Ronni all flutter their hands in front of their faces, mocking us. Zane roars. Jace whistles, looking all around the room but at us. Connor shakes his head and mutters, "Get a feckin' room."

Fee and her sous chefs put on an amazing eleven-course feast. We spend hours eating, drinking mocktails, visiting and enjoying one another's company. With absolutely no pressure. It's glorious. After dinner, we hang out in the lounge. Zoey and Alex are deep in what looks to be a serious conversation. Fee sits on Zane's lap, chatting with Ronni. Connor is content just listening but looks half-asleep. Jace tells me about an online accreditation program he's working on to get certified in equine therapy.

In other words, we've all taken a year off from the band, but our lives are fuller and more enriched.

Eventually, the night winds down. Zoey and I snuggle in the back seat of my car as Sergey drives us home. She rests her hand on my thigh. "Sitting back here with you on the way home from the new Mission is kinda like déjà vu. It reminds me of when I first met you and you shocked the hell out of me by jumping in my Uber."

"Best decision of my life." I stroke her shoulder and think back to that night. When I saw her in the crowd from the stage, something intuitive told me she would change my life.

I wasn't wrong.

Not by a long shot. I've got to remember this when I'm having self-doubt. My life with Zoey is worth everything I've ever suffered.

The second we're back at the house, I lead her straight to bed. Wordlessly, we kick off our shoes and strip off our clothes. "I love you so fucking much," I whisper, suckling on the spot behind her ear that drives her insane. "I can't wait for you to be my wife."

Zoey moans, "Ty, I don't think you have any idea how much you mean to me. How much I love you. I will never stop loving you."

I will never get tired of Zoey expressing her love. Telling me. Showing me. I crave it. How is it possible to have feelings this intense for another person? *How?*

After we make love, as we lay wrapped in each other, spent, I have a bit of an epiphany. Now that Jada's gone for good, maybe I won't carry that constant acidic worry around. She's not coming back. She can't hurt me anymore. There won't be a tell-all. Or more television interviews. She can't make up stories to sell to the press. Or worse, tell the truth.

I'm really and truly free of her.

Free to live a normal life with Zoey. Free to bury the past where it belongs. Free to purge myself of bad memories. Hopefully, one day soon, free to be a good parent to our kids.

Our kids.

Wow.

Maybe we just made a baby tonight.

"One more day, Ty." Zoey twirls a lock of my hair around her finger as she loves to do. "Then you're mine forever."

I pepper her face with little kisses. "I'm already yours forever, but I can't wait to make it official."

"Doesn't it feel good to know nothing will ever come between us again?" Zoey turns in my arms and blinks up at me. "After everything we've been through."

Like many times before, this could be an opportune time to tell her. Just drop my diagnosis into conversation like it's not a big thing. Like it's all under control because it is.

It *is*.

"Of course, nothing will *ever* come between us again," I say instead.

Just fucking tell her.

Zoey tilts her head up and kisses me. "Oh. My. God. Ty. We are getting *married*."

"We are." I swallow down my nerves and press forward. "Butterfly, I've been meaning to, um, tell you something.

Um. I don't want you to be worried because I've got it handled..."

She scrunches her nose. "Are you *cheating* on me?"

"*No!* I'd never..." I pull back from her in horror.

Zoey drags me back to her and plants another kiss on my lips. "Oh, babe. I'm sorry. I know you wouldn't do that. I was kidding. It wasn't funny."

My heartbeat subsides a bit as I settle back into her kisses.

"Do you have secret children?" she mumbles against my lips.

Now I'm onto her game. "Yep, that's it. I confess, I have at least a dozen kids scattered all over the world. That I know of."

Zoey swats me. Pouts dramatically. I boop her nose. She giggles and rolls over on her back. "Seriously, Ty. I trust you. If you want to tell me something you can. There's nothing that you could ever say or do that would change us."

Well...

"It's actually not *that* big of a deal."

"We don't need to do some big confessional right before we get married, Ty. What's in the past is in the past.

Getting married and raising our family is our future."
She nestles against me. "If you promise me it's no big
deal, then let it go. Let's leave all of the old crap in the
rearview mirror."

Thank fuck. You're off the hook.

"Okay. I promise it's not a big deal, baby." I close my
eyes and rest my head against hers.

Saying the words fills my stomach with acid.

Because I know my promise is a lie.

The thing is?

I'm willing to take the risk. All I need to do is turn it
into the truth without Zoey ever finding out.

Chapter Nine

THE DAY I'VE BEEN waiting for forever has finally arrived. I can honestly say, I've never been so sure about something in my entire life. It's eight a.m., I've been up for two hours. Sitting at the kitchen counter at my parents' house, trying not to drink too much coffee. The sky is beginning to brighten to a clear, crisp blue. It's not going to rain. Imagine, a November outdoor wedding in Seattle where the weather actually cooperates. I can't help but giggle.

Although, I am getting impatient waiting for my mom and dad to get up. It was my idea to spend the night at my childhood home. A little superstition about not seeing Ty on the morning of our wedding. Not that we haven't been texting all morning. He couldn't sleep either.

"Darling, why are you up so friggin' early?" Mom shuffles into the kitchen bleary-eyed. She pours herself a cup of coffee.

I pull my LTZ sweatshirt over my knees and shrug. "I'm too excited. I couldn't sleep."

"What time is Ty heading over to Zane's house?" She yawns. "I thought we'd leave here around one."

I nod. "That's fine."

"Hello, my precious girls." My dad is decidedly more awake as he makes his own coffee.

My parents give each other a look. Mom walks over to the cabinet above the desk and pulls out a small box. "Zoey, your dad and I have been saving this to give you on your wedding day. I hope you like it."

I take the box and open it. It's a beautiful antique diamond bracelet with intricate filigree. "Mom! This was grandma's. I've only seen you wear it on special occasions."

"When your dad and I got married his mother gave this to me and made me promise I'd pass it on to you when it was your time." My mom and dad surround me and I'm enveloped in hugs. "It's yours now. Years from now, you'll give it to your daughter or your daughter-in-law and the tradition will continue."

It's impossible not to cry. I love my parents so much. "Thank you. This is so precious. I love it."

"Let me put it on you." I turn and my dad clasps the bracelet around my wrist.

It's stunning. Subtle. Classy. I twist my forearm around to watch it sparkle. "Will you guys keep it for me until I'm dressed?"

"Of course, honey." Mom side hugs me. "Why don't we all go out for breakfast? It's going to be a long time before you eat again, so let's make sure you don't faint from hunger at your wedding."

I pick at my Buddha Bowl at Portage Bay Café when Ty texts me letting me know he's going over to Zane's earlier than planned. "*In case you want to get home to your own house to get ready."* Leave it to him to know I'm dying to be home. I send him a long string of heart and kiss emojis.

We finish breakfast and go back to my parents' house so Mom can quickly gather her clothes. An hour later, she and I walk into chaos. Caterers are setting up in the kitchen. Florists are putting together elaborate arrangements. A team of workers are outside constructing a pergola and stringing lights so we can get married against the backdrop of the Seattle skyline. Mom sees something that is not to her liking and dashes out into the yard.

Better her than me.

"Holy fuck, this is really happening." Jace walks in holding his darling towheaded daughter, Helena. I hug them hello just as Alex rushes in with her garment bag and a huge duffel bag.

I squcal and lurch myself at by best friend. "OMG! Can you believe this?"

"Of course, I can. I'm so psyched for today!" She cocks her head. "I've got champagne. I know you don't drink much because of Ty, but I thought you might like to have a little toast with the girls when they get here."

I sigh happily. "Yes. I'd love that."

Alex sends her family over to Zane's house and together we bring everything up to my bedroom. When I open the door, my breath is taken away. Hanging on the door to my walk-in closet is my wedding gown and veil.

"Oh!" I clap my hands to my mouth. "Wow."

"It's beautiful." Alex runs her hand down the silky ivory fabric. Immediately we clasp hands and squeal. Jump up and down like we're teenagers.

"Holy shit. Do you believe I'm marrying Tyson Rainier?" I'm beyond giddy, reverting into my seventeen-year-old self when Alex and I first saw LTZ live. "You're the only person who understands how monumental this is!"

Alex throws her arms around me. "Whooda thunk we'd bag the rock stars?"

"And keep them!" I twirl around my bedroom. Alex joins me. That's when I spot a card propped up on my nightstand. My breath hitches in terror for a second, remembering the note I left Ty to break up with him all those years ago. I push the fleeting thought out of my mind, rush over and rip it open.

Butterfly,

Don't worry, this is a good nightstand note.

The next time I see you, it will be minutes before you walk up the aisle to marry me. For the record, I hated waking up without you this morning. It's never happening again, I can't sleep without you in my arms.

Okay. That's cleared up.

Here's what I really want to say. I'm stalling because this is probably the most honest I've ever been. Here goes.

Meeting you changed my life.

Up until that day, I didn't think I was worthy of having love.

I wasn't sure if I was capable of loving someone.

I certainly didn't know what it was like to be loved by someone.

You opened up my eyes to all of these possibilities. Now I know exactly what it's like to love and be loved. Of course, you're not just someone, you are the most precious, beautiful, intelligent, giving, honest, trustworthy, sexy woman on the planet.

You're my butterfly.

And I will spend the rest of my life proving that I'm worthy of you. And the family we'll have someday soon.

I love you. I love you. I love you.

—Your soon to be husband, Ty

I clutch the note to my chest, sink down on the bed and bawl like a baby. What did I ever do to deserve the love of someone as kind, sensitive, and amazing as my Ty?

Alex sits next to me. "Is it a good note?"

"The best note." I nod vigorously. "I am literally bursting with happiness."

"Is it okay to come in?" Ronni peeps her head in the door.

I wave her in. "Of course. Be forewarned, I'm bawling my eyes out because Ty left me a beautiful note."

"Of course, he did. He's such a keeper." Ronni's dazzling smile lights up the room. "Fiona wanted me to tell you that she's going to get ready at her own house. Wrangling Mia and Lena into their flower girl outfits has proved to be a bit challenging. I left the twins with Connor and his family. I'm so happy to be *fuh-ree*. Give me a glass of that champagne."

Alex taps her finger on her chin. "Do you think I should I go help Fiona?”

“Don't be silly.” Mom walks in. “You're where you belong today. Jace is over there, he'll be fine."

I quickly send Ty a text telling him how much I loved my note. Then, we pop the champagne. The five of us spend the afternoon getting manicures and pedicures. We tell Ronni stories of the early days of LTZ. How Ty and I couldn't bear to be apart and drove the guys crazy with our PDAs. How Alex couldn't get Jace to give her a second glance. Ronni shares stories of how mad Connor used to get when she was fake dating Ty. We howl with laughter until it's time to get ready.

“What a beautiful bracelet.” Alex strokes my wrist after mom clasps my “something old” back in place. She reaches in her bag and pulls out an exquisite strapless bodysuit in ice-blue sheer tulle. It's detailed with smooth panels of embroidered lace.

I hold the lingerie up and hug my best friend. “This will be perfect under my gown.”

“Duh. And it's both new and blue.” Alex hip checks me.

“Here's my contribution.” Ronni hands me a black jewelry box. “Something borrowed.”

I open the box to find an absolute piece of art from Piaget. A dainty necklace of hundreds of glittering marquise-cut diamonds, in the shape of a rose. Easily worth tens of thousands of dollars. "Oh, Ronni. This is too much..."

"Stop, Zoey." Ronni laughs. "You're only borrowing it. Connor and I are really happy for you both. I thought this would be perfect for your dress."

Ronni is the next recipient of a ginormous hug. "It's beautiful. Thank you."

Mom looks at her watch. "Okay, we have old, new, borrowed and blue. Time to get you ready."

Hair and makeup show up. I've decided to keep my look very simple, with a slightsmoky eye. I'm wearing my hair loose because I know Ty loves it that way. It's going to be a bit more refined tonight, with two small loose braids secured at my nape where my veil will attach.

Ronni and Alex change into their champagne-colored bridal dresses. Alex's gown is body skimming with a high collar and balloon sleeves. It looks conservative until she turns around. The back plunges all the way down to her ass, revealing her toned back. Her shoes are Jimmy

Choo Saresa pointed-toe glitter pumps with a horseshoe crystal buckle.

Ronni's dress is a sophisticated, off-the-shoulder, mermaid satin number, stopping just above her ankles. She's wearing nude Louboutin Pumpaclou stiletto sandals, with a rivet-embellished ankle strap.

Mom emerges from my closet in her shimmery sheath dress holding a shoe box. "Ty told me where to find these. He said you don't have to wear them if they hurt your feet, but he had these made for you."

Yet again, my husband-to-be has gone out of his way to make our day special. I open the box to see a custom pair of handmade white René Caovilla stiletto sandals. I trace my finger along the toe band and up the strap that will wind around my ankle and up my calf. It's covered in micro-rhinestones and dainty butterfly appliques.

They're the most beautiful pair of shoes I've ever seen. I don't care how sore my feet are, I'm wearing these to my wedding.

Alex helps me into my bodysuit. Then my gown, which is a simple, silk body-hugging sheath with delicately lowered shoulders that twist around my décolletage. Mom secures the removable skirt with a long train to my waist.

Worn together, you can't even tell it's two pieces. My veil is simple with a thin lace edge. It attaches to the braids at my nape with a diamond butterfly clip.

Mom turns me around to look in the mirror and I gasp. Honestly, I never thought much about my own wedding until Ty asked me to marry him last Christmas Eve. I've been so happy to be in the moment with him, planning our wedding wasn't even on my mind until the past few weeks. I'm so glad I didn't waste all year on stupid bridezilla shit. Or spend time planning a big event where we'd have to worry about security and paparazzi.

Because our wedding is going to be perfect.

It's all come together just as it was supposed to. Everything Ty and I have been through to have our happily ever after was worth it. The good times. The pain. The separation. Our reunion. Even my accident. It's all led us here.

Two tiny dynamos burst through the door in light-pink princess dresses. Fiona follows, in a knee-length pale-champagne skater dress and flat satin slides. "I'm sorry, the little heathens couldn't wait to see you."

I crouch down to embrace Helena and Mia, the most darling flower girls on the planet. "Can I get a kiss?"

"Mama says I'm not supposed to mess up your make-up." Mia sways back and forth with her hands behind her back. Long, dark hair held back by a butterfly clip that matches mine. Lena stands next her, shyly mimicking Mia in her little white Mary-Janes. Her light-blonde hair is braided, and she also has a matching butterfly hair piece. The girls are beautiful. Just like their mothers.

"I don't mind, kisses are better than perfect makeup." I smile as I gather both girls to me, they kiss my cheeks.

Alex picks up Helena and takes my hand. "Z, are you ready? It's time, but I think you should come take a peek out the window."

My mom pushes the curtain on the floor-to-ceiling window overlooking our back garden. We all crowd together to get a peek of the scene. Carter, Ty, and my dad are standing at the altar in a three-way embrace.

They break apart, and my heart swells when my dad pulls Ty back into his arms. He cups Ty's head and whispers something in his ear. Ty nods and grips Dad's elbows. They have what looks to be a very special moment.

"Let's go, sweetheart." Mom kisses my forehead. "For the record, you're the most beautiful bride the world has ever seen. I'd say that even if you weren't my daughter. Let's get you married."

The six of us leave the room and find Jace, Connor, and Zane waiting for us at the sliding glass door. All looking so handsome in their suits. My ladies join their men and get ready to walk down the aisle.

Dad appears at the door and his eyes well up when he sees me. "You take my breath away, Zoey."

"I saw you and Ty through the window, what did you say?" I take his arm and watch the couples walk toward the altar to assume their positions. Ty shuffles back and forth on his feet, looking nervous.

Dad pats my hand. "Some things are between a father and his son-in-law."

We step onto the path lined with roses. When Ty spots me, he clutches his heart. Wipes tears from the corners of his eyes with his thumbs. Zane claps him on the shoulder, grinning from ear to ear.

I take the first step toward him.

All I can think is, *this man will never have to prove anything to me.*

There is no one on this planet more worthy of my love.

With my heart overflowing, I walk down the aisle toward my future.

Chapter Ten

IT'S ALL I CAN do not to faint when I watch Mike Pearson lead Zoey to the edge of the patio. My butterfly is absolutely breathtaking. Angelic. She leans up and kisses her dad on the cheek. He helps her arrange her dress, and she takes his arm.

Then she looks up and looks directly into my eyes. *Mine.*

Her radiant smile spreads across her face. I've never seen her so happy. So sure of herself. In this moment, I know, without any shadow of a doubt, that my purpose in life is to make sure she never loses that smile.

She floats toward me, and I'm smiling through happy tears. We've finally made it here. As she gets closer, I can't help but reach out my hand to her. Mike swats it away good-naturedly and everyone laughs, including Zoey.

Carter, who was Internet-ordained specifically to marry us, proudly presides over our ceremony. It's fitting, considering he not only was instrumental in breaking us up, but maneuvering it so we'd get back together. He's a man with many regrets, fuck-ups and foibles, but he's the closest thing I have to a father.

And I love him, for all his flaws.

Everything else falls away when Zoey and I say our vows. My eyes never leave hers and we clutch each other's hands tightly. We exchange our rings and just like that, she's my wife. I'm her husband. Our kiss sealing the deal is scorching. So scorching, everyone hoots and whistles. The second we break apart, our closest friends and family surround us in one giant hug. I truly can't recall ever feeling so completely comfortable in the moment at hand.

So this is what true peace feels like.

I like it.

Zoey and I split up to chat with our guests, huddled around heaters scattered throughout the backyard. Fascinated, I watch Zoey interact with the little girls, Lena and Mia. The two of them are in awe of my bride, petting her hair and rubbing their little hands all over her gown. Zoey cuddles them to her and giggles. Smooches their cheeks. I can't help but picture her with our children.

"You have no idea how proud I am of you." Carter snaps me out of my daydream, patting my back. I wrap my arm around his shoulder. He cleans up pretty well, in a smart black suit with his hair tied back in a leather string. "I've watched you grow up, Ty. You've overcome a lot to become a man of strength and conviction. To have a woman love you as much as Zoey has loved you for all these years? It's fucking rare."

I squeeze Carter's shoulder. "Not so rare in our group. We've all done pretty well. I'm just grateful I ever met her."

"I am too, I'm so sorry..." Carter's voice is wistful.

Nope. We're not going there tonight. Carter's interference with Zoey and me is in the past. I deftly cut him off and change the subject. "Where's Lianne tonight?"

"London." He nods. Sadly. "For a couple of months."

"You know, there's nothing keeping you from being with her." I cock my head and squint at him.

He gets a faraway look in his eyes before he shrugs and smiles. Doesn't answer me. I worry about him. In so many ways, Carter and I are a lot alike. Shockingly so. I probably would have ended up like him—heartbroken and alone forever— if Carter hadn't righted his wrong when it came to how he broke Zoey and me apart. His redemption story on overcoming a decades-long addiction has been such a great inspiration to me.

We're interrupted by Mia, who wraps her arms around Carter's legs and tugs at his sleeve. "Grampa, I love you."

Such perfect timing. Carter gazes down at her like she's his whole world. "Ah, my little Mia. I love you to the moon."

Meanwhile, Zoey returns to my side. We put our arms around each other and survey the scene. Connor and Ronni each hold one of their adorable infant twin boys. Jace picks up Helena and brings her over to Alex. Zoey's parents, Mike and Olivia, are talking to Zane and Fiona. Man, we are so lucky to have these amazing people around us.

Focusing my attention on my new wife, I steal a few little kisses. Zoey whispers against my lips, "I already love being Mrs. Rainier."

"God, I love that too." I touch my forehead to hers. "You've made me the happiest man, Z."

"Mr. and Mrs. Rainier, shall we take your guests into the dining room?" The head caterer gestures to the house.

Zoey elbows me and whispers with glee, "Didja hear that? We're *Mr. and Mrs. Rainier.*"

"Don't you ever forget it." I clasp Zoey's small hand in mine and follow the caterer. I'm actually relieved to get inside the house. As fortunate as we have been to have good weather, it's Seattle. In early November. It's fucking cold. I haven't eaten all day because of the nerves, so I'm also fucking hungry.

The little group of us herd into the house and sit around the dining room table that Zoey and I have only used one other time. Our engagement dinner. The caterers have decorated it beautifully in soft white and the pinky-tan color of the bridesmaid's dresses. We sit at the head of the table and everyone takes their seats around us.

After a delicious meal catered by our favorite restaurant, Altura, Zane stands and pings his spoon on his water glass. "Brothers, sisters, parents and awesome kids, it is time for the toasts. Each one of us will take a turn to tell Ty and Zoey—who have sickened us with their all-consuming love for a decade—how glad we are that they are finally fucking *married*."

Everyone laughs when I mutter, "fuckwad" under my breath.

"I, Zane, said *fuckwad*, will go last." Zane spreads his arms wide, and before he can say a word, Helena claps her hands excitedly and yells, "Fut-wat."

Mia scowls at her. "It's not Fut-wat. It's fuck-wad, Lena."

The entire table erupts in laughter. None of us can contain ourselves for a good few minutes.

"Jesus, man. You're corrupting my kid." Jace leans back and cocks an eyebrow when he recovers.

Alex swats him. "Pot calling kettle."

More laughter ensues.

Zane waves everyone off with a flourish. "That's enough. Carter, I think you should start."

Carter squints at his son but gets up and raises his glass of club soda with lime. "The fact that the two of you have kept me in your lives after my major fuck-up is a true testament to your forgiving natures. Ty, you are my son. Zoey, I love you dearly. I know I don't deserve to be here, but I'm beyond touched that I *am* here. Here's to a lifetime of happiness together."

Everyone at the table claps. Zoey wipes a tear from the corner of her eye and clutches my hand.

Fiona is up next. "Zoey, I've told you this before, but when I first met you there is no way in hell that I'd ever thought a shy little sweetheart like you would last with these heathens. Of course, you've proved me wrong. Tyson, you take good care of this one, or you'll answer to me."

"I will cherish her forever," I say before kissing Zoey to prove it.

Connor stands and holds out his hand to Ronni. They give each other a sweet smile and Ronni speaks. "It feels like a lifetime ago when Ty and I were set up by our publicists and looking back it's so weird, right?"

"Uh, yeah." Connor fake-glares at her. "It feckin' sucked."

Everyone laughs.

"When I got to know Ty, all he could talk about was Zoey. How she was the sweetest, most loving and supportive woman he'd ever met. How he only wanted the best for her." Ronni smiles at Zoey. "I'll admit, I was a bit protective of him, knowing how he felt about you and thinking you'd given up your chance with him. I'm happy to say, I was wrong. He was right. Together, you are two halves of a whole."

Connor nods. "Jaysus. I've got nothin' to add to that. Congratulations to the both of you."

"I'm next." Alex jumps up. "The night Zoey and I went to see the band at The Mission, we had every intention of making two of you LTZ boys fall in love with us. Little did either of us know we were actually going to manifest that shit. It's been a long road with a million twists and turns, but I'm just giddy that we are sitting here at your wedding."

More cheers and toasts ensue, but Alex jumps back in. "Ty, I'm just here to tell you that it was an absolute miracle the two of you ever made it on a date. I've never seen two people with so little game in my life. So, double congrats!"

"True that." Connor and Jace say in unison.

I shake my head and laugh at the memory. "It's *sooo* true, I remember being terrified of even talking to Zoey. Looking back at my twenty-one-year-old self, it's hard to believe how far I've come. Really, how far Zoey and I have come."

"Here, here!" Carter bellows.

Jace rises and smirks at everyone around the table. "I'm actually super thankful that you guys are finally married. Why? Hopefully I can finally fucking retire from managing your media shit. For once and for all. Talk about a thankless task. So, cheers. *Finally*!"

Alex smacks his ass.

"I guess it's our turn." Mike and Olivia stand, holding hands. Mike smiles and points at me. "You. I can say now that you put a ring on my daughter, as a father who is highly protective of his only daughter, I was terrified when she brought you home that night. A long-haired, bad-boy rocker is not who you envision for your child."

Olivia interrupts, "Except you won both of us over immediately. We loved you from the beginning, Ty, but the two of you were so young. We weren't surprised when things fell apart, and I think we both knew that Carter meant well."

"Watching Zoey suffer for all those years was tough," Mike continues. "When you found each other again, there were still a few more bumps in the road, but Tyson? You proved yourself again and again. There's no one else on earth we'd trust more with our precious Zoey. Welcome to our family."

"Oh, Dad. Mom." Zoey pops up and the three of them embrace. She waves me over and I join them.

That's when it hits me. Holy shit, I have in-laws. I actually have parents. I can't help but well up a bit. "Mike and Olivia, I'm so lucky to be part of your family."

"Ty, you're calling us Mom and Dad from now on, don't argue." Olivia kisses my cheek. "I've always wanted a son and look at what a handsome one I've acquired."

Zoey nestles back into me as we both sit down, whispering in my ear, "I'm so fucking happy right now."

"Okay, okay. Now it's time for mine." Zane pings on his glass again before I can reply. "I've been waiting all day to say— Ty, my brother, it's been you and me from the day we met. At first, I was confused, you're such a sexy beast I'll confess in front of all of you and Zoey—I had a bit of a man crush on you."

"We all did," Connor calls out.

"When we played that show at The Mission, and you saw Zoey in the crowd, me, Connor and Jace only hoped for one thing. That you wouldn't fuck it up. And somehow, you didn't and managed to snatch up a tiny high-school hottie, no offense, Mr. Pearson." Zane points at Mike.

"None taken." Mike chuckles.

"Anyway, you two belong together." Zane clutches his heart. "Zoey, you love Ty exactly how he deserves to be loved. With your whole heart. With your whole soul and with your extremely intelligent lawyer brain. He's lucky to have you, but you're also lucky to have him. And now you have us. We're all a big dysfunctional family, but we have each other. To Ty and Zoey!"

Everyone toasts us. I stand and pull Zoey up with me. "I can't believe we're fucking married! How many hours did I brood over losing this woman?"

"Eight hundred, forty-five thousand," Jace mutters.

I point at him. "You're about a hundred thousand hours short."

The entire table bursts into laughter again.

"I'm grateful to each and every one of you for being here with us tonight." Zoey looks up at me and cups my cheek. "I love this man and promise that your Mr. Broody is a thing of the past. I'm going to make him so happy; he'll never need to brood again."

Connor's grin is wide. "Thank feckin' Jaysus."

Everyone titters and giggles, as does Zoey. However, as much as the sentiment touches me and I join in jolly reaction to Connor's comment, a little part of my stomach seizes. Being perpetually happy feels like a ton of pressure. My head knows Zoey's comment is just in the spirit of the "slags," as Connor calls them.

My heart?

It's pierced with a shard of fear.

Shit. Even after her death, my mom's fucked-up legacy lives on inside me. Hiding my trauma from my friends—no, they're my *family*. God. Even on the happiest day of my life, this life sentence of emotional baggage fucks with my head. Can I live my entire life concealing such a big part of myself?

From Zoey.

From the guys.

Is it even possible?

Zoey leans up and kisses my cheek. "Ty, are you going to answer Carter?"

"Shit, I spaced out for a sec, butterfly." I nod to Carter. "What did you say?"

Carter repeats himself, "Should we take this to the living room and jam a bit before the cake?"

"Absolutely!" My voice sounds a bit more enthusiastic than I feel. "That's a great idea. Zane, Carter, come down to the practice room, we'll bring a few guitars up."

I kiss my bride before we go to retrieve the instruments. The look of absolute bliss on her face when our lips part softens the edges a bit. She loves me. I love her. That's what today is about. Our lifelong commitment to each other.

Nothing else.

I won't let it be.

Chapter Eleven

A Month Later

WHEN I DIP MY toe in the pool, the water is so refreshing I decide to plunge all the way in. It's unseasonably hot this December in Los Angeles. A swim is just what I need.

I'm so glad Ty and I decided to spend our first Christmas holiday as a married couple at our house in LA. Mom and Dad will join us in a few days. Ronni, Connor, and the twins will be here for Christmas Eve. For now, we have a few low-key days to look forward to before the celebrations start.

Gazing out over the infinity edge of the pool, the Hollywood Hills stretch out below me. I bob about enjoying the view, feeling peaceful. Content. And a bit sad. I got my period this morning. It was about five days late and I was getting so excited to pee on a few sticks. Now, it won't be necessary.

It's not for a lack of trying. I don't think Ty and I have ever had more sex than we have in the past month since our wedding, and that's saying a lot. He's insatiable. We both are. It's a bit of a bummer though. When I ditched birth control three cycles ago, I just figured... Well, it hasn't happened. Not that I'm in any rush or anything.

"There you are." I hear my husband's deep voice and find Ty sitting on a lounger to the side of me. "I got out of the shower and you weren't in the bedroom."

I shrug and paddle over to him. "One of the best things about having a pool is I can swim whenever I want."

"It's a great view." Ty lowers his sunglasses to look at my bare breasts bobbing just above the water line."

I press myself up on my forearms, squishing my boobs together. "You could join me."

"God, don't tempt me. I've got a melody in my head I'd like to get down. Would you mind if I work in the studio for a bit?" Ty replicated the Seattle recording studio on a smaller scale in one of the downstairs guest rooms. He's been in a creative mania, writing and recording at all hours of the day. It's really the first time since we've been back together that I've experienced this side of him. I'm the one who's woken up without him beside me quite a few times since we got to LA.

"Of course not. I have a few meetings for the foundation this morning." I push off from the edge and float away from Ty. "Not for a couple of hours though, so I'll just have a little pool time."

Ty stands. "Of course. You should enjoy, butterfly. I just wanted to check on you. This morning you seemed sad."

"Oh. Not really *sad*, sad. I got my period."

"Ah."

"I was a few days late." I draw in a deep breath. "I guess I just thought..."

Ty smiles, but it seems slightly strained. Or is it relieved? I second-guess myself when he waggles his eyebrows. "It will happen, baby. We are perfecting our craft. Holy hell. My dick is still sore from last night."

"Is it an Olympic sport yet? We could be champions." I splash him a tiny bit on purpose before he scuttles out of range and heads back into the house.

A few hours later, I'm done with my calls. I've not seen or heard a peep from Ty. Quietly, I tiptoe into the studio where he's seated at the mixing table. I don't want to disturb him if he's having a particularly genius moment. That's when I see him intently perusing what looks to be one of his old journals.

"Babe?" I rap on the doorjamb with my knuckles to alert him I'm in the room.

Ty slams the book shut and spins around. "Hey."

"Is that one of your old journals?" I approach him, a little taken aback by his abrupt reaction. I didn't realize he brought them down here with him. I thought he kept them locked in the guest room at our Seattle house. From way back when I first met him, he's been adamant that I shouldn't read them. I've always respected his wishes, of course.

"Yeah." He holds it up and sets it down. "I was just looking for some lyrics I wrote years ago."

I climb into his lap and stroke his silky hair. "Did you find them?"

"Nah." He wraps his arms around my waist and rubs his nose against mine. Nuzzles my cheek. Kisses my neck.

I reach down and cup his growing erection. Stroke him through his board shorts. He gasps, breath hot against my skin. Encouraged, I slip my hand under his waistband and feel his steely velvet length harden under my touch. My thumb rubs his sensitive ridge and slides over his tip. I slide out of his grasp onto my knees in front of him.

My eyes lock with Ty's as I tug on his shorts. He lifts his hips to allow me to pull them down his legs. His beautiful cock lays flush against his abs, which have more definition than I can ever remember. I grip the base and take him in my mouth as deeply as possible and worship him.

I love giving Ty head. I love rubbing his penis all over my lips. Licking him like a lollipop. Laving him from root to tip. Stroking him. Sucking his balls. Swirling my tongue along his perincum and sometimes when I'm naughty, like today, rimming his anus.

Ty's slumped low in the chair. I'm kneeling between his legs bobbing up and down, enjoying his drugged expression as he watches his cock disappear in and out of my mouth.

"Fuck, Zoey. I'm going to come," Ty moans and tries to pull out. Like always. Except today I just want to drink him down.. So, I double down and amp up my speed until Ty's too far gone to stop me. He bucks, cries out and spurts his hot release down my throat. I swallow everything he has to give. There's not a millimeter of his cock that doesn't get attention from my tongue and lips until he's clean.

When I'm done. I find him watching me. A strange look on his face. I ask saucily, "So, how'd that feel?"

"Amazing." He almost absentmindedly reaches down and strokes my cheek. There's something behind his eyes, I think. Still, I can't help but smile. Giving Ty pleasure makes me so happy.

Using his thighs as leverage, I boost myself up to standing. Ty pulls his shorts back up, then grabs my ass and pulls me toward him so quickly I have to clutch his shoulders not to lose my balance. "I fucking love you," he whispers into my ear. "It's my turn."

"Would you mind if we wait until tomorrow?" I straddle him in the chair and rest my hands on his shoulders.

"Oh. Right." He nods when he remembers about my period. "Except, I thought we were past all of that."

I reach back and caress the back of his head. "We are. Sometimes it's okay just to receive, baby. I saw you sitting there with your old journal and just wanted to make you feel good. I always want to make you feel good. Will you just let me do that for you?"

Ty tenses. Only for a second. Then leans up and kisses me softly. We stare into each other's eyes for a bit. Soaking each other in. When I feel him completely relax, I bury my face into the crook of his neck when he whispers, "Okay."

We venture back upstairs. I sit on a barstool at the counter while Ty cooks. Our usual routine. He whips us up some salmon and a cauliflower puree in record time. After dinner, we curl up on the couch to watch *Heartland*, a Canadian show that Alex loves about a horse ranch.

In this particular episode, the main character's boyfriend, whose name is "Ty" too, is struggling coming to terms with his abusive stepdad and alcoholic mother. My Ty doesn't say anything, but I can feel him stiffen every now and then during some of the scenes. When the show ends, I hit pause before the next episode starts and turn around in his arms.

"Now it's my turn to ask if you're okay." I peer up at him. "I'm wondering if you're going through some stuff. We launched head-first into wedding mode after Jada died. Is there anything I can do?"

Something passes behind his eyes again. I know it for sure this time. But it's only for a second, then replaced with a puzzled look. "Why would you say that?"

"Ty." I cock my head. "C'mon. We don't hide things from each other. You weren't looking for lyrics. You were reading your old journals."

He sits up and rests his elbows on his knees and buries his face in his hands. "Fuck."

"It's okay, babe." I rub his back.

Ty doesn't say anything for a long time. Eventually, he glances up on me. His brows are knit together. "Z. I can't."

"Can't what?" I'm a bit confused. "Tell me what's bothering you."

"No." He shakes his head.

My heart plummets and then smashes on the floor. "Why?"

"Please don't make this about you, Zoey. It's not. I...I...um. I just can't talk about it, okay? Can you give me some space on this? Trust me until I figure things out?" Ty's eyes are a bit frantic. While I'm empathetic he's clearly struggling with something, in the past his secrets have bitten me in the ass. Hard. Especially when he's this evasive. I'm concerned for him. But, I'm also scared.

Hurt.

Trying to find my equilibrium, I get up and head back upstairs. I truly don't want to say something I'll regret. If something is on Ty's mind and he's not willing to share with me, I'm bummed. Because we made a pact. We don't keep secrets. Ever. It's our *rule.* A rule I've honored religiously.

Anger takes over. By the time I'm in the master bathroom brushing my teeth, I'm seething. Ty joins me. "Look, butterfly..."

"*Don't* call me that right now," I say through a mouthful of toothpaste.

"It's not like before..." Ty protests.

I whirl around and my voice is much louder and harsher than I intend. "You mean the before when I knew there was something wrong and you blew me off? The before when I had the great privilege of watching a video of you coming down your publicist's slutty mouth?

I'm the one who nearly got hit by a taxi, Ty. When I recovered, you promised me there would never be any more secrets between us. You *promised*. So yeah, you are seriously scaring me. Why can't you tell me what the fuck is going on?"

He just stares at me, surprised at my outburst. "This is *not* the same," he finally whispers.

"How do I know that?" I brush past him on the way into the bedroom.

He follows, touches my arm. "*Please* trust me."

"Maybe *you* should trust *me*." I shake off his arm and go to my side of the bed. Begin throwing the decorative pillows on the floor while simultaneously wondering why the hell we have so many of them. They're stupid. I'm getting rid of them tomorrow.

"*Zoey*." Ty remains rooted to the doorway between the bathroom and the bedroom. He looks utterly anguished, which sends my brain into places I don't want it to go. "Please."

"All of this is sending up huge red flags, Ty." I sit on the bed. Stare him down.

"It has nothing to do with you and me." He begins breathing in and then letting breaths out.

I crawl into bed and pull the covers up to my chest. "For one, you should be able to tell me anything. For another, it's not that you can't tell me. It's that you *won't* tell me. Now I'm imagining the worst when it could have already been in the rearview mirror. There's going to be this thing between us now. For no good reason."

"There *is* a good reason," Ty bellows.

"Well, it better be, because you keeping secrets from me feels like shit."

Ty stares at me. His chiseled jaw sets stubbornly. "You want to know what feels like *shit*? Fine. If you *really* must know, I'll fucking tell you. Yeah. I'm struggling. Because I've been having terrible fucking nightmares about my childhood. Jada dying has brought it all back."

I notice my husband crossing his arms protectively around himself. My voice softens slightly. "What nightmares?"

"I *don't* want to tell you." His teeth are clenched so hard I can see his jaw tremble.

Undeterred, I jump out of bed and stride over to him. "Why? How would you feel if I said that to you? That I didn't *want* to tell you something. You'd lose your mind.

You wouldn't understand. You'd be as pissed as I am right now."

He just stares at me. I watch a myriad of emotions cross his face before he settles on one I've never seen before.

White. Hot. Seething. Anger.

It takes over his entire body and the Ty I know is gone. Replaced with someone else.

"Okay, *Zoey*. I'll fucking give it to you good. How about I tell you about the hundreds of times my mother verbally berated me just for being alive? Or the absolute terror I'd feel when I'd make the slightest mistake. Why? Because she beat the shit out of me. Do *you* know what it's like to live with a mother who's high on heroin or meth or whatever the fuck she could get her hands on? It fucking sucked. Every. Fucking. Day."

Ty continued, "It was *me* who had to clean her up when she'd shit her pants. It was *me* who had to undress and wash her when she vomited all over herself. Do you *know* how badly I wanted to scrub my eyes out when she'd fuck men right in front of me just to get drug money? How do you think I felt when she *made* me let a guy suck my cock for drugs? *Huh*?" Ty snarls. "Do you want more? Oh, I've got more. I could spend weeks telling you more about how badly she fucked me up. You've got yourself a real catch, Zoey. *Congratu-fucking-lations.*"

I can feel my mouth fall open. I'm in complete shock.

"Okay. So now you know. I've dropped the bombshell. But, are you *happy*? Did I do *okay?* Do you feel *better* now? I sure fucking hope so because I feel like *ass*. Did you remember when my *wife* said she wanted me to make me feel good earlier today? I fucking believed her. I'd stick to blowjobs from now on, Zoey. Take it from me, you give world class head." Ty storms out of the bedroom and slams the door.

I'm left standing there. Stunned at his outburst. In utter and total shock. What just happened? I'm utterly devastated. What have I done? I know from the deep pit in my stomach that all of that stuff really happened to him. In the back of my mind, I *knew* there was more to his story. But, I truly had no idea the magnitude of what Ty lived through.

Why did I have to push him so far?

I'm so overwhelmed with anguish. How could anyone treat their child the way Jada treated Ty? No wonder he talked to her at the hospital that way. No wonder he told the crematorium to destroy her ashes. She was pure evil.

Oh, how I desperately want to go to him. Take him in my arms and tell him I'll make it better. But I can't. Instinctively I know I'm the last person he'll take comfort from now.

I have no one to talk to about this. I have not a clue what to do.

None.

I swear, if Jada wasn't already dead, I'd murder her myself.

Chills run down my spine. Fear permeates my entire being.

As deeply as I love him, I have no idea how to handle what Ty just unloaded on me. How to process what my husband suffered. Or what this means for him. For us.

For our future.

Chapter Twelve

My neck screams out in pain when I open my eyes. Figuratively. Somehow, I've fallen asleep in my gaming chair in the studio. I move my head from side to side to ease the tension.

Taking stock of my surroundings, I'm confused. I have zero recollection of how I got here or what happened. Baskets full of cables are strewn about the studio. One of my practice guitars is smashed, splinters of wood litter the floor. Frightened, I get up and plow through the room. Searching for any sign of alcohol. Thank God there's no sign that I fell off the wagon. A nervous break-down I can take. Reverting to using substances to soothe myself would be a huge step in the wrong direction.

As I'm straightening up the room, I notice that my journal is torn to bits. I pick up the remnants and shuffle through the torn pages. Fuck. I vividly remember when I started to document Jada's abuse. It was after I met Zane. I was fifteen. Usually, I only skim a page or two before putting it away. Last night, I must have kept going. It would explain the destruction in the room, nothing good ever comes from me reliving the past.

Still, I can't help but read the words on the pages. Painful fucking memories flood back. Ones I wish would just disappear.

I met a guy named Zane Rocks. His dad is Carter Pope, the guitar player for Limelight. Carter doesn't even act like he's famous, he's sort of a boring old guy who putters around the house. He's talks a lot about being in recovery. I figure, if Carter can get clean, maybe she can too someday.

I let it slip to her about my friend Zane. I don't know how she knew Carter was Zane's dad, but she did. She said she knew the band before they were famous and they were all entitled assholes. Then she demanded I steal a bunch of Limelight memorabilia from Zane's house and give it to her to sell. She said the band owed her at least that. Whatever "that" means. Who knows. She said she needed the money. I know it's for drugs. There's no fucking way I'm stealing from two of the only people in the world that I like.

When I got home from work, she tried to smash me over the head with a cast iron pan. She was hiding behind the door to the kitchenette, so I didn't see it coming. She was too fucked-up to get a direct hit, but the edge of the pan split my forehead open just above my eye socket. This morning, both eyes are black and I have a knot on my eyebrow that won't stop bleeding. I can't go to school for a couple of days. They'd ask too many questions. I got some powdery stuff at the drugstore to stop the bleeding. I'm going to have a nasty scar.

Visons of my daily agony come roaring back. And the reason I wrote this shit down. I figured, if Jada killed me, maybe the police would find this journal. And know who to arrest for my murder.

How fucking sick is that?

Today I showed her pictures of my black eyes and head wound. I told her if she didn't leave me the fuck alone I'd move out. Mom cried and begged me not to leave her. She reminded me about my grandparents' trust and how the rent on the apartment would only be paid so long as I was living there. She promises to be better. But, I've heard it all before. At least now I have some insurance.

I found a card for an attorney in the back of the silverware drawer. I called her. She manages the trust that pays our rent. It's true. The trust is contingent upon me living here. She better get her shit together before I turn eighteen. After that, I'm leaving. I still have two years of being stuck here so I put three deadbolt locks on my bedroom door. I should have done this years ago. I'm sick of my shit getting stolen and sold for drugs. Zane's letting me keep my guitar at Carter's house.

I thumb through some of the pages that aren't torn out. A few pages are filled with stuff that happened to me when I was really young. Fuck. I forgot that I'd done this. Gulping down a breath of air, I forge ahead.

She came home from her job and was mad at me for not having dinner ready. She got a crazy look in her eyes. I was scared and hid under the bathroom sink. She found me and dragged me out by my throat. She wouldn't let go. I was choking. I almost passed out before she finally released me. I had bruises around my neck for two weeks. Nobody at school even asked me about it.

I was late from school because I missed the bus and had to walk. When I got home she punched me in the nose and it broke. She beat me so bad I broke some ribs. I couldn't walk or even sit up for a few days. She said it was because I kept going to school when she needed me at home. She wouldn't take me to the doctor because she said there was no way she'd let anyone report her to CPS. When I was healed enough, I went back to school. No one asked where I had been.

She was really high and yelled and screamed the house wasn't clean enough. She pulled everything out of the cupboards, closets, drawers and threw it all in the middle of the floor. She made me clean it all up and put it away. After I was done she said I hadn't cleaned fast enough. She beat the shit out of me and made me do it all again.

I was about eleven or twelve and we were homeless one summer and had to live in her car. She'd make me sit in the front seat when she'd bring men over to make money. They would put their dicks in her mouth and she'd suck them off. Sometimes they'd fuck her. I tried to leave but she told me I had to stay to protect her. I'd curl up in a ball in the front seat and try to plug my ears.

One morning I woke up and my dick was hard. She pulled down my pants squeezed it and laughed. She said I was a man now. Later in the day she brought some guy to the car and told me he was going to make me feel good. Before I could stop him, he pulled down my pants and put my dick in his mouth. I screamed and tried to push him off, but my mom said we needed *the money. My dick got hard when he sucked on it. I couldn't help it. I cried because I felt so ashamed. After, he paid Mom $500, gave her a baggie of something and thanked her for my virginity. I threw up.*

She brought another guy to the car. There was no way I'd let anyone do that to me again. I'd die first. I spit in his face. He smashed me in the jaw but I kicked him hard in his balls and ran away. I was found by a police officer in a park. When they found her, we were both put in a shelter together. I told her that I'd kill myself if she made me do that ever again. The next day we were in the apartment we live in now.

My heart breaks for myself. I know I shouldn't read this shit. It only makes me furious at myself that I didn't leave. Find a way to protect myself better. Why did I let her abuse me that way? I should have said something. Then again, I didn't think anyone would believe me.

She told you no one would believe you.

Lisa hasn't read the journal, but I've gone through most of the details with her. Just before Zoey and I got back together, dealing with my childhood abuse was our primary focus. Brutal, brutal sessions. Which, now that I think about it, was a big reason why I slowed down and then stopped therapy.

The day I left Zoey at the hotel in Laguna Beach in a rage? That was two days after an excruciating meeting with Lisa about the man in the car. It completely fucked with my head. After that day, I became convinced therapy was making shit worse. Dredging up the past wasn't worth risking my revived relationship with Zoey.

I still feel that way. Shit happened. I *know* I didn't deserve it. I *know* it wasn't my fault. End of fucking story. The past is where it belongs.

Right?

So why in the fuck am I sitting here alone in my studio reading all of this shit right now? Reliving it? These fucking memories *don't* help me. They make me feel horrible.

Like yesterday. Zoey came down here to make me feel good. And it kills me that every time Zoey gives me head, I can't fully enjoy it the way I wish I could. The way she wishes I *would*. Her blowjobs are amazing. Reverential. From way back when we first started fooling around, she has always worshipped my dick like it's her favorite prize. But a flashback of preteen me in the car threatens to interfere just when I'm about to come. Not always. But when it does, I feel sick and can't bear to finish in her mouth.

It doesn't help that our publicist gave me a blowjob without my knowledge and filmed it. Used it to try to drive Zoey and me apart in New York. And almost cost Zoey her life when she nearly got hit by a taxi running from the paparazzi who were stalking us.

Now, blowjobs are something I have mixed feelings about. Sometimes I love them. Sometimes I let Zoey suck me off because it makes her happy. Other times, when I can't handle it, I pull out and distract her with some other pleasurable activity before I'm too far gone.

It's not like I can tell her why I sometimes get so weird about her sucking me off. I just fucking *can't*. It's *mortifying*. I don't ever want her to think anything we do together sexually isn't pleasurable for me. Because it is. Even head.

Especially head.

That's when I remember.

Holy mother of fuck. Last night I *did* tell her.

Goddammit. How will I ever face her? What is she going to think? I mean, her knowing about the beatings is one thing. But *that?* I don't want her to ever think about *that* when my cock is in her mouth. But how could she not?

What have I done? I've just fucking ruined everything.

I shove the torn pages back into the journal then bound up the stairs to the kitchen with the intention of throwing it in the garbage. Except, I really can't do that. Zoey—or someone—will find it.

Ah, the fucking joys of being a celebrity. Always worrying about assholes sifting through your trash to try to earn a buck from a fake story. Maybe I should burn it? But where? No one has fires in Los Angeles. The fireplace in the living room has never even been used. I look down to see my hands, which are clutching the damaged journal, are shaking uncontrollably.

Is my mental health really this fragile? If it is, what in the fuck am I going to do?

"Ty?" I whirl around. Zoey stands in the entryway looking spooked. Of course, she is. Confessions aside, I lost my shit on her catastrophically. And it's not the first time. Maybe I am a worthless piece of...

Stop it.

When I see her face, so clearly concerned, full of love, I have a moment of clarity. Zoey was angry with me for keeping things from her. She was scared about another Sienna situation. Her anger triggered me, and I felt like a trapped animal. I truly didn't mean to yell at her. I can still see her horrified expression. And her tears. I can still feel how badly I needed to get away from everyone and everything...including her.

Holy shit. Last night, I think I actually blacked out from rage.

From fear.

My voice is raw, ragged. "I'm so sorry, Z. I didn't mean to react that way. Drop that shit on you. I..." Zoey tentatively takes a step toward me, and I give in to the pain. My eyes fill with tears. I place the journal on the counter and brace myself on the kitchen island for support. It feels like my legs are going to give way. I can't believe I lashed out at my beautiful wife when she'd never deliberately hurt me. All she wants to do is love me. Support me.

Help me.

"I love you, baby." Zoey wraps her arms around my waist and presses her cheek against my chest. "I shouldn't have pushed you last night. I'm the one who's sorry."

"I want to do right by you, Zoey. I want to let you in. There are just some things...fuck. Please?" I cling to her "I can't talk about that stuff right now. Maybe ever. It's too..."

"Shhh. It's okay. Shhh. I'm right here," Zoey whispers against my chest.

I sink onto the barstool, keeping Zoey pressed tightly against me. "I don't want to be this sad-sack emotionally reactive guy. Not when I've done so much work to keep my past where it belongs. We've had such a great year together. Full of so much joy. So many accomplishments. Now we're married and trying for a baby. That's who I want to be for you, not this...fucked-up mess. You're the most important thing in the world to me."

"I get it." Z blinks up at me with her piercing hazel eyes. "But, Ty? I just want you to be you. All of you. Because I love you. No matter what. You don't have to pretend you're okay when you're not. Never."

I nod. Snuggle her back closer to me. "My reaction was uncalled for. I'm sorry. I don't want to keep doing this shit to you and apologizing. It's not right."

"Well, there's two people in every disagreement. Even if I was hurt and scared, you didn't deserve for me to imply I couldn't trust you. It was wrong. I *do* trust you."

"I'm so out of my depth, Z." My voice is shaky. "I don't have a fucking clue what it feels like to have a parent who loves and supports me like your parents do for you."

She grasps both of my hands in hers and squeezes. "I'm not going to lie to you, baby. I don't know what to think about...that stuff you told me. We don't need to talk about things if you don't want to. If I could, I'd take every ounce of pain you've suffered away."

"Well, I'm just trying to fucking forget it ever happened. It doesn't define me, you know?"

"Of course, it doesn't." Zoey traces my lips with her finger. "So, you *do* trust me?"

"I do with my life, baby. And I want to let you in, I just don't know if I can." I point to the journal on the counter. "As you guessed, this particular journal is not filled with lyrics and poems. It's one I kept about the abuse."

Zoey's eyes well up with tears when she looks over at it. She looks back at me, questioningly. I run my finger along the spine. Take a deep breath. Pick it up and hand it to her. "Will you take it? Keep it for me?"

"What do you want me to do with it?" she whispers.

"If I'm honest, I want you to destroy it. Make sure it is obliterated so I'll never see it again and no one can ever read it, including me." I swallow a huge lump in my throat. "But, now it's yours. You can decide. If you really want to know what happened to me, it's in there. Just please don't make me say it out loud. And please don't pity me because of what happened to me. I'm a different person now."

She reaches over to the journal and hooks my finger with hers. We both stare at our joined digits for a while. So much heaviness in the last few hours. I hate that my CPTSD is like an invisible cloak permanently fastened to my back. A cloak I can't tell anyone I'm wearing, the irony of that fact isn't lost on me, considering the circumstances.

Zoey climbs onto the barstool next to me. Rests her head on her forearms and peers at me. "Why are you scared for me to read it?"

"I don't want you to see me as that abused kid I was before I met you. I want you to see me only as the man you saw on stage that first night. The rock god. The way you looked at me when we met, and now? It's what I live for. I still can't believe you trusted me enough to give all of your firsts to."

"I do see you as all of those things, Ty." Zoey grips my hand with hers. "It doesn't mean you are *only* those things. I really do love *all* of you."

My voice quivers. "Zoey, being with you gave me the courage to front one of the most successful rock bands in the world. Being with you inspires me to be a better man. With you, I'm a fun, carefree person who can joke and laugh and be silly. I *never* want you to look at me like I'm broken."

She bites her lip. Her eyes squinch together. Then she nods slowly. It's not really an acknowledgment. More like she understands where I'm coming from and wants to think about what I said. My analytical girl. Her gaze returns to the journal. I can picture the hamsters running on a wheel in her head. While she does her introspective thing, I grow contemplative too. Maybe I should just tell her everything. Get it all out there. Take a chance. Share my diagnosis.

My mouth opens, but no words come out because after all that's transpired in the past twenty-four hours, I just *can't.*

I'm completely depleted.

"For the record, no matter what, I'll never think of you as broken." Zoey's soft voice snaps me back to the present. "Just because you told me some of the more horrific details..."

"I screamed them at you in a white-hot rage, Z." I shake my head. "Not my finest moment. It's not who I am. Who I want to be."

Zoey strokes my shoulder. "Babe, I couldn't sleep last night after what happened. I did some research, if even one of those things you lived through was my reality, there's no way I'd handle it half as well as you do. I'd say an outburst here and there isn't the end of the world. At least now I understand it a bit better."

I swivel back and forth on my barstool. "You don't need to make excuses for me. The fact that my mom abused me doesn't give me the right to verbally attack you."

"Of course not, but don't you see, Ty? You are completely self-aware about your situation. Whatever you've been doing to cope is working. This doesn't have to be a forever thing for you." Zoey looks at me so earnestly I almost believe her.

Even though she's wrong, I'm going to do everything I can to prove her right. For now, that means reverting to what always works with us. I kiss her. Lead her to our bedroom and make slow, sweet love to my gorgeous wife. Spend the entire night into the morning showing her just how much I adore her. Over and over again.

Eventually, when we're spent and she drifts off to sleep, I make a commitment to myself. Now that she knows about what I endured, I'm *not* going to let the train go off the rails any more than it has.

The train being my brain, that is.

She's right about one thing. I'm self-aware. I know what I need to do. And I will. Because if I don't get my shit together soon, I'm afraid I'll never get myself back on track.

And where would that leave us?

Chapter Thirteen

THE PROSPECT OF A house full of people for the holidays somehow softened the impact of the truth bombs Ty dropped a couple of weeks ago. I'm not burying my head in the sand, but Ty and I have been distracted. Running errands. Decorating the house. Well, supervising the decorations. A professional team has adorned the inside and outside in the most beautiful silver-and-gold finery.

The exterior looks like something out of a fairytale. Silver snowflakes hang from every tree. White lights have been wrapped around every surface. Giant gold stars have been mounted along the entryway.

Inside is even more lush. Our main tree is twenty feet high. There must be at least ten-thousand sparkly lights wound around every branch. Giant pewter poinsettias are spread strategically throughout the tree. Dozens of hand-blown gold glass butterflies catch the light and are placed in between clear glass musical instruments. Hundreds of tiny crystal drops fill in the blank spaces.

"I think this tree is even better than the one we had in Seattle last year." Ty looks down at me from the top of the ladder. He's placing a custom Chihuly glass angel ornament at the top.

I peer over from the kitchen island where I'm wrapping gifts for the McLoughlins and my parents. "Last year you surprised me with an engagement party, I'll never have a more favorite Christmas tree."

"True." Ty is satisfied with the angel placement and descends the ladder. "Are you regretting not spending the holidays in Seattle?"

"No. I just want you and me to be together. We could be anywhere and I'd be happy." I loop bows around another present for the twins and set it aside.

Ty saunters over to me and inspects the present. "This looks awesome, you're a great present wrapper." Then he looks at me with a boyish grin.

If I'm honest, I've never known Ty to be so—light. Almost like a weight has been lifted after he told me what happened and gave me his journal. I haven't destroyed it like he asked. I haven't read it either. I've locked it in my jewelry safe in Seattle where no one but me and Ty have the combination. It's still unread.

Taunting me.

I'm not sure why Ty wanted me to have it. It's hard to figure out if he's testing me. Or if he really wants me to read it. I can't bring myself to clarify just yet. We had such a rough patch, however brief it was, but he was so distraught. Anguished. It would break me apart to see him that way again. For now, I've decided to let it go. At least until after the holidays.

"When do your parents get in again?" Ty moves behind me. Rests his chin on my shoulder. Wraps his arms around my waist and cups my breasts.

I shoo him off. "Don't start any funny business, I have presents to wrap."

Ty reaches over and grabs a strip of red ribbon. Ties it around his neck. "I'll be your present." He waggles his brows.

Lord, he's so fucking hot. I turn and look him up and down. Black tank. Black shorts. Red ribbon. Giant boner. The corner of his mouth curls up. Because he knows it's *on*.

Who am I kidding? It's always on.

We send Sergey to pick up my folks at LAX and spend the next couple of hours unwrapping each other. Even our sex is sweeter right now. There's been none of the porn-star fucking we've been at all year. Which is amazing, don't get me wrong. It's just...since his confession, every time we make love it's as though we're trading souls. Intertwining our hearts even further. Almost like all of the molecules of his body are infusing into mine and vice versa.

Like our love is deeper. Stronger.

We've achieved a new milestone in his ability to trust me with his past. Even if it's a baby step, I feel so incredibly close to him.

"Thank you, baby." Ty nibbles on my earlobe. He and I are spooning. There's no place I'm happier than being enveloped by my husband.

"For what?"

"My whole life I daydreamed of having a real family. A doting mother and father. Or two mothers. Two fathers. Any combination would have been fine by me. I *craved* any semblance of a normal life. I'd have given *anything* for someone to care about me." Ty seems calm, almost retrospective.

I look around at him. He bites his bottom lip. "I've been thinking a lot about things. Why I didn't leave. The thing is my mom always managed to pull her shit together when child protective services paid a visit. She'd make sure the apartment was tidied up. Food would miraculously appear in the cupboards. She'd dress me in a new t-shirt and jeans from Goodwill. Then she'd coach me on exactly what to do and say during the assessment."

I nod. Stroke his cheek. If he's going to open up further to me, there's no way I want to interrupt.

"I was afraid of the unknown, so I always did exactly what she asked. I was so desperate for her love, I thought if I pleased her things would get better. Can you believe I fell for her motherly act every goddamn time? She knew what she was doing. No one ever intervened. No one rescued me. No one placed me with a better family. All because I was too scared to tell anyone the complete truth."

"Does it feel good to talk about it?" I twirl a lock of his hair. Gaze into his gorgeous blue eyes.

His forehead wrinkles. "I wouldn't say it feels *good*. It's more like a relief."

"You're safe with me." I kiss his chin and then his lips.

"Even now, I sometimes can't believe I have a family," Ty murmurs between kisses. "You. Your folks. My band."

I grip his face between both of my hands. "You do. You're *my* family, Ty."

A few hours later we're all sitting around the kitchen island eating the dinner Ty's cooked for us.

"You never cease to amaze me, Tyson." Dad holds up a fork of homemade shrimp ravioli with a Gorgonzola cream sauce. "Incredible."

Ty laughs. "I had a lot of time on the bus over the years. I couldn't write tragic love songs all of the time, so I cooked. This is a much better kitchen though."

I take a bite of the pasta. Holy crap. "You've been holding out on me. This is the best thing you've ever made."

"I try to avoid carbs most of the time. Gotta watch my figure," Ty jokes as he pats his ripped belly.

"Before I forget, we swung by the house like you asked. You had a package sitting on the front porch, let me go get it, Ty." Mom jumps up and disappears into the guest room. She returns with a medium-sized box and an envelope and hands them to Ty.

I clap my hands and pretend to reach for the package. "Oooh, sneaky, babe. Sending my present to the Seattle house. Not so sneaky of you to bring it out a week before Christmas, Mom."

Ty raises an eyebrow at me but looks trepidatious. He glances at the return address, clearly not recognizing it. Shakes the box. Holds up the envelope. "Huh. Not sure what this is. There's no name. Seems like fan mail or something. Usually, management likes us to let them handle it. Too many crazies from the early days."

"Maybe Sergey can take a look?" I offer.

Ty nods. "Yeah. Good idea. First, I'll ping Katherine. Maybe she knows something about it. I'll be honest, I'm a little weirded out that it was left at our house. I hope one of the guards left it on the porch, that will make me feel better."

Fair point. We have pretty tight security, and the house is owned by an LLC, but the number of LTZ fans who manage to track down our address is sometimes alarming. In addition to Sergey, we have a team of rotating security guards that are there 24/7.

He sets the box aside and we finish dinner. Ty and I grab some tea and head to the theater room to watch a movie. My dad appears with a bottle of Old Rip Van Winkle twenty-five-year-old bourbon and holds it up. "I couldn't resist buying this at duty free. It's pretty special, but I don't want to offend."

"It doesn't offend me, I hope it doesn't offend you if I don't partake, though." Ty eyes the bottle, a hint of longing passes across his gaze. "If I were still drinking, though, it would be right up my alley."

"Put it away, Mike." Mom shakes her head.

"Seriously. Don't. Not on my account." Ty holds his hands up with his palms out. "When we're on the road, I'm around a lot worse. It's been a few years now since I've had any alcohol—or drugs—"

Dad looks wary, or maybe it's a bit guilty. He has a vague idea of Ty's former struggles, obviously. They were out in the public for all to see, after all. By the time we reunited, Ty had his addiction under control. I've never seen him waver once. "Son, it's not my business. I apologize... "

"Please. Mike." Ty shakes his head to dismiss the subject and sits down in one of the big comfy couches. I sit next to him; he wraps his arm around my shoulders and turns on the giant screen. My folks sit on the matching couch next to us. Dad sips his bourbon. Ty stares at the screen the entire time.

I can feel the tension emanating from his body. His breathing is a bit irregular, and I realize it's because he's doing his exercises. His knee bounces then relaxes. I squeeze his leg with my hand and snuggle in closer to him. He smiles down at me, but there's just...something off. He's completely zoned out and trying to hide it. When the movie is over we say our goodnights and head up to bed. Go through our evening routine. Climb into bed. Ty lies there staring at the ceiling. Finally, I have to just break the spell. "What's going on?"

"I was just thinking about the package." Ty turns to his side and runs the back of his hand along my jaw. Leans in and licks the seam of my lips. I open to him. His tongue meets mine, causing me to moan. I reach down between us to find his cock as hard as steel. I pump him a few times and hook my knee over his hip. All thoughts of whatever was bothering my husband are forgotten for now.

Ty grips my hips and rolls over on his back so I'm straddling him. I position him at my entrance and sink down. "Ahhh." I breathe out a gush of air when he's deep inside me. "Yeah," I sigh when he begins to move me back and forth so my clit rubs against his pubic bone.

"That's it, baby. Take what you need." Ty lets go of me and rests his head on his hands, his elbows flat against the pillow. I brace myself on his muscled torso, caging my breasts between my arms. He groans. I circle my hips in slow motion and then pick up the pace by swiveling then riding him until I find exactly the rhythm I need.

His eyes squinch shut. His mouth lolls open. He licks his lips and whispers, "Fuck, yeah, Z."

With the dual stimulation of my G-spot and clit, my orgasm sneaks up on me. I milk Ty's cock as hard as I can so he'll go over too. Instead, he flips me over onto my back and holds my legs wide open at my knees. With short, quick thrusts, he finishes and collapses, although he's careful not to crush me.

Ty's head is buried in my neck, I scrape his lower back lightly with my nails as his spasms subside and breathing regulates. Apparently, he's just getting started. Ty kisses his way down my body and buries himself between my legs. Hungrily, he laps up our release. Flicks his tongue back and forth on my clit. Then tiny circles. Then long, slow licks. Repeats. He keeps me on the brink for what feels like hours. I begin to float away where nothing matters but my ecstasy.

At some point, Ty slurps my clit into his mouth and sucks hard. Every nerve in my body fires. My scalp prickles. My hips thrust up and smash against his face almost involuntarily. I gush all over his lips.

I'm still floating when he turns me over and props me up on my knees. Spreads me open and rams into me deliciously, his arm banded around my belly to hold me up. Nothing matters except for the pleasure vortex of my pussy sucking his cock into my body as I come over and over again. He's brought me to the brink of sexual madness. Ty bellows when he comes, slamming his hips against my ass, his balls hit my clit. He grabs a handful of my hair in a tight ponytail at my nape. Pulls my head back and devours my neck, still pumping his release.

Eventually we collapse in a heap. Breathing heavy. Completely spent.

I guess we're back to porn-star fucking, and God it's so good.

Sweet Ty returns after a few minutes and cuddles me close. Tucks us under the covers. Exhausted, we both begin to drift off to sleep.

Boning my husband is my favorite thing to do. I'm not going to lie.

But lately, I can't help but wonder.

Did Ty replace some of his old addictions?

With sex?

Chapter Fourteen

ZOEY'S SOUND ASLEEP WHEN I slip out the door and pad into the kitchen. Usually after I fuck her senseless, she's out for a few hours, so I have a little time. It's nearly pitch black in the kitchen except for the eerie glow of the outdoor lights through the window. Which makes the goddamn package sitting on the counter look even more ominous.

A cardboard box of doom.

I knew it the minute Zoey's mom handed it to me.

I snatch it up together with the envelope and head downstairs to the studio. Sergey ran some sort of test on it, confirming the contents aren't dangerous. I mean, not technically dangerous. Ice runs through my veins as I turn the package over. Examine it. Set it down. Stare at it for a while. There's no way for me to sleep until I know what's inside. The thing is? I'm scared shitless to open it.

Fuck it.

I use a pen to puncture the tape, and then drag it lengthwise until I'm able to pop the box open. Another box rests inside, although it's not taped shut. The words "JADA ROGERS" are printed in all caps across the lid.

Immediately, I squeeze my eyes shut. Start breathing in. Breathing out. Surprisingly, I feel calmer than I thought I would. I decide to just get it fucking over with, so I pull out the smaller box and take off the lid.

There's not much inside. No shock there. It's not like she owned anything of value. There's a plain, wood container. A broken watch and a couple of cheap bracelets. Some used makeup. Three business cards, one for the bar she used to work at, one for The Mission and one for a lawyer named Alicia Spock.

Huh. The name rings a bell, but I don't know why.

My heart is still racing but I take the wood container out and study it. There's a dainty little clasp keeping it closed. I flip it open. Inside is a packet of Sudafed. A lighter. Two beakers. Bottle of nail polish remover. Jesus fuck. My mother was cooking meth? What the hell am I going to do with this shit? Who sent it to me in the first place? My hackles go up. *Am I being set up?*

Disgusted, I pick up the container and head outside through the garage. I'm about to dump it in the trash when I remember. Just like with my journal, I can't risk someone going through my garbage, finding meth work and writing some stupid story about me. I bring it back inside. Flush the pills down the toilet. I pull out the business cards and close the box. I'll have Sergey dispose of it together with the rest of the junk tomorrow.

My attention is now focused on the envelope. Carefully, I rip it open and dump out the contents. A couple pieces of folded paper fall out together with three photographs.

The first is a polaroid of my mom. She's heavily pregnant standing in front of the Space Needle wearing a huge smile. My God, she really was beautiful. My memories aren't completely fucked-up. Although, I have virtually no recollection of ever seeing her happy. When I turn the picture over, there's no writing on it. I suppose the baby must be me. Huh.

The next picture is tiny. Only about a square inch. It's a picture of a wrinkly newborn. On the back it says, "Tyson Rogers September 16." Wow. I've never seen this before. It's obviously me right after I was born.

The last one is of Jada wearing a blue floral dress, holding a baby in a white gown. Me again, I guess. It looks like the picture was taken in a church. There's an older man and woman standing behind us. On the back, all it says is "Tyson Christening." I scrutinize it for a moment. The couple must be my grandparents. I barely have any memory of them. My mom only bitched about how awful they were. In the photo, Jada actually looks fresh-faced and content. I certainly never saw her look so good.

Next, I look at the two pieces of paper. One is a list of men's names that I don't recognize. The other is a flyer for an old Limelight show at The Mission. On the back of the flyer all of the band member's names are neatly written in block lettering. Weird. I nearly toss them in the box of garbage but think better of it. Tuck the pictures and the business cards back into the big envelope.

Now that the mystery about what's in the box is solved, my first inclination is to hide the envelope. Then I think, why? Habit probably. Instead, I bring it upstairs with me. When I open the door to the bedroom, Zoey is still asleep. I place the envelope in the top drawer of my nightstand, take off my shorts and crawl back into bed with my wife.

When I wake up the next morning, it's late. Zoey isn't next to me, but I can hear a bit of commotion in the kitchen. Pots and pans clanking around. Animated conversation. I open the drawer to my nightstand and rifle through the pictures and business cards again. Put them away. I decide to take a shower before I face the in-laws. By the time I've dried off and thrown on a pair of board shorts, Zoey has joined me. She sits next to me on the bed and takes my hand. "I sent my folks out Christmas shopping so you could have a little break. Did you have trouble sleeping last night?"

"Yeah." I glance over at her. "I had to see what was in the box."

She puckers her lips, then releases them. "And?"

"How about I just show you."

Zoey sits on the bed while I retrieve the envelope from the nightstand and hand it to her. She opens it and sifts through the contents like a detective. She holds up the tiny baby picture. "Oh my God, you are adorable."

"I'd never seen these before last night." I take the picture from her and squint at it.

"What is this?" Zoey holds up the list of names. "It's all dudes. I wonder…"

I grab the list from her. "Do you think one of these guys could be my father?"

"Maybe?"

It's too much to think about. I gather everything up and shove it in the envelope and place it back in the drawer. "I'm not really sure what I want to do about all of this. All I know is I need some time to process it."

"Wouldn't it be nice to know who your biological father is?" Zoey's voice is tentative. "I mean, if not for our own kids' sake? Don't you ever wonder?"

"Nah." My entire life, Jada was consistent about reminding me she had no idea who my dad was. She joked about it. Used it as a weapon. Sometimes, she even cried about it if she was particularly wasted. At some point, I became a bit desensitized. "Truthfully, I never even considered the possibility I'd find out who my dad was. I'm really not sure that I want to know. My mom was a monster. I don't want to find out my father is just as bad or worse."

Zoey looks heartbroken. "Yeah. I didn't think about that. I'll drop it, baby."

"Thank you." We hear noises from down the hall. "Your mom and dad must be back."

I follow her down the hall to the living room to find not only Mike and Olivia, but Ronni and Connor with the twins, Tristan and Torin. Olivia is making googly faces at the infants, who stare up at them.

"Hey, man." I clasp Connor's hand and we do that side bro-hug thing.

Zoey hugs Ronni and joins her mom in ogling the twins. "May I?" she asks Ronni.

"Of course." Ronni gestures toward the boys. "Pick a twin. Any twin."

I certainly can't tell if she picks Tristan or Toran up, because the babies are dressed the same, but when Zoey snuggles the little one close, my heart swells in a way I never knew possible. My eyes are glued to my wife as she strokes his little head. Kisses his cheeks. Let's his tiny hand grip her finger.

She looks over at me with the most adorable grin. "I need one of these, Ty."

"Uh." My eyes are wide as I look over at her parents. Mike waggles his finger at me and shakes his head. Olivia laughs.

"You are more than welcome to take one of these lads off our hands for the night," Connor jokes. "They seem calm and sweet now but get 'em both going and holy bejeezus."

Ronni picks up the other twin. "You aren't giving my babies away, no matter how hard you try, Connor."

"Damn." Conner takes his son from Ronni and places him in my arms before I can protest. "Here, Ty, don't listen to her. He's yours."

Laughing, I awkwardly take the baby from our bassist and hold him up under his armpits away from my body. Ronni dashes over and gives me an assist. "Just support Tristan's neck and place him against your chest."

Once he's situated, I glance at Zoey, who just beams while rocking Toran. "You're doing great, babe."

I look down at the little guy and think about the picture of myself at the christening. I couldn't have been any older than the twins are now. He looks up at me innocently. Trustingly. And I know, without a shadow of doubt, nothing on earth would ever make me harm this child. And he isn't even mine.

Why did my mother hate me so much? What did I do to her? I've asked that question so many times.

At least I know now that I'm not the same kind of monster my mom was.

With Zoey by my side, I think I can be a good dad.

No, I *know* I can.

Chapter Fifteen

I'M SO FREAKIN' EXCITED, I can barely stand it. The past two months have been amazing. The funk Ty was in seems to have waned. The holidays were really fun. We've avoided the dark Seattle winter months and Ty and Connor worked together to produce his brothers' band's album. Padraig and Liam, Connor's twin brothers, practically moved in during the month of January. The music is amazing, and at long last Fireball is getting some traction.

Meanwhile, I've helped the foundation open up ten more schools for the program.

And now I have even better news to share with my husband. He's down in the studio in an LTZ band meeting. A Zoom call with management and their booking agency talking about what's next. As much as I'm dying to interrupt, I have to wait. Fidget. Wait. Fidget. Finally, I get sick of myself and open my laptop. At least I can answer a few emails while Ty's occupied.

Two long hours later, Ty shuffles into the kitchen looking exhausted. His hair is disheveled like he's been raking his fingers through it over and over. At least he smiles when he sees me. "Hey, babe." He embraces me from behind and kisses my cheek.

"You look a bit rough." I swivel in my stool and wrap my legs around his to pull him close. "What's going on?"

He grips the back of my chair on either side of my head. "Hourglass has run out. Management wants us to start recording. We can't figure out whether we'll do it here in LA or back in Seattle. Obviously, I don't really care. But Connor won't commit to a schedule until they know Ronni's shooting schedule. It's been a long-ass conversation and there's no resolution."

"It's tough when there are kids involved." I touch my lips to his. He takes the bait and we kiss a few times.

Ty wraps his arms around my shoulders. "Yeah. Except, it's more about Ronni, I think."

"Oh?" I'm surprised. Ronni's never struck me as someone who ever held Connor back. "Why do you say that?"

"Her show got picked up at Netflix. Connor really can't leave with the kids being so little."

I nod. "Well, that's awesome. And also, understandable. Zane wants to be with Mia when Fiona's working. Alex told me Jace is pretty settled out at the ranch."

"Yeah, and they're all in Seattle." Ty sits down beside me. "Our lives are changing, I get it. We agreed to take a few extra months—I mean, I was the biggest proponent of more time off, so I'm fine with it. We do have to get back to LTZ work, though. At least plan things out. Otherwise, fuck it. I want to start producing some of the projects I've been offered. Maybe even do a solo record."

"Well, I have something to tell you that might throw a wrench in the discussions. Actually, I have two pieces of news."

Ty raises an eyebrow. "Should I stay seated?"

"Yes. I'll be right back." I dash into the bedroom and return with a small, flat box wrapped in silver paper. Tied with a black chiffon ribbon. "This is a gift for you that I had made specially."

Ty takes the box and eyes me skeptically. "I'm intrigued. Is this an early Valentine's Day gift?"

"You could call it that." I shrug as nonchalantly as possible.

He rips open the paper to find what looks like a jewelry box inside. He purses his lips and squints at it before taking the top off. He finds two plastic sticks inside, both with double pink lines. His eyebrows nearly fly off the top of his head. "Does this mean..."

"Yes! I'm pregnant!" I fly into his arms. "Are you happy?"

Ty buries his face in my neck and squeezes me tightly against him. "I— Wow. Butterfly. Is this for real?"

I cup his face in both hands and kiss him full on the mouth. Stare into his deep-blue eyes. "Yes. It's for real. I booked flights for us to head back to Seattle this weekend so we can meet with my doctor and get the official results on Monday."

"Holy fucking shit." Ty shakes his head. His smile wide. "I'm gonna be a father. We're having a baby! Do we call your folks?"

"No, I think we get confirmation and probably wait until my first trimester is over. Just in case."

The expression on his face indicates he's clueless. "In case of what?"

"Not all first pregnancies make it, babe. I don't want to tell anyone until we get through the first three months." I take his hand and place it on my belly, then tip my lips up to his for a kiss. "For now, it's our little secret."

"Wow." He stares at his big palm across my lower stomach, which still has the tiny stubborn pooch but definitely isn't any bigger yet. He rubs up and down. Shakes his head. "Wow."

"You can't be all that surprised. Your dick practically lives inside of me."

He looks up at me, a naughty grin spreads across his face. "Nah. I guess I'm not. But it's nice to know my boys are swimmers."

Ty pulls me against him again tightly. His entire body enfolds mine. One hand cups my ass. The other is wrapped around my shoulder. We rock back and forth.

Me standing between his legs as he swivels on the barstool. I'm so happy at his reaction. Not that I didn't think he'd be excited. Part of me wondered if he'd freak out a bit, though. If I'm honest.

"So, I have some other news. I'm worried you won't take it quite as well, but I hope you won't be mad at me." I back away but keep a grip on his arms. "I looked up that woman from the business card in that envelope you got, Alicia Spock."

He squinches his nose and gives me a puzzled look. We really haven't talked about the contents in a few weeks, so I'm not surprised when he says, "Who?"

"The lawyer. From the envelope."

Ty's jaw sets. His face closes down. "Oh?"

"I called her." I bite my lip. I have no idea how he's going to take this.

Not well, apparently. He stands and looks out of the sliding glass window to the pool. His back is toward me. "Why would you do that, Z?"

"I wanted to surprise you." Suddenly, my well-intentioned query doesn't seem like it was the best idea. But, I dig myself in deeper. "I wanted to give you some closure about your mom."

Ty whirls around and shouts, "Closure? Do you really think I'll ever have any fucking closure after what I went through? You're delusional, Zoey."

Whoa.

"What was the purpose?" He advances toward me. His eyes blazing with anger. "After I trusted you with my journal, did you ever think that this was something you should have talked to me about? Maybe considered my feelings on the matter?"

"I thought—" I sputter.

"I lived through it. Why would I want to open another can of goddamn worms?" He stops in front of the counter. Crosses his arms protectively around himself. God, he looks absolutely crushed.

"Baby, I'm sorry. I overstepped. I really thought..." I reach for him but he pulls away.

"This is supposed to be an awesome day. The day we find out we're having a baby. Now, it's tainted." Ty stalks off toward our bedroom.

Wait, *tainted*? My eyes sting with tears. "Hey. That's really harsh, Ty. You *know* I wouldn't do anything to hurt you."

"Do I?" He whirls around. "Why wouldn't you talk to me about contacting her first? Maybe I don't want to open up a can of worms. Did you ever think of that? I'm still trying to process all of this shit."

"Fine. You're right. I should have talked to you first. For some reason, I thought it would be a nice thing to do." I slump against the wall. "I don't really know why I did it now that I see your reaction. I'm sorry I hurt you."

Ty's face softens. "I keep telling you I want to leave my past in my past. You have no fucking idea how hard it is for me to be *normal.* To fit in to some world that I can't begin to understand. If I talk to this person and learn something else that...uh. Fuck. Zoey. I'm hanging on by a thread. Don't you see that?"

"You *are* normal, though. Why would you say that?" I'm worried. I thought we had worked through most everything but he's *hanging on by a thread?*

"How is my life normal?" Ty approaches. His hands in the air. "Tell me. You know about how I grew up. I'm in a band with my best friend, who happens to be Carter-fucking-Pope's son. Now I'm this weird famous person that everyone wants a piece of. They think they know me. Like I'm some mythical rock god. 'Take your shirt off, Ty.' 'Sing us a song, Ty.' 'Sign this autograph, Ty.' It's fucking bizarro-land. You and I can't even go to the grocery store to get ice cream without some sort of mob scene."

"Yeah, but what is *normal*? You have friends. You have me. We are geeks who sit and watch Netflix all night. We can't keep our hands off each other. We talk about our hopes and dreams. No one is really normal, but this is *our* normal."

Ty shakes his head. "Sure, but there is a big part of me that needs to be on stage, Z. I love the feeling that I'm invincible. When I'm in front of our fans, it's really the only time I feel fully in control. It's like I'm someone with superpowers to make people happy. When it's just me? I know all of my flaws. I'm super aware that I'm on the verge of fucking up everything at any given moment."

"Do you really feel that way? That you're going to fuck things up?" I go to him and take his hands. "I don't see you that way. Ever. It breaks my heart to hear that you do."

He just shrugs.

"Do you still talk to Lisa? I haven't heard you mention her in a really long time." Part of me is starting to feel a bit nervous. "Maybe that would help. With all of this? Your past?"

Ty looks away. "Nah. Not for over a year."

Wait, what?

Somehow, I know to tread lightly. "Do you want to?"

"No. I really don't. And I don't want you *nagging* me about it either. Is there a way we can stop this conversation? Please?" Ty folds his arms across his chest. Sighs like he's annoyed.

"Yeah. I'm done. I just want to make things better, and I've made it worse." I absentmindedly rub my belly. Tears spill down my cheeks. I hate it when Ty and I fight. I hate it even more that he's struggling. I hate walking into landmines. Feeling like I'm intruding on something I don't understand. But I *need* to understand because these outbursts seem to come out of left field.

Ty's hands join mine at my belly. "I'm sorry, baby. I wish we could just focus on the future. Whenever I look backward, it bites me in the ass. I'm not mad at you. Not even a little bit. Mostly, I'm mad at the situation. I learned a long time ago, I can't fix myself. I've got to live with what's happened and move on. Look forward to the good things in life."

"That's what I want." I lean my head on his shoulder.

"You're my future. That shit in the envelope is my past. Can we leave it there?"

I nod, but now I'm sad. God, this day has gone so completely different than how I planned it in my head. I should have talked to him first and not charged ahead. What matters is the little baby I'm carrying. Our son or daughter.

It's just that... Crap. I'm so scared. He wouldn't even let me tell him about the conversation I had with Alicia Spock. What do I do? My emotions are all over the map. He needs to know, but now is certainly not the time. He's upset. I'm upset.

"I love you, butterfly." Ty's voice snaps me out of my spell.

I cling to his hands. Look up at him. Hope he feels how much he means to me. "I love you too, babe. I'm *really* sorry."

"We're fine." He presses his forehead to mine. "I'm so excited. Really. We're finally pregnant. This isn't tainted, forget I said something so stupid. Today is a miracle. Let's focus on that. Let's be happy."

"Okay." I smile at him.

Wishing I believed everything was fine, when all I can feel is a swirling sense of doom.

Like I've set something into motion I can't take back.

Chapter Sixteen

ZOEY'S SICK AGAIN. NAUSEA. Throwing up. It's been brutal. Headaches but thankfully not aura migraines.

Pregnancy hasn't been her friend, and we're finally through her first trimester. I'm waiting for her to get ready so we can go see her doctor. I'll admit, I've been on pins and needles. I'm reading too many internet medical sites in the middle of the night and freaking myself out. Zoey assures me her symptoms are par for the course.

"I'm sorry I'm running so late." Zoey's wearing leggings and one of my sweatshirts. Getting dressed has been a struggle for her on the bad days. Today is one of them. Secretly, I'm relieved she's having symptoms on the day we have the appointment. I want her doctor to see first-hand what she's been going through so she can fix it.

I help her into her raincoat. "Sergey will get us there on time, butterfly."

An hour later we're in the waiting room after Zoey's been through a battery of tests. Dr. Sabel joins us, looking at her chart. "Well, good news. Everything looks fine. Your blood pressure is within a normal range. If anything changes, especially if you get any bad headaches you need to let us know right away. We'd prefer you don't develop preeclampsia since you're already a bit of a higher risk for strokes because of your history with migraines."

"What can we do about the nausea? And the throwing up?" I hold Zoey's hand tightly. When she's feeling bad, I can't stand it.

"A lot of medications aren't safe for you to take while you're pregnant," Dr. Sabel warns. "Tyson, you can really help by keeping Zoey calm and stress-free."

Got it. Keep your shit together, Rainier.

Zoey squeezes my hand. "Dr. Sabel, what about sex? We ordinarily have a fairly active sex life, but it's been nearly a month since we've, um... Ty's worried about hurting the baby."

"*Zoey?*" My face turns red. She's not wrong, I am worried. I didn't expect her to be so blunt about it.

Dr. Sabel laughs. "For now, you should be fine. Intercourse is fine. Oral is fine. Even anal. I'd just say, please avoid anything too strenuous."

Got it. No porn-star fucking.

On the way home, Zoey and I hold hands in the back seat while Sergey drives. She leans in and whispers to me, "All I can think about is getting home and getting naked." She rubs our clasped hands across my cock, which springs to life. "This inside me would make me feel pretty damn good."

"Well then, I'm going to make you feel really, really good, baby," I say before pressing my lips to hers. We make out for the entire drive home, separating only when we pull into the driveway.

Once we're inside, I pick Zoey up and take her to our bedroom. Undress her. Spend twenty minutes eating her out. Savoring her tanginess. Licking and suckling her to oblivion. Making her come like it's my job because, according to her doctor, it kinda is.

She climbs on top of me and rides my cock like a greedy cowgirl, resting against my bent knees. God, how I've missed being inside her. She reaches back and strokes my balls, causing her back to arch and her heavy tits to jut forward. I cup her breasts, which are fuller, even more lush. Pregnancy has caused her nipples to darken into ripe, dark-pink berries. They're incredibly sensitive. Just little strokes over the tips causes them to tighten so deliciously. When I pinch them lightly, she grinds her clit against my pubis and moans through her orgasm. Watching her come apart sends me over the edge too.

We lie cuddled together in a bliss cocoon. I'm dozing off when my phone buzzes with a text. I see the number, but it's not one I recognize. So few people have this number, I decide to read it.

Ty, this is Alicia Spock. I have paperwork for you that needs to get finalized. Your manager gave me this number. Please call at your earliest convenience.

What the actual fuck. I'm furious. "Z, did you talk to that Alicia Spock woman again?"

"No, not since you told me not to," she mumbles, half-asleep

I try to control my reaction. I don't want to cause Zoey any stress, but it's hard. I'm triggered. Just like every other time my past comes up. Which is one of the worst parts about living with CPTSD, because I literally cannot control my reactions. But today, I'm not going to act like an asshole. I'm certainly not going to put my pregnant wife through any more bullshit, so I manage to keep my voice calm. "She just texted me. Apparently, Katherine gave her my number."

"You never wanted me to tell you about our conversation, so I dropped it. I never contacted her again." Zoey sits up. Studies me. "What's going on?"

I close my eyes and breath in. Breath out. My scalp tingles. "She says she has paperwork for me."

Zoey nods but stays silent.

"Would you please tell me what happened when you talked?" I get up and put on my shorts. I'm not having this conversation naked.

Zoey pulls on her underwear. Looks around for my sweatshirt. I hand it to her. Once she has clothes on, she sighs deeply. "She's legit. A lawyer at a medium-sized firm. She didn't tell me much, only that she had something for you at her office."

"Did you tell her it's me? She could be a star-chaser, Zoey." I throw my hands up. "Don't be so naive."

So much for not being an asshole.

She winces. "Give me a little fucking credit. I told her Jada passed and I was a lawyer in possession of some of her things, including Alicia's business card. All she told me was she had some paperwork to give to Jada's next of kin. Your name didn't even come up."

"Oh." I immediately regret my reaction. I always do. "God, babe, I'm sorry I got a little aggro."

Zoey finds her leggings and puts them on. "Ty, I've got to get this off my chest. Any time anything about your past comes up, you bite *my* head off. It hurts my feelings. I know it's hard for you. So, I try to respect your wishes and avoid the subject. Don't think I don't notice when you are bottling things up inside. You might think you're hiding it, but you're not."

"Your point being?"

She winces. "Fine. I was shocked to learn you aren't still working with Lisa when she's been so instrumental to your recovery. I'm not judging, but I will say this.

You owe it to our child to deal with your past and find out anything you can about your background. It's about more than just you and me now. I realize I'm not showing yet, but I feel this little baby growing inside me. He or she will be here before you know it. This is happening. There's no more time for this shit. Seriously."

She leaves the bedroom, not exactly in a huff. But holy hell, I'm on notice. No doubt about it. Truth be told, she's right. I can't lash out at the one person who is there for me. One day, I'll push her too far and losing her would end me. For a few minutes, I do my breathing exercises until I feel calmer. Then, before I can talk myself out of it, I text Lisa, asking her to set up an appointment.

My phone rings not a minute later. I shut the bedroom door and go into the bathroom. I don't want to hurt Zoey, but this therapy shit is between me and my therapist. If she's still my therapist, that is.

"Tyson." Lisa's soothing voice instantly makes me feel foolish for thinking she'd judge me for aborting our sessions. "I'm glad you called, I've been thinking about you and wondering how things are going."

I give her the quick rundown of the past year or so. I don't leave anything out. Jada's death and all of the shit surrounding Alicia Spock. The band, and the uncertainty about how we're all going to make it work now that we all have our own families. Zoey's health issues. Our marriage. Pregnancy. I unload about the severe anxiety I've been dealing with. My triggers. The blackout. My fear of letting down my wife and child.

"That's a lot to unpack, Ty. Last year when I agreed you could go off anti-anxiety medication, we were supposed to double up our sessions so I could monitor your progress. I haven't talked to you in over a year. Considering all you're balancing and dealing with, frankly, I'm worried about you." Lisa's admonishment feels pretty tame, thank God. "May I ask what you have told Zoey?"

I can't help but sigh. "Nothing."

"Nothing?"

I stare out the bathroom window to the pool. Zoey's lounging on a lawn chair with her laptop. Her hair is tied up in a knot. She's chewing on a thumbnail while staring intently at the screen. My heart cracks a bit. I hate lying to my beautiful wife. "Well, nothing about my CPTSD diagnosis. Or that I was on meds. I told her about the abuse, but..."

"She doesn't know the entire picture," Lisa finishes.

"No. But she's worried. I've lashed out."

"Ty, it's been a while, but what I'm about to say bears repeating. Growing up, you endured severe ongoing trauma. The abuse and repeated betrayals when your mother was supposed to be your caregiver trained your brain to cope with the inevitability of more trauma. Fear of intimacy. Trust Issues. Abandonment. I'm saddened but not surprised you haven't let Zoey fully in. What you are doing and feeling is common when you aren't managing your CPTSD," Lisa reminds me. "You do need help, and I'm not telling you anything you don't know."

Shit.

"Lisa, I do trust Zoey, I just can't seem to *tell* her. All of this shit with my mom dying? It's fucking with me. I haven't gone back to substances, but I can't seem to control when I lash out. I've hurt her feelings. More than once. I can't risk doing that to her when she's pregnant."

She sighs audibly. "Ah. Ty, it's also not surprising when you're triggered you default to reacting emotionally. Sometimes even irrationally. You're attempting to protect yourself by pushing your wife—who only wants to be closer to you—away. We made tremendous progress on your own internal belief system, but we were just scratching the surface about your CPTSD when you stopped therapy."

"It's true. I do feel strong about knowing my worth and all that."

"Well, at least that answers my question about what happened to you. When I didn't hear from you after reaching out several times, I'd hoped you'd found an- other counselor. Someone in the Seattle area, perhaps." Lisa sounds worried, but she keeps her professional de- meanor intact.

"I do appreciate your concern, Lisa. But, up until the past few months, I've felt great," I protest. "I *really* thought I was okay. Zoey and I took nearly a year-long vacation. Traveled. Had a lot of fun. Relaxed. Had lots of sex. It was the first time in my life I had no responsibility. And it was glorious. I didn't feel like I *needed* any help. Or maybe, I just wanted to live a little. Not be such a headcase all of the time."

"Ah, Ty. Of course, you deserve to live a wonderful life. It sounds like you've had a great adventure this year. A whirlwind of exciting experiences. All of which keep your endorphins high." Lisa's voice is softer now. "It's easy in those moments to push what you've been through out of your mind. But it's all still there, unfortunately. Now, all of your dreams with Zoey are coming true. You got married. You're having a baby. You're settling into real life. You reached out to me for a reason. Tell me how I can help."

All I know is getting back into therapy isn't what I want. "I was thinking that, for now, I'd like to go back on the anxiety meds."

There's a long silence.

"How do you expect that to help if you're not dealing with the root issue?" Lisa queries. "I'm not being judgmental, I'm sincerely curious about your mindset right now."

"I don't think I can handle that kind of deep therapy right now. And I don't want to tell anyone about the CPTSD, Lisa. Not even Zoey," I confess. "If I can just get my nerves under control, she and I can focus on the baby. I won't have outbursts and that will help me make sure Zoey's not under any stress."

Lisa is silent again for a few seconds before replying, "Ty, I'm empathetic to where you're at, but now I'm going to set a boundary. I will not prescribe anti-anxiety meds for you unless we start having sessions again and I can monitor you. If that isn't acceptable, I'm afraid you'll have to find another doctor. Meds alone will not fix what is going on with you. If you are willing to set up some official time, then we can continue this conversation and decide if, and when, you should be prescribed something."

"Oh. Shit." I'm completely deflated. I didn't even consider that I'm essentially treating Lisa like a drug dealer. Giving her no fucking respect. I'll just have to nut up. "I apologize, Lisa. I didn't mean to overstep. Truly. Let me check Zoey's schedule. I'll text you sometime when I'm free."

"Is it your intention to keep this from Zoey?" Lisa asks.

"Um—well."

"Ty, I look forward to getting our sessions scheduled. Before I go, there are two things I want you to remember. First is, you, as a survivor of complex trauma, have a tendency to look for any indication—or sign—that someone is trying to harm you. You'll fight. You'll flee. Or you'll freeze. Until we can get scheduled, pay attention to how you're feeling when there is something triggering. Try to breathe and use the tools I've given you before you react."

I'm floored. She's nailed it. I've been doing all of these things. "Okay, what is the second thing?"

"Please reconsider telling your wife. Partners of people living with CPTSD have a very hard time understanding what is happening when you exhibit behavior you can't always control. Consider that Zoey probably *really* is trying to figure out how to help you. When you react to a trigger, she probably also feels like she's doing something wrong." Lisa's voice is soft, without any pressure whatsoever. "Telling her might be stressful for *you*, but consider whether her knowing will actually be less stressful for *her*."

"But how do I know that? What if knowing her husband has a mental illness makes her more stressed?"

She takes a minute before answering, "Well, here's something else I can offer. I'm happy to set up some sessions with the three of us. To help explain and ease her worries. I truly believe if you can find a way to trust your diagnosis is safe with her, you'll be surprised at what you might gain."

All of what Lisa says makes sense.

Every single thing.

I only hope I'm strong enough to take her advice.

For my sake, and for Zoey's.

Chapter Seventeen

ALEX IS WAITING FOR me at the end of the gravel drive. My BFF hasn't changed at all. She wears her uniform of a black t-shirt and jeans. Black Frye boots. Her honey-colored hair is in two braids. Stunning. The woman can't be called anything else.

The second she sees I'm coming up the drive, she bounces up and down excitedly. When I pull up and park, I barely put on the brake before she's yanked the door open. "Get your ass out here, woman. I cannot believe you'd keep this from me."

"Alex, you know I had to. But, we're telling everyone this week. We're due late this year." I hop out of my SUV and squeeze her tightly. "I've never been so excited."

We start walking toward her house. What started out as a pretty modest place when Alex bought it a couple years ago has turned into a sprawling, modern ranch house. Jace's sister Jennifer and her girlfriend, Becca, are caretakers at the ranch. They live on the property in their own small guest house and are former construction workers who helped Jace and Alex build a separate wing with several guest rooms, as well as a big practice space for the band.

Alex opens up the fridge and pulls out some meat and cheese, but doesn't touch it, even as I chow down. "Jace was a little bummed that the band decided to take three more months. I think he's getting worried that LTZ is calling it quits."

"Ty is getting anxious to go back, too. But I don't think Jace should worry. The timing makes logical sense. The restaurant opens soon. Ronni's on a three-month shoot, so when that's over, Connor should have more flexibility." I pat my belly. "I'll be huge by the time they start recording, most likely."

Alex chews a bite of cheese thoughtfully. "I'm looking forward to all of that. Your baby bump. Recording. It's been a long time since I've been around Jace during the recording process, isn't that a trip?"

"Not since we were teenagers. Speaking of Jace, where is he?" I look around. "Where is everyone?"

"Becca and Jen are gone for the weekend. They are finally getting married, so they're visiting a couple of venues. I offered the ranch, but they want to go somewhere where they can be pampered. Who could blame them?" Alex laughs. "Jace and Lena are out at the grocery store. Getting the fixings for a peanut butter pie. It's a new thing. He makes pies."

"Pies?"

"My mom taught him." Alex rolls her eyes. "Just when I thought I was through with all that."

"Oh, God." I shake my head. "The sexy drummer from LTZ is making pies. The hot singer knocked up his wife. What happened to those bad-boy rockers we picked out at The Mission?"

"I'd bet Ty still has an eight-pack just like Jace. They were workout buddies for a long time." She wags her finger at me.

"It's true. Ty's in the gym more than ever right now. Sometimes he works out for three hours a day." I take the empty plate to the sink and rinse it off. Stare out the window for a sec. As much as I'm tempted, I'm not going to talk about my worries about Ty with Alex. Not anymore. I've grown up. I talk about it with him, or not at all.

Right now, it's not at all. I'm afraid of walking into another landmine. I figure, we can sort things out after the baby is born. It's not like either of us are going anywhere.

So, I change the subject. "Show me the new horses, I'm dying here."

We spend the afternoon with her newest animals. Ty made me promise not to ride, but he didn't say anything about brushing and grooming them. It's so relaxing out here in the peace and quiet. On this beautiful property. I swear, I've never seen Alex happier than she is on her ranch. Especially with her family. Jace. And Helena.

By the time we return to the main house, the two of them are in the kitchen working on the pie. The room is an explosion of pastry. It's a disaster. It's impossible not to gasp.

When Jace sees the look on Alex's face, he saunters over to her. Kisses her cheek. "We'll clean it up, don't worry."

Lena is covered in flour and runs up to Alex. "Mama, we're making a pee-butt pie!"

"I can see that, so keep the grubby little mitts off me until your dad cleans you up." Alex grabs a couple of bottles of water from the fridge and gives Jace a smooch on a clean part of his cheek. "We're going to sit out under the heater on the porch, babe."

Jace grins at us and redirects Helena to the pie-making task at hand.

I snatch a couple of cozy throws from her couch before we head outside. "I'm always freezing right now; this pregnancy hormone thing is whack. You sure you don't want to get yourself married and knocked up too?"

Alex turns the heaters on and takes a seat. Curls her feet under her. "Married? Yeah. Probably. Knocked up? Not a chance. We're not planning for any more kids."

My bestie never wanted children. After Jace went through hell with Helena's mother's family, they adopted her. The little darling may not be their biological child, but she couldn't be more loved. Part of me thought that Alex might change her mind. Especially once I got pregnant. My visions of us raising babies together are not to be, I guess. "I get it. You've always known what you want."

Alex nods. Looks out across the pastures. Tightens her blanket around her. I reach over and clasp her shoulder. "Is everything okay?"

"Uh, yeah. Of course," Alex says too quickly. "I just miss this. Whenever you and I have time together, it makes me realize how little we see each other anymore."

"Adulting is weird. Of course, having a lot of sex with the guys we love is definitely *not* weird. It's awesome. I'd never want to go back to being seventeen."

Alex laughs. "That couldn't be more true. Oh, I forgot to ask. Are you guys going to the friends-and-family opening for Fiona's restaurant?"

"Of course. Do you really think the guys will be able to pull off a secret show at The Mission?" I'm so excited to see LTZ play live. It's been over a year. "I heard the guys are coming out here for a weekend to rehearse."

Alex wrinkles her nose. "They are? I didn't know about it."

"Um, I didn't realize..."

"Gawd. That man. Do you mind if I have a word with him?" Alex stands up and then sits back down. She looks pale.

"Are you okay?" I reach over to touch her forehead.

She shakes me off. "I'm fine, I stood up too fast when I haven't eaten enough today. I'll be right back." She doesn't wait for my reply as she pushes through the door into the house.

Five minutes later, she returns with Helena, who is now clean and wearing a new outfit. "Lena, can you show Zoey the new chickens?" Alex shoots me a pleading look. I take the hint. She needs a moment, and I'll give it to her.

When Alex disappears back inside, Lena and I go hang out with the chickens. I take her for a walk around the property when my BFF doesn't return right away. I'm completely confused about what's going on, but I'll always have my best friend's back. Hanging with her daughter is a joy, anyway.

After thirty minutes, Jace finds us. His hair is haphazardly piled on his head. He's still caked in pie dough. On top of that, he looks depleted. Not a good look for a guy who's as laid-back as LTZ's drummer is. "Hey, Alex isn't feeling that great. She's lying down. She told me to tell you she's sorry but she's not up for any more today."

"What's going on, Jace?" My heart can't take knowing something's wrong with Alex. It's not like her to act like this. Plus, I've got the market on drama. Not her.

He sighs. He picks up Lena and tilts his head to his daughter, indicating it's not something he can discuss in front of her. We walk toward my car. When I get in, he gestures for me to roll down the window. "It's something she and I need to work through, I hope you understand."

"Yeah. Okay. Tell her I love her." I wave to Jace and Helena and leave. Feeling a bit blue. As I head toward the ferry, I call Ty.

He sounds like he's out of breath. "Hey, babe. I'm in the middle of a run, what's up?"

"Again?" I'm a little annoyed, honestly. Hormones. Everything bugs me right now. Especially Ty's work-out schedule.

"Wow, what's wrong?" I can hear him shut off the treadmill.

I press my palms to my eyes. "I'm sorry. That came out wrong. Things got a little weird here. Something's up with Alex and Jace, so I'm on my way home. I'm feeling edgy."

"Oh, shit. That sucks. How about I start dinner so it will be done by the time you get here?"

God I love this man.

We hang up. Rather than go up on the ferry deck, I stay in my car and think about the past topsy-turvy months. We've had so much to deal with. But I'm not sure why Ty has started such an aggressive work-out routine. He's always taken care of his body, but right now it's insane. You'd think he was training for a marathon or something.

It's like his obsession with exercise has taken over his obsession with having sex with me. Even after we got the all-clear from Dr. Sabel, sometimes we go four or five days without being intimate. And then, it's only when I initiate.

I'm trying not to takc it personally, but it sucks. He used to not be able to keep his hands off me. I still want him as much as I ever have. More, probably. Pregnancy makes me incredibly horny.

As I'm sitting in my car alone, suddenly I feel ugly. And fat. My boobs have gone up an entire cup size. None of my pants except leggings fit. My face is fuller. My body is just changing.

Meanwhile, he's ripped and as gorgeous as a super-model. Hell, he's the face of half-a-dozen designer ad campaigns. We were just in New York last week for a Prada photo shoot. My husband really *is* a supermodel.

And I'm just...plain old me.

By the time I get home, I've worked myself into a state. True to his word, Ty's plating up dinner. Homemade pasta with gorgonzola pesto sauce. Carbs and fat. I've been craving this meal so much, he makes it at least once a week now. His face lights up when he sees me. "Hey, butterfly. I made your favorite."

"I appreciate it, but I'm not hungry." I kick off my shoes and dump my purse on the counter. Then huff to the living room and flop down on the couch. Sulk. I know I'm being a hormonal psycho, but I can't help myself.

Ty follows me and sits down too. "Oh, babe. Don't be upset. Alex will be fine. It was just a bad day. Come eat. You're growing our baby, you need some nutrition."

"*No*. I'm full of nutrition. So much nutrition that I'm fat and ugly." I burst into tears. "And you won't even have sex with me anymore."

His eyes nearly pop out of his head. "What? You're so beautiful. The most beautiful girl in the world. Why would you think that?"

"All you do is work out. All day. All night. Or you're in the studio. I'm watching my body change and you don't want me the way you used to. If you're not attracted to me now, what's going to happen when my belly gets big?"

"Oh God, butterfly!" Ty takes my hand. Pulls me against his body. "I can't wait for you to have a huge belly. It's going to be awesome."

All I can do is cry. And cry and cry. Ty rocks me until I settle a bit. "I need to be close to you, and I feel like you're pulling away. Ever since I found out I was pregnant, it's like I'm not your sexy wife anymore. All I am is a baby vessel."

A myriad of emotions pass across Ty's face. He's clearly concerned about my state of mind. But he's also...scared? Maybe guilty? I can't focus enough to analyze. I'm too caught up in my own shit. Ty wraps his arms around me and squeezes. "I love you, baby. What do you need from me? I'll do anything."

"Just you." My voice is small. I feel so insecure.

Ty pulls off my shirt and throws it on the floor. Unclasps my front-clasp bra. Works it down my shoulders and tosses it on top of my shirt. Gently, he lays me back on the cushions. Begins to worship me. Kisses my entire face while rubbing his hands on every part of my exposed body. My collarbone. My upper arms. My forearms. My wrists. Each finger. My palms.

With both hands he cups my breasts and pushes them together. Swirls his tongue on my nipples until they are tight and needy. Satisfied, he strips off my leggings. Then my socks. Rubs his hands over my feet. Calves. Thighs. Hips. Stomach. Then back up my arms, breasts, and neck. He follows his caresses with soft kisses on each body part. By the time he reaches my lips, he's literally kissed my entire naked body. He looks at me like I'm the sexiest woman on the planet. "Better?"

I nod. Tears well in my eyes. This time, happy tears. He kisses them away before standing and stripping. I watch him in awe. He's like a marble statue. Every muscle on his body pops. His granite-hard cock is flush against his tight abs. His hair flows around his shoulders, halfway down his back. It's been months since he's had it cut.

God, he's even more beautiful now than he was ten years ago.

I reach for him and he kneels between my legs. He spreads them by pressing my knees apart with his palms. Hoists my calves over his neck and scoops up my ass to bring my pussy to his lips. With one hand he grabs a cushion and places it under my hips. At this angle, I'll be able to watch every single thing he does with his mouth. I can feel moisture run down my thighs just thinking about it. He peers at me through my spread legs. "Watch me love you. So you never, ever have any doubt about how much I want you. How much you turn me on."

Ty tastes and savors me. He doesn't leave one millimeter of my pussy unexplored with his tongue. And lips. And fingers. Our eyes remain locked as he shows—not tells—me how much he loves me. I'm a multi-orgasmic, blissful mess. Then, he throws the pillow on the ground and guides his cock inside me. Fucks me. Loudly.

Our bodies slap together. The smell of sex permeates the living room. He rubs my clit furiously, and when I go over yet again, he yells, "Fuck yeah" and spurts his release all over my tits. Runs his finger through his come and feeds it to me. Then, gentle Ty returns. He cleans me up with a warm washcloth. Tenderly sucks my nipples. Kisses my neck and eventually my lips. Showers me with every ounce of affection I could ever hope to have from my husband.

"I don't want you to ever think I don't want you, baby. Because I do. I always do," Ty whispers in my ear as I lie satiated in his arms. "I'm so sorry you thought I was pulling away. Everything I do is for us. For you."

I run my finger down his chest. "I'm so sorry I'm a hormonal time bomb. But we only get to go through this first time once. I just want you present. So much."

"Yeah." He stares off into space. Another thing he's doing more and more of. "I'll do better."

I choose to believe him.

Despite our incredible lovemaking, I ignore yet another nagging feeling that something is off with him. With us.

Because, what choice do I have?

There's no turning back now. We're having a baby soon.

I just hope he's ready.

Chapter Eighteen

IT'S IN THE MIDDLE of the night, and I can't sleep. Again. Zoey rests peacefully beside me.

There's so goddamn much on my mind.

Some good things, though. It feels incredible to finally have an agreed-upon schedule with my band. For fuck's sake, it's taken long enough. The opening of Fiona's restaurant, *Gus*, is the catalyst. We're kicking off LTZ business by playing a show for two hundred select guests at The Mission, including a bunch of kids from my foundation. A few super fans. Friends and family. It will be great.

Connor and Ronni arrive from LA in a few weeks. I have a surprise cooked up for Zoey. I'm telling her all of the guys are staying at the ranch overnight to rehearse. In reality, we'll be at our house when the ladies throw her a baby shower. I nearly derailed the whole thing when I told Zoey we'd be practicing out at the ranch. My feeble attempt at a distraction backfired. Alex thought Jace had forgotten about the shower.

Jace texted me to let me know Alex was mad at him. She made up an excuse that she wasn't feeling well, which is why Zoey came home early that day. Seems weird and very unlike Alex and Jace, but who am I to argue?

In any case, Zoey's pregnancy hormones were not something I factored into the equation of me trying to get my own shit together. Especially since I started my sessions with Lisa again. Two horribly tough hours each week. One hundred and twenty minutes of mind-fuck. Delving into the shit drains me mentally, and because the anxiety meds haven't completely kicked in yet, the only thing that keeps me functional afterward is exercise.

Up until last night, I'd actually been proud of how I'd been handling things. Sure, I've been working out a lot more. What Z doesn't know is two of the hours I'm supposedly in the gym are actually my sessions with Lisa. I thought I'd been doing everything in my power to take care of my wife. Cooking nutritious meals. Rubbing her feet. Giving her massages. Not putting any pressure on her to have sex.

I couldn't fucking believe it when she actually thought I didn't find her attractive anymore.

As if.

It's been added back into her care routine. Not that making love to my wife is a hardship. I love her changing body. She's so fucking hot. Her curves are lush. She positively glows. And, she's so incredibly orgasmic right now. When she comes, her entire body relaxes. She sleeps so restfully. Like now.

I just wish I had the same benefits.

It's the therapy. After a session, fucking is the last thing I feel mentally capable of doing. Let alone sleeping. It's not only the subject matter. It's the guilt about keeping such a huge part of my life from Zoey. And now more guilt because of how much time I have to devote to this shit in order to keep Lisa off my back.

Time I should be spending with my pregnant wife.

The least I can do is make her feel beautiful and wanted. Her well-being is the most important thing in both of our lives right now because she's the one carrying our baby.

Lisa continues to encourage me to tell Zoey we're working together again. And about the CPTSD. But I'm stubborn. I *know* what's best. Now is not the time. Not when our child's health is at stake. Not when my wife needs me to be strong. I'm doing something right. Her blood pressure is normal, which it most certainly won't be if I dump more of my shit on her now.

So, no way am I doing that. It's not even a question.

Tomorrow we're finding out if we're having a boy or a girl. It makes all of this so real. Zoey's already connected to our baby because it's growing inside her. She may not realize it, but she always cradles her belly now. Instinctively protecting our child. Loving our child. I'm not jealous, exactly. It's just I can't help but wonder.

When he or she is born, will I feel the same connection?

Seven hours later, I hold Zoey's hand at the doctor's office. I'm exhausted. Last night my brain wouldn't fucking shut off. Breathing didn't help. I couldn't get up and exercise in fear of waking her up. Consequently, I didn't sleep a fucking wink. I'm trying to be present. I really am because I realize it's monumental to find out the sex of your first baby.

But, I can admit it. At least to myself. I'm just going through the motions. Staring at a weird monitor while the doctor coats Zoey's stomach in goo and swirls some sort of device all around it. The whirring sound nearly lulls me to sleep. In fact, I think my eyes even close for a second when Zoey grips my hand and jolts me awake. She's beside herself with excitement. "Ty, pay attention. We're going find out..."

"Sorry, Z." I blink rapidly and force myself to smile. "I'm ready."

A few seconds later, Dr. Sabel looks up and grins. "It looks like you're having a boy."

Everything falls away. All of the exhaustion is replaced with joy when I see the little alien-looking 3-D image of my son. I kiss Zoey's forehead. "A boy," I whisper. "Wow."

I'm on cloud nine when we leave the doctor's office through the back door. Zoey is more subdued, although she seems to be excited to see Sergey waiting for us. Zoey hugs him. "We're having a son," she tells him as soon as the door to the car is closed.

"That's fantastic." He pumps his fist. "I'm so happy for the two of you."

I cuddle Zoey close to me on the ride home. Listen to her call her parents. Alex. Fiona. Even Ronni. Through the phone, I hear all of the excitement and congratulatory squeals. I repeatedly kiss the side of her head, staring out the window, lost in thought. Freaking out a bit. What the fuck do I know about being a father to a baby boy?

"Ty?" Zoey waves her hand in front of my face.

She comes into focus and I shake my head to clear the cobwebs. "Sorry, baby. I was zoned out for a second. What were you saying?"

"Never mind." She twists out of my embrace and looks out the window.

I close my eyes and sigh quietly. Mentally chastise myself. I touch her shoulder. Come up with a truthful, but lame explanation. "Z. I didn't sleep well last night. I was so excited."

"It's fine," she says without looking back at me.

So, it's *not* fine.

When we get home, Zoey changes into sweats and logs on to her computer. Doesn't really talk to me, instead buries herself in work. I head down to the gym and run six miles. Take a quick shower and head back into the living room. She's still on her computer, staring intently at the screen.

"Did I do something to piss you off, Z?" I sit next to her. Glance over at what she's so engrossed in. She has a search open to marriage counselors. "Ah. So, this is where we're at."

She takes a deep breath. Steels herself and looks at me. "Yeah, I think it is."

My heart thunders in my chest. She's fucking leaving me. Holy. Fucking. Shit. I look down at my clasped hands, which are resting on my thighs. A lump forms in my throat. I know, without a shadow of doubt, that I will die if I lose Zoey.

"What can I do?" I whisper. "To make you stay."

"What the hell are you talking about?" Zoey pushes on my arm, somewhat playfully. Somewhat seriously. "Are you crazy?"

But those words.

Those words.

Set. Me. Off.

I jump up and begin to pace. Then turn to her and scream, "So, what if I *am* crazy? Will that give you the excuse you need?"

Zoey's mouth drops open. She presses the palm of her hand to her stomach. "What? What excuse?"

"Nothing. Forget about it," I snarl.

"Ty, do you *really* think I'm trying to find an excuse to leave you? That's what you meant, right? Because of what you told me? Because I know about your abuse?"

I just look at her. I don't answer. I just seethe.

"You know what, Ty? Ever since you told me, I've researched and tried to learn all that I could so I could be a good partner to you. I've tried to do as you asked. Not bring things up. Let the past stay in the past. But

I can't anymore. Not for my sake. Not for your sake. Not for our son's sake. We need help to navigate this. To communicate. *That's* what I was doing. Finding us a counselor. Because I *want* to be with you *forever*." Her voice is calm, but firm. "I *promise* I'm not leaving you. I just want you to trust me. If you can't, Ty, what do we have to hold on to?"

My perfectly crafted house of cards tumbles down all at once, and it's almost like an out-of-body experience when I hear myself bellow, "There *is* something going on. Four years ago, I was diagnosed with a mental illness. CPTSD. No one but Lisa knows about it and I want to keep it that way."

Clearly, she wasn't expecting to hear me say that. Her eyes are wide as saucers. "Wait, what did you just say?"

I repeat myself. Verbatim.

Zoey tilts her head, her eyes still bugged out. "Four *years* ago?"

"Don't worry about it. I've got it under control. Ask Lisa. I'm back in therapy." I cross my arms petulantly.

"Don't *worry* about it?" Zoey curls her feet under her. Grabs a pillow and hugs it in front of her belly. "I'm trying to be calm, but what you just said? I've never been so scared in all my life, and I want to understand exactly what you're telling me."

"Wait here." I jog back to our bedroom and return with my journal from Zoey's jewelry safe. I angrily toss it on the couch next to her. "Don't you remember? It's all in there. My mother left me a legacy of shit to deal with. It's so fucking *awesome*."

She looks down at the journal. Then looks at me. Pats the sofa next to her. "Ty, I've never wanted to read your journal. I want you to *talk* to me."

That's when my mind catches up to what happened. I blew up *again*. At my pregnant wife.

All my anger drains out of me and is replaced with fear. And resignation. And shame.

She knows.

Holy fuck.

I plop down next to her and bury my face in my hands. It takes me several minutes of doing my breathing exercises before I can look at her. "It's mortifying. Five years ago, Zane and Carter took me to rehab. After working with Lisa for a while, she diagnosed me with Complex Post Traumatic Stress Disorder. It was brought on by my childhood trauma."

"When you told me about...all of that stuff, I assumed Lisa was still working with you. To cure you."

Zoey's so blissfully ignorant of my shame. I wish I could keep her that way, but now the cat's out of the bag. I'm dragging her down with me. My son too. Exactly what I never wanted to happen. She might as well know what she's dealing with. "No, that's where you are wrong. I'll never be cured."

"Never?" Her eyes fill with tears.

I shake my head.

"But why would you keep this from me?" She looks so lost. Vulnerable. Sad.

Without hesitation, I unload the truth. "When we first got to know each other again, I thought I had my shit handled. No, I *did* have my shit handled. Lisa thought so, too, and I went off my anxiety meds. I didn't tell you because I thought it would upset you. Then you had the accident. I just couldn't get the words out. Then too much time passed, and I felt guilty. Recently? The past few months have been..."

"Overwhelming." She takes a deep breath. Wipes the tears from her eyes with her sleeve.

"Yep."

We sit on the couch together for long time. Neither of us moving. Neither of us talking. Finally, Zoey gets up and disappears into the restroom. Returns. Grabs a bottle of water from the fridge and pads over to where I'm still sitting and stands in front of me. "I'm not going to do anything dramatic, Ty. We're married. We're having a baby. That means we're tied together forever. I've got to be completely honest with you. I'm so incredibly hurt right now. I can't even find the words. And so we're clear, it's not that you are dealing with..."

"CPTSD," I help her out.

"CPTSD," she repeats. "I'm hurt because you lied to me. For nearly two years. Even after everything we've been through. After the promises we made. Still, we're married. I'm pregnant. I take my vows to you seriously. But, right now? I can't even process. I actually don't know how to unpack this level of deceit. It's making me question everything we have ever been to each other. Who we can be."

She's right. I did this to us. *Me*. I can't even look at her. I hang my head in utter and total shame. How could I have thought I was protecting her?

It's all so clear to me now.

"Ty, look at me, please. This is important."

I do.

Zoey's expression is softer. I can see she's frightened. But strong. "The thing is, I love you. Deeply. You're my guy. Rather than jump to all sorts of conclusions. Rather than issue ultimatums. Or storm out of here. Or call my mom. Or take you in my arms. Or fuck you. Or tell you to fuck off. Rather than react at all, I need to sit with this. Analyze. Ponder. Whatever you want to call it. Right now in this moment? I have no idea where we go from here. All I know is we have to address this. Immediately. You and me. Or we won't make it."

"Don't say that, Z. We're going to make it." I'm in agony.

She shuts her eyes. Sighs. "There's nothing in the world I want more, babe. It's just...I would like to have a discussion with Lisa. Can you set it up for tomorrow? I need to have more information about..."

"CPTSD."

"Yeah, CPTSD."

"Yes." I look up at her. Now that she knows, I will literally do anything she wants to make sure she doesn't leave.

Zoey looks confused. "Yes, what?"

"I'll set it up now." I pull out my phone and send Lisa and Zoey a text making an introduction and request for a meeting. "Done."

A tear escapes and rolls down her cheek. "Thank you. Can I ask you one thing?"

"Anything."

"Is any of this real for you?" She gestures around our house and then points between me and her. "Because, I believed in us. I believed we could get through anything."

"*Everything* between you and me is real. It's always been real." I reach for her, but she takes two steps away from me. "Zoey, *please*..."

"No, Ty. I need some time on my own. Because you and me doesn't feel real at all right now. But, do you know what *is* real?" She cups her stomach. "He is. So everything I do from now on is with our son in mind. And everything *you* do should be the same. Right now, I need to go relax. Calm down. Take care of him. Alone."

She grabs her laptop, and my journal. Then turns and walks away from me to our bedroom.

I hear the door lock.

That's when it all sinks in all the way down to my toes. Life as I've known it is over.

After tonight, nothing will be the same with Zoey.

Ever again.

Chapter Nineteen

WHEN I WAKE UP, it's nearly ten a.m. I'm exhausted. I spent the entire night crying about what happened with Ty. Reading about CPTSD. Medical sites. Blogs. Survivor stories. I pored over everything, except his journal, until I finally passed out a couple of hours ago.

I can't pretend that I'm processing what Ty told me, I'm not. I can't pretend that I'm not terrified, I am.

I'm also brokenhearted. Over the past twelve hours, I've read enough to know how badly my husband must have suffered to be diagnosed with CPTSD. How it's affected everything he's ever done. Every thought in his mind. Every decision he makes. Every relationship he has.

I'm so angry at him for lying to me. The betrayal is agonizing. But, I'm beginning to understand. Not excuse. Just understand.

I can't help but feel proud of my husband for surviving. He's resilient. Brave. He's turned out to be a sweet, caring, kindhearted person. He put himself out there with me. Not all survivors of CPTSD can do that.

On the other hand, I also realize that he's been in hiding for his whole life. Not just from me. Not just from LTZ.

From himself.

I roll over and peek through the gauzy curtains to see Ty sitting in our back garden overlooking the city. He's not gazing out at the view, he's facing me. He peers up at our bedroom window, almost like he can feel me watching him. I can tell he hasn't slept much either. His hair is disheveled and his clothes are wrinkled. I want to go to him. Comfort him. Tell him it's going to be okay. That we'll get through this.

But, I can't. Because I'm not sure that's true. Not anymore.

I know some of his reactions aren't his fault. From my extensive reading last night, I've gleaned the trauma he suffered as a child rewired his brain. He doesn't think like I do. Actually, he doesn't think like most people. I had an "aha" moment when I read a survivor blog describing how CPTSD manifests in real life. It was eerie.

Spacing out. Losing focus at the weirdest times. Like at our baby's ultrasound.

He's also emotionally overreactive. It's always been like that with him. Ecstatic. Angry. Hurt. Loving. Attentive. Creative. Happy. Sad. Reactive. Considerate. Enthusiastic.

Sexual.

I attributed these characteristics to his artistic mind. Never in a million years did I think "mental illness." In my mind, it's not a stigma. Or, it shouldn't be. It's just that...fuck. Ty's my husband. I'm not an expert. Not from one night of reading. I can admit, I'm in way over my head.

But, I am determined. I will figure out a way to get my family through this. I owe it to Ty. I owe it to me. Mostly,

I owe it to our son. I'll do whatever it takes. Starting with an emergency Zoom session with Lisa later tonight.

For right now, in this moment, I need to take care of myself. And my baby. Put the oxygen mask on, as they say. After a long, cool shower I slather myself in lotion. Moisturize my face. File my nails. Pluck a few errant eyebrow hairs. Put on a little makeup. Find something comfortable, but pretty, to wear. Dry my hair.

When I get to the kitchen, Ty is plating up an omelet and home fries. "You need to eat, Z." His voice is devoid of emotion as he sets it on the counter. "At least let me still feed you."

"Come here, babe." I hold out my hand to him. He looks at me with confusion. I wiggle my fingers. Tentatively, he approaches. I place his big hand over my belly. "Say good morning to your son."

He looks up at me with tears in his eyes.

"I want to get through this, Ty. I *hope* we can. But honestly. I don't *know* how we can. We *won't* if you continue to keep things from me. Lying is a hard no. Talking with Lisa later will hopefully clear up some of my questions, but this is going to be a long haul. Our blissful, idyllic year is officially over. Now the hard work on our marriage begins."

"I know." He pulls out the barstool for me to sit, so I do. "Now that I've told you, I don't know why I ever kept it from you in the first place."

I take a bit of the delicious eggy goodness. "As you probably guessed, I immersed myself in CPTSD all night."

"I figured." He nods.

"What happened to you isn't your fault." I cock my head. "I'm sure you know that."

He squeezes his eyes shut. "I do. Did you read it?"

"If you're referring to your journal, no." I take another bite. "But I'm beginning to think I should. Would you read it with me?"

He looks up and out the window. Breathes in. Breathes out. I recognize these exercises as one of the tools Lisa gave him to cope. All of the things he's religious about? Exercise. Sticking to a routine. It's all so clear to me now. Except the past year has been a giant upheaval. Me coming back into his life. The band's hiatus. Jada's death. Our wedding. The baby. It's a lot for *anyone*. So, yeah. I'm willing to cut my husband a little slack.

As long as we can come up with a path forward. A healthy path.

"I'm not sure I can handle that, Zoey," Ty finally answers. He's clearly forlorn. Like he wants to do it to please me. "Some things..."

"It's okay. I don't want to do anything—or ask you to do anything—that will be harmful to you. Please know that you can always be honest with me. I won't judge you. If something feels too hard, tell me. Just like you did now." I slide off the stool and stand in front of him. Place my hands on his forearms. Squeeze. "I'm going to do whatever I can to be your safe place."

"I hate this. I hate being broken. You deserve so much more." Ty's voice cracks.

I put my finger to his lips. "You are *not* broken. I love you. All of you. Thank you for breakfast. I didn't sleep last night, so I'd like to lie down before our call with Lisa. I won't forgive myself if I don't keep this little guy healthy."

"Can I nap with you?"

I hold out my hand. "Of course."

He takes it and we go to our bedroom. Sleep overtakes me immediately when he cuddles me close and we curl up together. When I wake up a few hours later, Ty's still wrapped around me, his hand rests protectively on my belly. I arch my neck slightly to study him. He's peaceful. I look at the scars in his eyebrow and feel sad that his biggest scars are inside of him.

"Creeping?" He opens his eyes slowly. Blinks at me.

"Yeah."

He squeezes me against him. "I'm glad."

An hour later, we log into the Zoom call with Lisa. I'm so anxious, I can barely breathe. I feel like my entire relationship is riding on this call. Which is irrational. Nonetheless, it's my truth. Ty and I sit together on the couch. He hasn't talked much. I sense he's nervous too.

Lisa's face finally appears on the screen. She's the epitome of cool. Maybe eight or nine years older than Ty. Long dark hair. Edgy but professional-looking. Kind eyes. "Zoey, it is so wonderful to see you again."

I look over at Ty and back at the screen. "Uh. Thanks."

She laughs. "I forget, you have been the topic of many a conversation while you only met me that one time."

"You got me there. Plus, I only learned about Ty's diagnosis yesterday." My knee bounces nervously.

She starts our session by addressing Ty. "Tyson, I'm very proud of you for having the courage to tell Zoey the truth about your diagnosis. It was brave. It was necessary. I know you've struggled with how and when to tell her. Or whether to tell her at all. But, I think in taking this step, you are heading down a more positive path."

"I hope so, Lisa. I'm scared shitless." Ty grips my hand tightly.

"That's natural. Now, the reason we're here today is for me to answer Zoey's questions about your CPTSD. Hopefully by the end of the call, we'll have a list of things we can work on individually or as a couple." Lisa peers through the screen at both of us. "What's most important to me tonight is boundaries. Ty, I will not breach your confidence, and Zoey I'll ask you not to put me in that position. I'm here to help you understand the diagnosis. What it means for you as a couple and to potentially come up with a plan to move forward."

I glance at my husband. He takes a deep breath. "Lisa, I want to give you permission to tell Zoey anything. I don't want any more secrets. As she reminded me last night, I can't expect her to trust me if I don't trust her."

And there's the Ty I know. Self-aware. Rational. Intelligent.

"I hear you. For now, I'll give the floor to you, Zoey." Lisa gestures for me to begin.

I suck in my lips and puff them out. Not sure where to start. "I've not had much time to process, but I've read a lot of stuff online. I'm scared because my entire world has been tipped. Ty and I have had a whirlwind year. With so many life-changing experiences. I'm trying to figure out...everything. I'm at a loss about what I should be doing. Or shouldn't be doing. I just want to help my husband."

Lisa smiles at me through the screen. "Zoey, I commend you for taking the time to prepare for this call. I want to address what you might have read about CPTSD, which is not officially recognized as a mental disorder like more traditionally recognized disorders such as anxiety, depression, bipolar, narcissism, or codependency. CPTSD is specifically related to trauma from being subjected to extremely dysfunctional parenting. Many clients with Complex PTSD are misdiagnosed with a lot more mainstream disorders. For instance, when I first met Ty, he was seeking help for addiction to drugs and alcohol. It took a year or so to realize that his substance use was how he coped. Drinking and doing cocaine soothed and distracted Ty from the mental and emotional pain of CPTSD."

I look over at Ty, who just nods at me. "Wait, Ty doesn't have addiction issues?"

"No, but I was heading in that direction. The reason I stay away from alcohol and pot is because of my CPTSD, not the other way around." He looks into the screen at Lisa. "Right?"

She nods.

"Lisa, I'm trying to figure out what that means for us. I can't help but worry that I'm doing everything wrong." I grab Ty's hand. "I love Ty. I've loved him from the first time I saw him. Can we get through this?"

Lisa's kind smile immediately soothes me. "You can. But I want to be honest with you, just as I've been honest with Ty. Healing from CPTSD is also a long, gradual process, which requires relearning how to interact with the world around you. For most people, it is exceedingly difficult to accept that recovery is never complete. Survivors have a hard time noticing their progress. When life happens, new events, stresses, things like marriage, babies...sometimes there is some regression. Leading to shame. Fear. Depression. Despair."

"Ty, are you feeling any of these things?" I look over at him. His expression says it all.

He shakes his head sadly. "I've been struggling. I'm excited but I'm also so afraid that I'm going to suck at this." He caresses my belly. "I don't think I have the tools to be a good dad."

"Ah, Ty. You've got to remember. Recovery typically progresses in a way that can feel like two steps forward and one backward. Sometimes it might even feel like five steps back. Or, like when you and Zoey got back together, five steps forward." Lisa sits back and shuffles through some papers. "Telling Zoey about your diagnosis is huge. It means you're admitting it to someone other than me. You're not hiding behind the addiction thing."

"What can I do, Lisa?" I clasp Ty's hand in mine.

"I'd like to set up a treatment plan so the two of you can develop tools for your family. Things you can use to manage this." Lisa gets straight to the point. "Think of CPTSD as a chronic illness. Like arthritis. Or diabetes. The two of you can have a full and rewarding life if Ty's CPTSD is efficiently managed. Communication and working together is the key. The authentic connection you two already have will be so much deeper and richer than most people get to experience."

Ty puts his arm around me. Kisses my head. "I want that, Zoey. I've been so scared. I'm not afraid to admit that to you."

"I love you, baby. I'm scared too." I run my fingers through my hair and look back at Lisa. "Lisa, we will do whatever it takes. What are our next steps?"

"We need to work on some of the hardest stuff. First and foremost, identifying triggers of Ty's CPTSD and developing skills to manage them. External triggers can be anything. A tone of voice. A location. An event. A facial expression. Anything that reminds Ty of his original abuse." Lisa starts taking some notes.

Ty sighs. "It's a lot of work, Z. Are you sure I'm worth it? It feels overwhelming."

I lean into him. "You're worth everything."

Lisa smiles at us. "Ty, you know your worth and now you have Zoey's support. Over time, you two will become extremely proficient at managing Ty's triggers, which will alleviate his anxiety and eventually things will even out."

"He'll have me right by his side." I throw my arms around my husband. "We'll do this together."

We work out a therapy program. Intense immersion at first. An hour every day for the next two weeks leading up to when the band starts rehearsing. Then we'll come up with a more practical and manageable schedule in the months leading up to our son's arrival.

"I don't know what I'd do without you, Z." Ty pulls me back against him after we end the call. "I had so many scenarios in my mind about what would happen if I told you. This wasn't one of them."

"Us working on it together?" I bring his hand to my little baby pooch.

"Yeah."

"We can do anything together, Ty. We're going to get through this. I promise."

We lie on the couch for a long time. Caressing our child.

Believing.

Hoping.

Not knowing that our biggest obstacle is ahead of us. One that threatens the very fabric of our lives.

And the lives of the people closest to us.

Chapter Twenty

SURPRISINGLY, THE WORLD DIDN'T end when Zoey found out about my CPTSD.

But, I can't lie to myself. I'm drained. Like everything else she sets her mind to, Zoey is super focused. Right now, her attention in one thousand percent on my well-being. I love her for it. I do. It's just I feel a lot of pressure to...well, I'm not sure. I mean, my life hasn't really changed much. Other than my wife knowing my deepest, darkest secret.

And that's the issue. She's like a machine. Reading everything she can about it. Constantly checking in with me. Asking me questions.

Jesus fuck. All of this combined with the intensive therapy sessions with Lisa and Zoey I'm being subjected to? I've got nowhere to hide. It's exhaustive, immersive work. It feels like they are scooping out my brain with a spoon. It's fucking hard. Having all of this attention directed at me and my condition is not what I wanted.

It's what you feared.

It's just not the same thing as the attention I get for being famous. That I'm used to. People want to be close to me because I'm the lead singer of LTZ. Taking selfies. Getting filmed while out in public. Squealing fans. Meh. All part of the gig. None of these people know me. They know the version of me I choose to reveal. The rock star version. Even though I *am* actually a rock star, it's still like I'm playing a role.

"There you are." Zoey flounces into the kitchen in a black dress. She twirls. "What do you think?"

I'm not sure why she's all dressed up. "You look stunning, butterfly. Where are you going?"

"*We're* going to lunch with Austin Andrews." Zoey takes my arm. "Did you forget? Ah, it's okay. The meeting is today about the grant for the foundation. Can you go throw on something a little nicer than joggers?"

It all comes back to me. Austin Andrews is the CEO of Hungry Llama, the biggest gaming company in Seattle. Zoey wants to pitch gamifying music curriculum for our program. Possibly getting some sort of donation. "Uh, sure. Give me five minutes."

An hour later, we're in the middle of lunch at the Metropolitan Grill. Half a dozen men and women in business attire have approached our table for my autograph. Austin, a muscular man with the most intense light-brown eyes I've ever seen, isn't overly impressed with my fame. It's kind of refreshing, truth be told. I never really know what I'm going to get when I meet with someone new.

"Zoey, your proposal really intrigues me. I wonder if the Rainier Foundation would consider using my grant money to expand your programming into tech. We have a serious shortage of programmers now, and it's getting worse every year. Aside from that? My biggest concern is diversity. We need to include women. The BIPOC and LGBTQIA+ communities." Austin leans back in his chair.

Zoey taps her black-tipped finger on her chin. "Austin, I love this idea. Let me counter. As you know, there is a huge perception in the Seattle arts community that tech is pushing out venues, museums, and galleries. If you would consider giving a generous unrestricted donation to the foundation, I promise we will work on a plan to unite tech and arts and implement that into our work."

I'm listening to the ping-pong negotiation back and forth. I'm not quite sure exactly what Zoey has in mind, but I trust it's something lucrative. At some point I lose track of what they're talking about and start thinking about the upcoming show at The Mission. The rehearsals. Our upcoming doctor's appointment. Lake Lyon, a young guitar virtuoso I want to produce.

In other words, I'm completely zoned out on the conversation I should be paying attention to.

"Ty?" Zoey touches my arm. Catches my eye. Shit. Obviously I missed something.

Austin holds out his hand. "I said, congratulations on the baby."

"Uh, thanks, man." Look around to see a couple of diners pointing their phones at us. "Z, we probably need to text Sergey. Looks like we're being posted on social."

She looks around and sees what I see. "Austin, I'm sorry but we'll probably have to cut this short. We haven't made a public announcement about the baby, and whenever we're out in public it seems we're on the radar. You probably understand we need to control the narrative here."

"Of course. No worries. Great first meeting, let's continue the conversation." He stands, shakes my hand and kisses the top of Zoey's. The manager of the restaurant escorts us out the back where Sergey is waiting. Once we're safely in the car, Zoey rests her hand on my thigh while she checks email on her phone.

"I'm sorry." I place my hand on top of hers. Squeeze.

Zoey looks up at me. "Why?"

"I spaced out back there."

She kisses my cheek. "Oh, no biggie. I had it covered."

"You don't have to cover for me, you know." I pull Zoey toward me. "I'm not an invalid."

She sets her phone down and pats my thigh with her palm. "I *don't* think that."

I grab her black-tipped hand and move it down to my cock. Stare into her beautiful hazel eyes as my dick gets hard under our combined touch. I lean down to whisper in her ear, "Then show me. I want to fuck you so bad, baby. I want us to be us."

Zoey's breath hitches. I suckle her neck. Stroke her hair and I continue to move our hands over my growing erection. I capture her lips and slip my tongue inside her mouth to dance with hers. Her body relaxes against me, she's lost in a place we both understand. Our passion. Our incredible connection.

One we haven't explored much since we started therapy with Lisa.

We pull apart when Sergey parks in the driveway. I catch his eye in the rearview mirror. He's pretty intuitive and heads inside. Zoey and I don't move. She leans her head on my shoulder and looks up at me. "I love you, so much. You know that, right?"

"I do." I bend down and kiss her again. Start slow. Grip her shoulders and lay her down on the back seat. She moans when I reach under her thigh and trail my fingers toward her panties. She's wet for me. I smell her sweet arousal. "I miss you, babe. I need to be inside you. I need to feel connected to you."

Zoey lifts her hips, allowing me to pull down her panties. "I want that too."

I push her skirt up over her belly. Her bump's not hugely noticeable under her clothes yet, but her pooch is definitely visible now. I kiss her stomach. Smooth one hand over our baby boy. Zoey groans and shifts so her legs fall open. I trail my finger down to her mound, push her panties to the side and stroke her. Use her juices to lubricate her clit. Rub and circle. Just how she likes it. Her hips rock and buck until she cries out and comes all over my hand.

So beautiful. I shift my position so I can kneel between her legs. Undo my black jeans, yank them down and stroke my cock a few times. Press inside her wet heaven. Zoey moans. Bites her lip. My hands grip her hips so we can grind on each other with more friction.

I work my knees under her ass to thrust higher. Deeper. I know exactly when my crown hits her G-spot because she cries out, "Oh, My. God."

Once I've got her where I want her, I'm relentless. I want to see her lose control, and I'm not disappointed.

She comes with a squeal. That's all it takes. I pulse inside her for what seems like forever.

I needed this. I needed her.

Badly.

Zoey giggles. "I can't believe I'm fucking my husband in the back of our car like a teenager."

I grab her panties from the floor and clean her up. Stuff them in my pocket after I pull my pants back up. "It's kind of a first, isn't it? You're so sexy when you conduct business. I just couldn't wait another minute to fuck you, butterfly."

"Oh yeah?" She taps her finger to her lip. "Come to think of it, we fooled around a lot in my old RAV4, but you're right. We've never done the actual deed in a car before. How is that possible?"

"Thank you." I don't answer. I just press my forehead to hers.

She grips my face in her hands. Kisses me. "Never thank me for sex. I'm your wife. I'm a sure thing."

"I meant, thank you for sticking with me." I pull her up into my lap. "All of this shit is pretty, um, tough. It takes a lot out of me. I'm sure it takes a lot out of you. Let's not forget to have fun. To fuck. To live. That's what's going to get us through it, you know."

Zoey throws her arms around my shoulders and buries her face into my neck. "Am I being super intense, babe? Tell me the truth."

"I've been living with this for a long time." I stroke her back. "The only difference is now you know. I don't have to pretend with you anymore. It's freeing. I just don't want everything we do to be about this shit."

She pulls back to look at me. "I don't either."

We cuddle a bit before we pull ourselves fully together to go inside. When we get through the front door, Sergey is waiting. He holds out the bat phone and my heart sinks. "I was just about to come find you. There's a phone call for you."

"Oh, shit. The bat phone?" Zoey looks up at me questioningly. "Should I get it, or do you want to take it?"

My entire body tenses up. Fuck. Double fuck. I can't catch a fucking break. I freeze and the world stops for a second. I shake the cobwebs out of my head to see Zoey now has the phone up to her ear. Nodding and muttering "uh-huh" repeatedly. When she sees me, she hits speaker and a voice from my past fills the air. "So, as I was saying..."

Zoey interrupts, "Ms. Spock? May I interrupt you? Ty is with me. Could you repeat what you just said?"

"Of course. I've been trying to get in touch for a few months now, ever since your mother died, Mr. Rogers."

What the actual fuckery? Does this shit never end? "Ms. Spock, with all due respect—and I don't mean to be rude when I say this—but I truly do not want anything to do with my mother. Destroy whatever it is you have and please leave me and my family alone."

Zoey bites her lip and looks at me. I can tell she wants to jump in and say something but fuck it. We have enough going on right now. I don't want this shit.

"Mr. Rainier, I don't represent your mother. I'm the estate lawyer for your grandparents. When your mother died, the final terms of their trust kicked in. You are the beneficiary of a substantial estate. Now that Jada has passed, the non-disclosure agreement is void and I'm authorized to release the results of your paternity. There's a few other minor loose ends..."

I hear nothing else. Paternity? I sink to the floor and slump against the refrigerator. My mind is an actual vortex. My entire head feels like it's encased in cotton. I can't do anything but stare straight ahead. I feel Zoey next to me at some point. Her arms are wrapped around me. She's cupping my head and pressing it against her collarbone.

"Ty, baby," she soothes. "It will be okay. I'm right here. I told her we'd call her back another time."

"Did you know?" I choke out.

She pets my head. "Know what?"

"Did she tell you when you talked to her before? Have you been keeping this from me?" I'm just devastated. Unable to even process what is happening right now.

Zoey grips my chin and turns my face so I'm facing her. I refuse to catch her eye. She moves her face in front of mine so I don't have a choice. "Listen to me. I. Do. Not. Keep. Things. From. You. When I talked to her before, all she said is that she had paperwork for you. I would never hurt you, baby. I promise."

"Okay," I say weakly. She doesn't deserve my trust insecurities. Zoey is not my mom. She's always come through for me. Fuck. I need to focus on putting into practice what Lisa is working on us with. I try the exact truth. "I'm just...overwhelmed."

"Well, that's understandable. It's shocking to me too, so let's just let it sit for a bit. It's not like we can unhear what Ms. Spock had to say." Zoey sits next to me. Our backs are against the fridge. She puts my hand on her tiny little bump and covers it with hers. "Remember the bigger picture, Ty. Little Rufus needs you."

I caress my little son inside Zoey's belly. "Rufus?"

"I like it. Rufus Rainier." Zoey kisses my temple. "Has a nice ring to it."

I laugh. She's nearly snapped me out of it. "What should I do?"

"Do you want to find out about your father?" Zoey threads her fingers with mine. "It could be a good thing for our son. If for no other reason, we know more about your health background."

My heart beats a little harder. It's so hard to process what this Spock woman has just dropped on me. As if I haven't had enough to deal with. What the fuck do I do? "Z, do we really want to add this shit into the mix? We have no idea who this prick is. I mean, does he know who I am? Has he known all this time and never bothered the fuck to find me?"

"I honestly don't know." Zoey leans her head on my shoulder. "It seems like if he knew about you, he'd have come forward. Everyone knows who you are."

"But, can I handle it?" I whisper.

Zoey rubs our hands over her belly. "Babe, you may not see it all the time, but you are the strongest man I know. I'll be right by your side. Whatever you decide."

"Maybe we should talk about it with Lisa on our call tonight."

She looks up at me. "Yeah. Wouldn't hurt to get her perspective."

I already know what Lisa's going to say. I'm not sure if I'll be on board. I don't really see how adding in some unknown asshole into the mix is going to help me with therapy. Getting ready for our son. Starting LTZ back up again.

I'd love to be a glass-is-half-full kind of guy.

It's just hard when every fiber of my being knows opening up this new can of worms is going to be a disaster.

Chapter Twenty-One

A WEEK LATER, I'M staring out at the city from our living room. Drinking a cup of herbal tea.

Ty's getting ready to leave for Poulsbo for the night. Alex will be here soon. A long weekend of hanging out with my BFF will be just what the doctor ordered after two weeks of intensive therapy with Lisa. When Ty and I learned about his grandparent's trust and the paternity situation, Lisa recommended Ty enroll in a month-long intensive program for PTSD survivors. Which scared me. I really hoped that our Zoom sessions would be all he'd need.

For me, they've been really helpful. And eye-opening. So much of his behavior over the years makes sense. I think back to when we first got back together and he left me at the hotel in Laguna Beach. His outbursts when he'd make assumptions about me leaving him. So much about CPTSD is heartbreaking. His abandonment issues were exacerbated when I broke up with him a decade ago. It's not his fault that it's a trigger now.

Now that I know what he's dealing with, as his partner, it's my job is to support him through his healing process. Help him identify when he's spinning and practice mindfulness. His meds seem to have kicked-in to Lisa's satisfaction. We've incorporated thirty minutes of meditation each day together. Ty's using a bunch of sensory objects to help with his anxiety. We have squishy balls. Fidget pens. Stuff like that. Mainly, I've realized that the exercise and time he spends writing and creating music are his best medicine. Techniques he used to soothe himself even before he knew about his CPTSD.

Lisa has also worked with me one-on-one. Because I'm pregnant, Ty and I realize my main priority has to be following my own doctor's orders. Keeping myself free of stress, which has been nearly impossible for the past few weeks. She's encouraged me to recognize my own limitations so I don't burn myself out. I'm learning new communication techniques so I can tell Ty what type of treatment I expect from him. I know he's going to lash out sometimes, but it doesn't make that behavior right.

In other words, I've got to find my own set of boundaries and be able to talk to him about it. Figure out a way to take care of myself when Ty can't be there in a way that I'd like him to be.

It's all worth it. Even though we're at the beginning of navigating his mental health journey together, he and I are closer than we have ever been.

"I'm all packed." Ty comes up behind me and wraps his arms around my middle. Cups Rufus with both hands.

I've popped. There's no hiding my pregnancy now. Luckily, a bunch of new, trendy maternity clothes arrived this morning, I'm wearing my first pair of pregnancy-panel jeggings. A cute flouncy black blouse. I turn and tilt my lips up to his. Ty leans into our kiss. His hair falls in front of our faces like a grapefruit-scented curtain. "I'll miss you tonight."

"You'll survive one night." Ty waggles his eyebrows. "I'll more than make it up to you tomorrow."

I turn in his arms. "Are we going to talk about this program?"

"Nothing to talk about, butterfly. If you think I'm leaving for a month while you're pregnant, you're wrong." Ty pulls me toward him. "Don't you think things are better?"

He's got a good point. His mood is dramatically different. Our sex life is back to where it was before I got pregnant, just a little tamer. "You're sure? If you need something more than these Zoom calls with Lisa, you can tell me."

"I told you, butterfly." Ty runs his fingers through my hair. "The stress of not being honest with you is what the problem was. Now that you know, it's like an entire weight machine has been lifted off my shoulders."

I stare deeply into his eyes. He bugs them out, causing me to laugh. "Fine, I trust you. I also trust you to let me know if things change."

Providing honest expressions of my trust are important in our process.

"We have about an hour before I leave, wanna relieve a little stress?" Ty brings my hand to his junk.

Um, always.

We make the most of the sixty minutes, but time passes quickly. Sergey texts Ty that he's waiting. We quickly get dressed and before I know it he's kissing me goodbye. Not ten minutes later, Alex bursts through my front door. We squeal and cling to each other. "Holy shit, Z. Look at this! Alex rubs my bump. Have you really been impregnated by the lead singer of LTZ?"

"Do you think he'll notice me if I have his baby?" I cock my hip and fluff out my hair before sticking my belly out. We burst into laughter. Our jokes about our star-struck teenaged selves never get old.

"I'm really sorry about when you were over." Alex winces. "I should have told you I wasn't feeling well. You just came all that way."

I shrug. "It's all good. Is everything okay now?"

"Hey, Fiona texted me. She wanted us to pop over to her house for some appetizer she's testing out. I'm kinda hungry, and, well, it's Fee. Should we go?" Alex doesn't answer me, she buries herself in replying to Fee.

Deciding to let it go for now, I grab my light jacket from the hall closet. "Yeah, it's perfect actually. I'm supposed to walk thirty minutes a day, can we take the scenic route so I get my exercise in?"

Alex and I meander around the neighborhood until we finally arrive at Zane and Fiona's place, where there are balloons in every shade of blue adorning the walkway. A giant blue-and-white balloon arch has been placed in front of the entryway. "Surprise!" Alex claps her hands excitedly.

We go inside to find my favorite women are throwing me a baby shower. Ronni and Fiona are there. So is my mom. Alex's mom. To my great delight, Lianne is also among the guests.

Fee's done an impeccable job. From the five-tiered topsy-turvy cake covered in light-blue-and-green fondant argyle to the mini-cupcakes topped with extraordinarily cute zoo animals. A huge banner spells out "Baby Rainier" in block letters with little Ty, Zoey, and baby boy characters.

"Oh my God, you guys." Tears fill my eyes. My pregnancy emotions are nuts. "This is amazing."

Fiona claps her hands and shoos us into the dining room. "Okay, ladies. Now that you're here, lunch is served."

It's a veritable feast. Honey-roasted chicken salad. Crumbly cheese biscuits. The most stunning charcuterie tray I've ever seen. A ton of little tartelettes. Goat cheese and fig. Spiced lamb and chutney. Roasted eggplant and feta. It's just beautiful. We sit around the modern dining room table and eat and drink for a couple of hours.

Ronni stands and uses her spoon to tap on her glass. "Zoey, on behalf of all of us here, we welcome you to the mother club. It's an experience like no other."

"Absolutely. And to your third trimester. Heartburn, constipation, giant tits, and the inability to ever get comfortable," Fiona toasts.

I laugh and cup my boobs. "I'm up two bra sizes."

"I'm sure Ty's not complaining." Alex rolls her eyes.

"He's not." I shrug.

"TMI." Mom swats me. "The last thing you want to hear about is your child's sex life."

"Mom, I'm pregnant. How did you think it happened?"

"Divine intervention," she retorts.

Lianne squinches her eyes shut and shakes her head. "Zane has always been TMI with me."

"Ah, well that's Zaney." Fee's eyes go half-mast. "You did a good job with my guy, Lianne."

Lianne embraces her. "He's always been your guy."

We all oooh and ahh. It's so true.

Alex stands and gestures to the living room. "Enough of the sappy shit. Presents. Now."

When I get up, suddenly I'm lightheaded. I sit back down again and take a breath.

"Are you okay, honey?" Mom puts her hand on my forehead.

I stand again. Luckily, the episode is over. "I'm fine. That was just weird, I felt like I was going to faint."

"Let's get you into the living room. Once that belly pops, the discomfort starts. Get used to it." Mom takes my arm and walks me to the couch.

"You should have seen my belly when I hit five months." Ronni's eyes go wide. "I never thought I'd look the same again. Well, I don't, but man. I was twice your size. The twins, God love them, have fucked-up my body big time."

Alex sits next to me. "You're gorgeous, Ronni. But, to your point, I can't say I'm envious. I didn't have to go through any of that shit and I have a beautiful daughter."

Fee brings in a tray of faux-mosas. Orange juice and seltzer. "With those stupid migraines, I'm so glad you're taking such good care of yourself, Zoey. When I was pregnant with Mia, I developed preeclampsia. I don't want that for you. Not with all of the complications that go with it. It fucking sucks."

"Yeah. Well, Ty's taking really good care of me." I smile "He cooks for me every night. Massages. Foot rubs..."

"Sex." Alex laughs as does everyone in the room except my mom, who hides her eyes.

As if on cue, my phone buzzes. It's Ty..

Ty:

Were you surprised.

Me:

You were in on it?

Ty:

Did you really think we're over at Jace's?

Me:

Um...

Ty:

We're down in the studio at our house. Have fun see you later. Love you.

Me:

Love you too.

I spend the rest of the afternoon opening gifts, surrounded by the most phenomenal women. Baby Rufus is going to be dressed to the nines. Plus, I have a high-end night nanny service, a mini Ferrari electric car, and a private jet voucher for a babymoon with Ty. Ronni's giving Rufus a role in the second season of her sitcom. All in all, the haul is out of this world.

With bags and boxes in hand, me, Alex, and Mom start the five-block trek back to my house. On the way, I have to stop a few times due to some heavy-duty cramps I'm having. Eventually, we get back home with the gifts. Alex dashes into the kitchen to get me water while Mom settles me on the couch.

"I'll head to the studio and get Ty." Alex dashes down the stairs.

Mom sits next to me. "It's normal to cramp, don't stress."

"I'm not."

Liar.

Ty's upstairs like a shot. He sits next to me. Looks into my eyes. "Z, what's going on?"

"I'm just a little faint. Slightly nauseous. Had a few cramps on the walk back home." I give him a look that I hope is reassuring. "And, now I've got to pee."

Ty helps me up. "I'll go with you."

The powder room is the closest bathroom. I don't let him in to watch me go, of course. A girl's gotta have some boundaries. When I finish, I happen to look down at the toilet paper before I toss it in the bowl and notice it's slightly pink. I take another sheet and wipe myself. Also a little pink. Suddenly, I'm even more anxious. No, I'm super fucking scared. I pull up my pants and open the door, hoping to keep calm. The last thing I want to do is upset Ty.

"What's wrong, you're white as a ghost." Ty grips my shoulders.

"Don't freak out, but I think I'm spotting."

Ty's eyebrows squish together. "What does that mean?"

"I have a bit of blood. Down below." I keep my voice neutral. Will him to stay calm.

"Fuck." Ty grabs his phone and punches some numbers. "Sergey will take us to the hospital."

"Okay, I'll call Dr. Sabel." I head into the living room to retrieve my phone. Make the call.

The rest of the guys are now standing around looking concerned. When they find out the plan, Zane and Connor head back to Zane's house. Jace, Alex, and Mom stay put. Ty cradles me in the back seat as we head to the hospital. He's calm and loving. My OB-GYN meets us just beyond the back entrance. Within forty minutes, I'm gowned-up, in a private room with my feet in stirrups getting prodded, Ty sits next to me holding my hand.

"Zoey, as you are aware because of your migraines we've been monitoring your health more regularly to prevent preeclampsia. The ultrasound looks good. As a precaution, we're going to run some blood tests. I'll need to get a urine sample today and tomorrow. Is there anything that's causing you extra stress right now?"

Ty and I look at each other. I cryptically explain that we're going through some family issues. Ty looks pretty devastated. I'm sure he's blaming himself right now.

"Look, Ty. I'm not going to tell you how important it is for Zoey to keep her stress down," Dr. Sabel admonishes.

"I know," he says glumly.

"Wait a minute. Ty's doing a great job. He's *not* to blame. I do want to mention we had sex earlier today, could that be why?" I'm not going to let him take any of the blame. Not when he's doing everything he can to take care of us. "Ty's um, well...large."

Ty buries his face in his hands. I don't mean to embarrass him, but he *is* huge. He can't help but hit my cervix when he's inside me.

"Possibly. Zoey, your cervix will change slightly in position during pregnancy. Your cervical discharge will also change in consistency and color. Why don't I take another look." My doctor resumes poking and prodding. Ty clutches my hand tightly throughout.

She stands and removes her latex gloves. She shows me a cotton swab with just a hint of the pink. "I think you're fine. But, I'll run the tests to be sure. Meanwhile, maybe lay off intercourse. There are lots of other options..."

"We've got it." I hold up my hand.

She laughs and shows us to the door. As we leave she touches my arm. "I mean it about keeping stress free. I'll call you with the results as soon as I have them, but you're at the stage where we need to be cautious."

"She won't have to lift a finger." Ty slings his arm around my shoulders. "I won't put my penis anywhere near her, don't worry."

On the way home, I lie against Ty. He entwines his fingers with mine. "This was scary."

"I know." I close my eyes and nestle into his chest. "But, I think we're fine. I'm glad we took it seriously. Better safe than sorry."

"Yeah, definitely." Ty kisses my head.

"Ty?" I look up at him. "Thank you. I couldn't ask for a better partner. I love you so much. In case you ever doubt it, there's no one in this world that I'd rather be with. You're it for me. Through thick and thin."

He kisses me softly. "Thank you. I needed to hear that, butterfly. I feel the same way."

Lying against my husband, all I can think is together he and I can get through anything.

Chapter Twenty-Two

AFTER ZOEY'S AND RUFUS'S little scare, I made a decision. Well, it was really made for me. My son is relying upon me to keep him safe. Which means, I need to man up and pay a visit to Alicia Spock. Today's as good a day as any. I want to get it over with.

I'm scared shitless.

"Are you sure you don't want to wait until after the show?" Zoey pulls an oversized silver blouse over her head. "Or after the baby's born?”

"Rufus?" I pull a black zipped hoodie off the hanger.

Zoey laughs. "Babe, we've got to stop calling him that. It was a joke."

"It was?"

"You're right, it's an excellent name." Zoey shrugs. "We'll go with it. Are you ready? I don't want us to be late."

Alicia's office is in the Smith Tower, Seattle's oldest high-rise. Once the tallest building west of the Mississippi, now it's dwarfed by almost every other commercial space downtown. Sergey escorts us up the elevator to the thirty-fifth floor. We're greeted by a perky forty-something receptionist who is clearly starstruck. I'm surprised she doesn't ask for an autograph.

"Mr. and Mrs. Rainier. So pleased to meet you. Please come this way." She leads us into a small conference room with a big view of Puget Sound. The table is old-school cherry wood. The upholstered chairs look like they've been here for thirty years. I guess they have. Maybe longer.

Who the fuck cares about the goddamn chairs.

I get Zoey settled and sit next to her. Sergey exits to wait outside the door.

"Are you doing okay, babe?" Zoey rests her hand on my thigh. "We can reconsider."

I cover her hand with mine. "Tell me the truth, do you think I'm making a mistake in being here? This is a huge fucking deal."

"I'm just worried." She cocks her head.

"About me? Do you think I won't be able to handle it?"

She cups my cheek. "You have handled way worse than what we're going to find out here. Just remember that. And remember I'm right here. I'm not leaving your side."

I'm giving her a kiss when Alicia Spock enters the room. She's easily seventy years old. Silver hair cut in a blunt bob. Blue suit. Blue flats. Reading glasses secured by a chain around her neck. She carries a thick stack of files. "Mr. Rainier. Mrs. Rainier. Thank you for coming."

"It's Ty," I say. "My wife's name is Zoey."

She nods. "Ty. Zoey. We have two matters at hand. The first is your grandparents' trust. As you may remember, we spoke many years ago. Your grandparents set up a trust for your care..."

"Look, I don't really want a rundown of the past. The trust was bullshit. It forced me to stay with my mother. Who knows, maybe they believed they were doing the right thing by me. But I did not have a great childhood. Not by a longshot. I don't have any feelings one way or the other about my grandparents. They might as well have been strangers. I'd really like to just get to the point of what you need from me."

Zoey speaks up, "What my husband means is you mentioned he is a beneficiary of this trust. We'd like to know more. And you mentioned paternity."

"Let me briefly explain. Your grandparents had three children at the time of their death. Your mother. Her twin sister, Jemma. And their older brother, Lawrence who passed away when he was only ten years old. When they died in the car accident, you were..."

"Twelve," I mutter.

"Yes, and Jemma and your mother were the sole beneficiaries of their estate. However, for your mother, there were stipulations." Alicia flips through some paperwork and turns to show me the document. "To gain access to the money, Jada had to be clean for five years, with regular monitored blood tests. She never managed to comply with that condition."

Zoey reads the document. "Huh. Seems logical."

Alicia hands us another thick folder. "Your grandparents never stopped monitoring your mother's activities. A team of private investigators surveilled your mom from the time she ran away from home at fifteen until your grandparents died. These are the reports, so in a nutshell, Jada was estranged from her parents but they kept tabs on her."

"Jesus. Who the fuck were they? That's the most fuckedup thing I ever heard. It's disgraceful they wouldn't have helped me." Ty flips through some of the pages and tosses them back on the table. "I can't really comprehend this."

"Your grandparents were Noah and Miriam Rogers. Noah was the sole heir to the Rogers Media Group, which owns television, radio and print..."

"Holy shit." Zoey's eyes are wide. "My old law firm Finney Cooper used to manage some of their ancillary businesses."

Alicia nods. "Miriam was Miriam Johnson, heir to Johnson Development Holdings."

"Double shit. That's Mia's paternal father's family. Fiona was represented by Finney Cooper too. They gave up all rights to her." Zoey grips my hand. "I have to say, they sound like terrible people. Especially in the way they treat their children."

Alicia taps her pen on one of the files. "I can't comment on that. I'll say, they're a complicated family. My firm has represented the trust for many years."

"Well, let's get this the fuck over with." I lean back in my chair, somewhat disgusted by the entire situation.

"Some of this is very sensitive information, so if you'd like me to stop at any point, please let me know."

I pull my hand away from Zoey and cross my arms in front of me. Lean back in my chair. Fix my gaze on Ms. Spock. "Just tell me."

"Your grandparents gave Jada and her siblings every advantage in life. Losing Lawrence devastated the family. Jada was never the same. Jemma managed to thrive. In fact, she's gone on to take over Noah's responsibilities at the company. As I mentioned, your mother ran away from home and was living on the street in the University District. She was addicted to drugs when she got pregnant with you, Tyson. Noah and Miriam got her into rehab and she was clean for a while. The family reconciliation was brief. Jada disappeared with you when you were about two. Your grandparents tracked you both down, and they resumed surveillance. It was tough love. They tried to get her to go to rehab." Alicia shakes her head sadly.

"Did she say no, no, no?" I snark. I catch Zoey's eye. She purses her lips. Yeah, not the time or place. I shut up.

Alicia sighs. "Tyson, Jada couldn't—or wouldn't—live by even the most basic rules. She put her parents at risk. She put her sister at risk. There was nothing they could do."

"They could have raised Ty," Zoey mutters. "So, he wouldn't have suffered at the hands of someone like Jada."

Alicia pulls out another folder. "Well, that brings me to your paternity. Jada identified a man she *claimed* was your father. He was a married politician serving on City Council. Turns out it wasn't him. But there were numerous, well, possibilities. She hung out with a real party crowd. Drug dealers. Musicians. Motorcycle gangs. Tattoo artists. She also turned to prostitution for money."

I shake my head in disgust. "Sounds about right. You also have no idea how often she threw the fact she didn't know who my father was in my face."

Alicia's brows furrow sympathetically. "I'm sorry to hear that, Tyson. As far as I know, Jada never knew who your father was. But your grandparents did. The PI kept a dossier on every man she had sex with."

"A dossier?" Zoey's eyes are wide. "That's incredibly strange."

"They had to know what they were dealing with. Noah had hopes of running for governor. With a child, like Jada, running wild. Well, that was their reasoning."

"It's bullshit." I snarl.

"The PI was able to get DNA from all of the men. Including the councilman. When the DNA results came in, your biological father was not a person they wanted to be associated with." Alicia taps the envelope with her finger. "They never told her about the PI. Or the DNA tests. Or the paternity."

Zoey squints at Alicia. "But, why? Maybe Ty could have lived with his father."

"Zoey, remember that Jada was only fifteen. Sixteen when she gave birth. They were deathly afraid of the blowback the family would receive. It would have been a huge scandal." Alicia doesn't exactly endorse the position, but she clearly has some fondness for my grandparents. I don't trust her. At all.

I knock the table with my knuckles. "Sounds like my father's identity would fuck up grandpa's plan to be governor."

"Your grandparents resumed basic financial support for your mother, and you. You had an apartment. Eventually, she got a job." Alicia ignores my comment. "As I said, your grandparents were trying to practice tough love with Jada. Hoping she'd turn her life around. It was their great agony. It didn't happen before they were killed. If she had ever managed to get clean? She would have inherited half of their estate."

"If they had a PI on Jada, how did they not know about her abuse of Ty? About when they were homeless? I thought they were paying for a place to live." Zoey cradles her bump protectively. "I just cannot imagine this level of dysfunction. It's incomprehensible."

I shoot her a glare. I'm pissed. How could she say that out loud? I breathe in and breathe out. Zoey notices and takes my hand. I realize my anger is not at Zoey. It's... *What if my grandparents knew...everything? And didn't help me?*

Alicia looks off into the distance. "The PIs were the ones who found you in the park. Took you to the police. That's when they put the trust together for the apartment. They thought by making sure you had a place to live, it was helping. I'm not going to pretend to know all of the motivations behind what the Rogers family decisions were. After they died, concern for Jada fell by the wayside."

"For me too. Actually, I take that back. I was never a consideration," I scoff. "This is a fucking joke. I don't want anything to do with this family, Ms. Spock. I'll be honest, I'm pissed that I'm even here. Why dredge all this shit up for me?"

Alicia points to the envelope. "Let's get you on your way then. As I mentioned, the DNA obtained by the PI was instrumental in identifying your paternity."

"Let me guess." I pull out the paper from my pocket and slide it over to her. "It's one of these guys? This list was in an envelope and package I received. Did you send it?"

She takes the paper and studies it through her reading glasses. "I haven't sent you anything. My guess is that your aunt Jemma sent it. She's wanted to get in touch with you throughout the years. Especially after your interview about your mother last year."

"Wait, Jemma knows about Ty?" Zoey leans forward on the conference table and turns to me.

"Yes. She learned a lot of this information when her parents died. Until Jada passed, the records were sealed. After her sister's death, Jenna contacted me to meet you, Tyson. She's a discreet person. You're well-known. She didn't want you to think—"

I wave her off. "Too late. I'm *already* thinking it. No thank you."

"Well, if you change your mind, her contact information is in the files." Alicia slides the sealed envelope to me. "All I'm here to do is fulfill the terms of the trust. Upon Jada's death, the conditional trust terms relating to your paternity expired. Those are the DNA results. I have only been the keeper, I have no idea who your biological father is. If you choose to open this and find out who he is? I'm not your lawyer, but I'd advise you to consult with someone before you contact him. He may or may not know you exist. It could be very awkward."

"Wait." Zoey holds up her hand. "What bothers me is how Ty's grandparents got DNA without permission.

Wouldn't all of these men have some clue why they were giving samples? Seems like a lawsuit waiting to happen."

Alicia squints. "I'm actually not sure."

"Fuck me." I toss the envelope on the table. "Why would I open this and completely ruin some guy's life?"

Zoey looks over at me. Caresses my shoulder. "Maybe, just maybe, it would be the opposite."

My wife. Glass-is-half-full girl. I can't help but smile at her. She's literally the best thing that has ever happened to me.

"What you choose to do with the paternity results is up to you. My final order of business is distributing the trust. I've completed its administration, including the final accounting. There are no disputes. There are no creditors. Therefore, I'm able to wire the funds directly to you." Alicia puts her reading glasses back on and checks the document before handing it to me.

Zoey peers over my shoulder. We look at the paperwork together. Then we look at each other. Mouths open. Holy fuck.

Over a hundred million dollars.

"I don't understand." I point to the number. "What does this mean?"

"Your grandparents' trust is now worth one-hundred twenty eight million dollars." Alicia peers up over her readers at us. "You'll want to consult with your business manager as to whether you'd like to create your own trust. All of the financials are there for your review, including the fact we have retained a sum of one-hundred-thousand dollars to finalize our fees. After you consult with your advisors, we'll wait for your direction."

Moments later, Zoey and I leave the office in stunned silence. I thought I was well off when I walked into the meeting. Now? Holy fucking shit. The question is, do I even want this money? As far as I'm concerned, it's fucking tainted. I can't even wrap my head around all of the shit I just heard. So many feelings. Anger. Rejection. Skepticism. Disbelief.

Also? Numbness.

"Are you okay, babe?" Zoey squints up at me. We're on our way home. "I'm feeling all over the map right now, so I can't imagine how you're processing."

I shake my head and look out the window. "I don't have a lot of empathy for Jada, you know that. She fucked me up badly. But, it sure sounds like my grandparents were no big tickle to deal with."

"I can't imagine ever doing anything to hurt this little guy the way your grandparents hurt your mom. The way your mom hurt you." Zoey rubs her bump. "Oh, Ty. Feel. He's moving."

I reach over and press my hand over hers. Sure enough, I feel a flutter. I look up at her in awe. "I'll never do anything to hurt this guy, babe. I promise you."

"Of course, you won't." Zoey leans on me. "You're going to be the best father in the world."

The drive home is fairly short. Tonight I have one more rehearsal at Zane's before the show tomorrow. I get Zoey settled in front of the TV before I head out. "I'll be home in a couple of hours."

"I'll be here." Zoey smiles up at me from under her snuggly blanket. "But Ty?"

"Yeah."

"Are you going to open the envelope?"

I shrug. "I dunno."

"Give it some thought." She blows a kiss at me. "Let's talk to Lisa first, but I think she'll encourage you to do it. Then everything is out on the table, at least. We can focus on the future, not the past."

I catch the kiss and put it on my cheek. "Okay."

"Whatever you decide." Zoey's so fucking awesome. The way she's concerned about me. It feels good now. Not overpowering anymore. "I'll support you. No matter what. It's you and me." She points at herself, then points at me.

"Me and you." I mirror her gesture.

Then I head over to Zane's.

We have the most incredible rehearsal. Full of creativeness. Fun. Joy of playing together. Excitement at being in front of a crowd again tomorrow. Our hiatus has done its job. We're rested. Rejuvenated. Ready for LTZ to resume world domination.

Fuck my grandparents. Fuck my mother. Fuck my poor unsuspecting bio-dad. On my way home, I make a decision.

All of that tainted money is going into my foundation. That way I can use it for some good. To help kids like me who come from fucked-up families like mine. Maybe even add in that programming shit Zoey was talking to that game developer about.

I'm not touching it. I don't need it. I don't want it.

As for the envelope?

I'll admit. I'm curious. I don't want to fuck up some guy's world. A man who has his own family. Who probably won't welcome me as part of his life. And why would he? He has no idea I even exist.

If it were me, I'd want to know. I'd want to be with my child. But this guy isn't me. Besides, how would Zoey feel if some rando woman showed up on my door with my kid? My whole body shudders. I don't ever want that to happen.

I guess I have some thinking to do.

Hopefully, I'll figure it out sooner rather than later.

Chapter Twenty-Three

GOD, I'M HAVING THE best erotic dream.

I'm lounging naked by our pool in LA. Ty's licking me from my anus to my clit. Plunging his tongue into my pussy. Spreading my lower lips between his fingers so he can give my clit full suction. His little nibbles are so gentle, but so precise. My thighs quake. I grasp his head to keep him right where he is.

"You like that, baby," he hums against my core, sending sparks through my entire body.

I hear a buzz. My eyes fly open when I feel a vibrating pressure directly on my nub. Ty smiles up at me from between my legs. Of course, my bump obscures a clear view of his lips. The only reason I know he's smiling is his eyes. They're happy. Calm. The sexy look Ty always has when we make love. Like I'm the only thing that matters in the world.

Shifting up on my elbows, I strain to see what he's doing. He holds up a tiny little bullet vibrator and then reapplies it to my clit. Begins to lick and suck my outer lips. He inserts two fingers into my channel and curves them to find my spongy little pleasure spot. The combined stimulation is my favorite thing, next to having his cock inside me.

Something we can't do after my spotting a couple of weeks ago.

I collapse against the pillows. My hands clutch the sheets. My hips buck and writhe, I can't help it. Every single thing Ty is doing to me builds and builds and builds. Then I explode. Ty backs off and sits back on his heels. Sets the vibrator down and taps the crown of his cock against my pulsing clit. Pushes his tip inside, shallowly. Repeats. Tap. Tap. Tap. Thrust. Thrust. Thrust.

I bite down on my knuckle when I come again. Ty pulls out and spurts all over my round stomach with a shout. My entire body melts into the bed. Ty flops beside me after he wipes me off with his t-shirt.

"Good morning." He nips my earlobe. "I ate you out for a quite a while before you woke up."

I stretch and roll over on my left side. Ty spoons me. "Ohmygod. I thought it was the most amazing erotic dream I'd ever had. How lucky am I that it was real?"

Ty's big palm splays over my bump. "I'm so lucky to have the two of you. When I woke up a bit ago, I couldn't help but feel all of the loves. I'm feeling great. Despite how completely fucked-up all that information was, surprisingly, yesterday wasn't as bad as I thought."

I'm glad he's in a good spot, but it was a lot of information. Part of me wishes we waited until after the baby was born to pile on more family drama. "I love you, babe. You handled yourself like a champ."

I think about my personal sessions with Lisa. How she's reminded me that as much as I can support Ty, it's his responsibility to manage his own triggers. My job is to try to learn them and help avoid events or situations when he's not in a good headspace. In our joint sessions, we're working on ways that Ty can cue me when he's in distress. So, I can help get him out of upsetting situations. Or help soothe him if leaving isn't an option.

Considering all the things we learned at Alicia Spock's office yesterday? Crazy fucked-up shit. I was resigned to the fact today would be challenging for my husband, with so much to process. But, I've got to take him at his word. I'm so happy he's feeling good because tonight is the opening of Fiona's restaurant. LTZ's private show at The Mission. Lots of fun things to look forward to. Great friends to hang out with. Maybe it's enough.

I wiggle my butt against him. "I'm so proud of you."

"All morning I've been giving it a lot of thought. Don't you think it would be an asshole move to open that envelope? Track down this dude and disrupt his life?" Ty strokes my belly, stopping to feel when our little guy flutters against his dad's hand. "It's not really fair when he has no idea I even exist."

"Yeah, I hear you. On the other hand, wouldn't you want to know if you had a kid out there somewhere?" I say this quietly - because it's a fear of mine. Ty went through years of promiscuity when we were broken up.

He's silent for a long time. I almost turn over to see if he's sleeping when he whispers, "I would. But, I'd never want anything to fuck my relationship up with you, butterfly. When all that shit went down with Jace and Alex, he went through a rough time."

"But they got through it. Lena is just as much Alex and Jace's child as if she were biologically related to them."

Ty moves away from me and gets out of bed. He walks around the bed and sits by my side. Smooths my hair from my face. "I know, baby. I don't want that for us. Please don't worry, I don't have any other kids. I promise."

"Okay." I smile up at my husband. "But, your biological dad does."

He stands "True. Well, anyway. I've got to get a move on. As far as the envelope? I'll think about it. There's no rush, right? We're going to talk to Lisa first."

"You're right. We can discuss it with her tomorrow in our session, babe," I reassure.

Ty's meeting the guys at Zane's for a quick check in with their management. Then they'll all head over to the club for rehearsal. I'll meet Ty over at The Mission around five to do some foundation promotional stuff.

We'll head to the soft opening of *Gus* at six with the rest of the band. After dinner, LTZ will play an acoustic set before the main event. Three bands from the foundation will take the stage at the club.

Lake Lyon, the guitar whiz. Candy Crushed, an all-girl glam-metal band, and Velocity 7, a group of siblings with the most amazing harmonies I've ever heard. A new generation of musicians. The cycle repeats.

After Ty kisses me goodbye, I get up for the day. Despite the earlier orgasms, I'm not feeling great. I didn't want to worry Ty. Not today. It's such a big night for everyone and it should be fairly low-stress for me. The show is private, invite only. We'll know everyone there. Once I'm at the restaurant, I'll just sit down and relax. We're in a VIP booth at The Mission, so I won't get jostled around during the show. I'll be fine. Protected.

Just before I get in the shower I stand in front of the full-length mirror. Twist from side to side. I can't believe how much my body's changed in the past month. My breasts are now two full cup sizes bigger, my nipples are larger and darker. My belly looks like I have a beach ball inside it. I trace my fingers along a few stretch marks, thinking about how Ty licked and kissed them last night.

He told me how beautiful they were because my body was doing all of the hard work keeping our baby safe.

I love this part of my pregnancy. Hormones aside, I feel confident again. Ty makes me feel beautiful. I truly feel we have achieved some real milestones. Our love is deeper now. More authentic – if that is even possible. I just feel it.

Lisa was right. The past couple of months of therapy with him has made us closer. Our trust in each other is solid. For a snap second before I learned about Ty's past and his diagnosis, I didn't think it would even be possible. But, if how he reacted to yesterday's meeting with Alicia Spock is any indication, all of the things we've put into practice are really making a difference in his well-being.

After a long, cool shower, I leisurely get ready. And by leisurely, I mean I take a nap. Then read for an hour. When I see that it's nearly four p.m., I grab my phone and see a text came in from Ty a while ago.

Ty:

> I love you. I'm feeling so excited for tonight. In fact, I've never felt better, butterfly. Hurry and get here, I miss you and Rufus.

Glancing around my closet, I decide to dress for comfort. An extra-long spandex black tank top. Black moto maternity jeans. Chunky platform boots. A long, black chiffon off-the-shoulder blouse. Dark-pink lipstick. Neutral shadow. Cat eyeliner. I twirl in front of the mirror and head out to the living room. I'm ready. I look good. I need to. With all of the press lined up to cover this event, my bump is making a public debut. The world's about to find out Ty's going to be a father.

"Mrs. Rainier?" Omar, our new security detail who is Sergey's second-in-command, is waiting for me. "Are you ready?"

I grab my purse from the counter. "Yep. Thank you for taking me, Omar. Please call me Zoey."

I try Ty's mobile from the car, but it goes right to voicemail. Ditto Alex. I figure they must still be doing soundcheck, so I close my eyes and relax against the seat. Omar answers a call, I can tell someone is agitated on the other end of the line but can't hear what is being

said. He doesn't react, just nods and repeats, "I understand. No problem."

Right about then, my phone starts pinging.

Alex:

> Hey, where are you?

Me:

> Fifteen minutes out

Alex:

> Okay

Alex:

> Hurry

Me:

> What's going on?

Alex:

> I'm not quite sure, but the band is all yelling at each other. The door is locked, Ronni and I can't get in there.

Me:

> I'll text Ty.

I actually call Ty again first, but he doesn't answer, so
I text him again.

Me:

> Babe? I'm almost there give me a call?

When I don't get a reply, I call Alex back.

"Dude? What's going on?" I say before she can get a word in.

Alex sounds out of breath. "I'm trying to listen, but I can't hear a thing other than yelling."

"Wait, what?" I've never heard the band get angry with each other. It's weird. "Have you talked to Jace?"

Alex shushes me. "One second. Uh, shit. There's more shouting. It's really loud. Sounds like Ty. Hold on I think the door's opening. Nope. Oh...yeah it's opening. It's Jace. Hold on, Zoey. Jace? I'm right here. What's going on?"

"Fucking chaos. It's a fucking disaster." I hear Jace in the background. Then there's a loud crash, like something huge has fallen over.

"Ohmygod," Alex yells. "Jace, get him outta there."

The phone goes dead.

By now, I'm freaking the fuck out. I yell for Omar. "Can you call Sergey? Something is happening at The Mission."

"Sergey has instructed me to take you back home, Mrs. Rainier." Omar begins to slow the car down to turn around.

Um, no fucking way. "It's *Zoey*. You take me to my husband, Omar. *Now*. I don't want to be an asshole, but I'll get out right now and call a Lyft if you don't drive me."

"As you wish." I hear Omar call Sergey back, who doesn't sound happy. I don't give two fucks. I need to get to Ty to find out what the hell is going on. My heart is racing.

I try Ty again. Nothing. Alex. Nothing. I call Ronni. Nothing. No one is answering me and I'm about to lose my mind when I notice we're only a couple of blocks away. My head starts to pound. Up ahead, I see blue-and-red flashing lights. Not just one set, it's like the entire block is filled with police. I scream, "What's going on, Omar?"

Something is terribly wrong.

Omar crawls along because traffic is completely stopped because of the police activity. I throw the car door open and run toward the venue, clutching my belly. As I get closer, I see Zane in the back of an ambulance cradling Carter, who looks semiconscious. From the distance, I hear sirens. Jace and Connor are in a heated discussion. Ronni and Alex stand close by to their men. Fiona is visibly crying. There's no sign of Ty.

God, please don't let him be gone.

I suck in a breath and both of my hands fly up to my mouth. Did I really have that thought? Oh God. I hurry toward the chaos, screaming for Ty. Alex rushes toward me and hugs me. "Zoey, shhh. Calm down."

"How am I supposed to calm down? Where is my husband?" I'm bawling. So unsure of what's going on. So incredibly scared. "Where is he?"

That's when I see him being led out of The Mission with his arms behind his back. In handcuffs. It's like all of the life has flooded out of him. I rush toward him. "Ty. Baby?"

He looks over, almost in slow motion. He has a black eye. His nose is broken and bleeding. There's a nasty scrape down his cheek. He stops. His eyes are blood-shot. Bleary. He doesn't say a word when the cop pushes his head down and places him in the back seat of the police vehicle. When the door is shut behind him, Ty peers out the window at me through devastated blue eyes. Then he looks away. Stares straight ahead at the seat in front of him as the vehicle drives away.

"What is going on?" I cry. Sink to my knees. My head is spinning. It feels like my entire world is falling apart.

Alex is once again by my side, her arm wrapped protectively around me. "I'm trying to get to the bottom of it. You look really pale, Z. Please come inside and sit down. You don't want anything to hurt the baby."

I look up at my best friend. She's right. Something is wrong. "Alex, please help me. I've got to protect my baby..."

And then the world goes black.

Chapter Twenty-Four

The Same Day

LIFE IS SO FUCKING good.

I mean, how can you beat a day like today. I'm playing a show with my band for the first time in over a year. My best friend's wife is opening her fancy restaurant tonight. And oh, I'm so fucking in love with Zoey. We're having a *son*.

Fuck yeah, I feel great. I meant what I said to Zoey. In the light of a new day, yesterday wasn't as bad as I thought it would be. Weird, sure. It's not every day you find out you have over a hundred million dollars, but I've already earned enough on my own to take care of myself and my family for the next several generations. The money from my mom's fucked-up side of the family? I'll put it to good use.

I pull out the envelope with my paternity results from my jacket pocket. Part of me wants to leave it alone. A big part. On the other hand, I've finally unveiled all of my secrets and the world hasn't collapsed. Why not just figure out who this asshole is and be done with it? Move on with my life.

With Zoey by my side? My band? I've got it all. For the first time in my entire life, I truly believe it. Deep in my gut.

I text Zane that Sergey and I are out front. He bounds down the walkway and jumps in the back seat with me within seconds.

"Hey, my brother." Zane holds out his fist.

I tap his fist with mine. "Ready, my brother?"

We chatter about some of the songs we've been writing together. Various band matters, the biggest one is our management. After ten years, all of us are ready to move to a different team. The plan is to head down to LA in a few weeks to meet with our first choice, Isis Management. They've been doing great things for Fireball, Connor's brother's band, who we just produced. As much as we love Katherine, she's pressuring us to do all of the things that burned us out in the first place. It feels like the time is just right to make a change.

After all, we're all family men now. But that doesn't mean we don't still want to play music. By the time we get to The Mission, Zane and I are pretty psyched at having new blood on our team.

Jace is setting up his own gear when we get inside. "Well, this feels like déjà vu. Other than this, Mission is a hell of a lot nicer." Zane hops up on stage to give him a hand.

Pokey, Zane's guitar tech waves him over to test out his setup. Connor appears from backstage, his bass slung low against his hips. "Hey, my brothers. Feels feckin' good to be back up on stage, not gonna lie."

I sit on the edge of the stage, writing a set list. My heart is bursting with fucking joy. I can't keep the smile off my face. Jace kneels down and flicks my cheek. "What's got you so happy?"

"Life, man." I cheesily grin up at him. "It's fucking awesome."

A flicker of anxiousness passes over Jace's face before his usual cool-cat demeanor takes over. "Yeah, sure is. Hey, you forgot to include *Butterfly*, we should play that tonight."

"Yeah. We should." I write it down as the encore. "Good?"

"Yep." Jace stands and heads back to finish setting up his drums.

I check my phone, Zoey must be taking a nap. She does that a lot right now. I shoot her a quick text.

Me:

I love you. I'm feeling so excited for tonight. In fact, I've never felt better, butterfly. Hurry and get here, I miss you and Rufus.

As the guys finish setting up, I consider whether I should tell them about my CPTSD. Zoey and I have discussed it with Lisa, and ultimately it's my call. It makes me nervous to share my diagnosis, but I trust these guys. They've had my back unconditionally for years. I think I'll set aside some time when we're in LA. It will be easier and less traumatic to tell everyone at the same time.

Yeah. That's exactly what I'm going to do. Zoey will help me figure out exactly what I should disclose. I don't think I'll be up for telling them specific details, but it's not like the fact I was abused so badly will come as a big surprise.

Sergey taps me on the shoulder. "Omar said Zoey is in her bedroom with the door shut. Her phone is on the kitchen counter, so she probably didn't get your text yet. Give it a half hour."

Okay, sure. I'll admit it. When Z didn't text me right back, I worried.

Jace clacks his drum sticks together and starts beating out a rhythm. Connor plucks a few low bass notes. Zane begins fiddling on his guitar. Ah, sweet, sweet music. God, I've missed this. I jump up to the microphone and tap it. "We're fucking back, my brothers."

"Feckin right we are," Connor booms into his mic.

We've been rehearsing at my house and Zane's, but nothing is like being on stage. We end up running through the entire hour-long set. The artists from my foundation watch. After we're done I chat with them briefly before grabbing my phone to check on my wife.

Love you too. I just woke up from a
nap. Miss you too. I'm just getting
ready. Rufus and I will be there
soon! xoxo

When I look up from my phone, I see Carter is walking toward me. It gives me a great idea. He's the closest thing to a father I've ever had. "Hey. How's it goin?"

"Eh? I'm pretty good, all things considered." Carter stands next to me. Crosses his arms.

Zane sees us standing together and joins us. "We sounded dope, man."

"You did." Carter pats him on the back. "How does it feel to be back on stage?"

"Amazing." Zane's beaming from ear to ear. "Tonight is going to be perfect. As excited as I am to play, I'm so proud of Fee. She's worked so hard for tonight to go smoothly."

"Can I talk to the two of you about something?" I look from Carter to Zane.

Carter raises an eyebrow. "Anytime. What's up?"

"It's kind of private, but I'd love to get your advice." I gesture to the dressing rooms. We go into the LTZ dressing room and lock the door. I sit across from Zane.

Carter sits to the side, facing both of us. He looks around at the state-of-the art flat screen, oversized couch, and catering area. "I can't get over how high-tech this is. It's nothing like the old Mission, that's for damn sure."

"Well, it's thirty years later, Carter." Zane claps his hands. "Okay, Ty. What the hell is up?"

I tell them briefly about my meeting with Alicia Spock. Explain what I learned about my mother and her family. "I've inherited some money. Apparently, my grandparents left it in trust for Jada if she ever got clean. Obviously, she didn't. Now it's mine."

"Holy shit, Ty." Zane slugs me enthusiastically. "That's fucking nuts. All that time you struggled, and your grandparents were rich?"

"Yep. And I'm going to do good things with their stupid money."

"Is that what you wanted to talk to us about?" Carter leans back in his chair.

"Uh, no." I pull out the envelope from my pocket. "Apparently, the grandparents also had my mother followed by a PI for most of her life. I learned she ran away from home when she was fifteen. Hung out on The Ave. Slept with all of Seattle and got pregnant with me. She never knew who my father was, but my grandparents did. They kept it secret my entire life. But, these are the paternity results."

"Whoa." Zane's eyes are huge.

"Yeah." I nod. "Whoa."

Carter leans forward. "Did you open it?"

"Nah. But I've seen some photos of her when I was a baby. It was with her shit." I take out my wallet and pull out the folded picture of Jada holding me at my christening and hand it to Carter. "She also had a Limelight flyer for one of your shows at The Mission."

"Holy shit," Carter purses his lips when he sees the photo. "She looks really familiar. I'm pretty sure she hung out at The Junkyard back in the day. Shit, Ty. When I went to see her when I first met you, I never put two and two together. They don't even look like the same person."

"Well, she was a junkie. She was only sixteen when she had me. She was a little worse for wear by the time I was in high school." I shrug.

"She looked—and acted—pretty rough, but I remember thinking at the time she seemed vaguely familiar. Huh." He squints. "Maybe I'll know the dude. You're, what? Three months older than Zane? So yeah, Limelight was still playing the clubs around then."

"I wanted to tell you something that happened when I first met you both. Jada demanded that I steal some Limelight stuff from your house. She said the band 'owed' her." I cringe at the memory. "I promise, I never did."

Carter scoffs. "Of course, you didn't."

Zane nods. "I'd never think that."

"Is there any reason she'd say that? Before I open this, I thought I'd better ask if she knew the other guys in the band? I mean, you were with Lianne, right?" I gulp. This is so awkward.

Carter leans back in his chair and looks nervously over at Zane. "Fuck. Those days are a blur. It's true, I had my eye on Lianne around that time, but she played hard to get. We were only together for a few weeks before she got pregnant with Zane. I cleaned up for a while. She was worth it to me. Before that? I was no angel. None of us in the band were. There's a reason I lectured all you guys about wearing condoms. We all fucked everything that moved. We snorted anything there was to snort. Smoked anything there was to smoke. Drank copious amounts of alcohol. I remember very little of it. Fuck, man. I'm surprised we were productive at all."

"I didn't mean anything by it, Carter. I just don't want to ruin some guy's life. Especially if it was someone in your band." I feel really bad bringing up past shit. I know how much I hate reliving my own stuff. Carter was way worse than I ever was.

"It's fine, Ty." Carter clasps his hands together. "You can't change the past, you have to own up to it. I fucked up a lot of relationships. With Lianne. Zane. My band. But back then, it was nonstop partying and fucking. None of us cared about consequences. We didn't even think about them."

I can relate. Luckily, I never got caught up in the hard stuff. Like Carter. Like my mom. I can't imagine putting Zoey through all of the shit Lianne and Zane went through. What I went through. Addiction is a destructive, selfish way of life. I wave the envelope. "Well, these are my paternity results. As I said, I'm afraid of fucking up some guy's life who has no idea he has a kid. Or another kid, as the case might be. I thought, since you are both dads, and you're basically my dad, Carter. What do you think?"

"*You're* gonna be a dad." Zane socks me in the arm. "What do *you* think?"

"I'd wanna know." I nod and repeat, "I'd wanna know."

"Me too," Zane affirms.

Carter stands. "I'd want to know. But, you're right. Once you find out, you'll have to decide how to approach it."

"Should I open it? Right now?" I wave the envelope. "Rip the bandage off?"

Zane comes up beside me. "Maybe you should do this with Zoey."

Carter shrugs.

"I'm still having sessions with Lisa. Zoey and I discussed talking it over with her first, but I think she'd actually be okay with me doing this with you guys. In fact, I think she'll be really proud of me." I walk over to the catering table and grab a plastic knife. Slit open the top of the envelope. Turn and face Carter and Zane. Pull out the paper and shake it loose. I've never seen one of these things before, it's a couple of columns and a bunch of numbers. I squinch my eyes and pore over what it says, and it all becomes clear. There's a column with Jada's name on it. A column with my name on it and a column with my father's name on it.

CARTER POPE.

PROBABILITY OF PATERNITY 99.9996%

The heat starts at my neck and floods my brain, my spinal column, my chest. It's like I'm becoming supercharged. Supercharged with rage. The kind of anger that no amount of anxiety medication can stave off. Pure. Utter. Fury.

The terror.

The anguish.

The shame.

The horror.

Every single emotion I've ever felt about the abuse I suffered manifests into an explosion of flammable gas.

I charge Carter, screaming, "You cock-sucking motherfucker. What have you done? *What have you fucking done?* How could you sit there and have that conversation with me? *How?* This is insanity. You knew I was your son all along. *Didn't you?* You did! You fucking knew all of these years and didn't say a fucking word. Who the fuck does that?"

Before he can get a word out, I pummel him into the ground. Beat his face to a pulp in my blind madness. At some point, Zane pulls me off and does some sort of ninja move, which has me in a headlock. He smashes my face so hard I see stars. His knee comes up and breaks my nose and I crumple to the floor.

All hell breaks loose. Connor and Jace rush in and pull Zane back. Carter lies unconscious on the floor. Zane rushes to him, screaming like a little child, "Dad. Daddy."

"What the fuck?" Connor looks around at the trashed dressing room. "What happened?"

Zane points at me as he frantically does CPR on his father. *My father.* "He fucking killed Carter. You're so fucked up, Ty. Seriously. Stay the fuck away from us."

EMTs rush in and load Carter up on a gurney. Zane points at me and yells, "Fuck you," on his way out.

"No, fuck *you.* And fuck *Carter.* You are both fucking *dead* to me," I roar.

Jace comes over to me. Reaches out to touch me, but I'm a live wire. "Don't you fucking touch me, you have no idea how sick to death I am of you treating me like a fucking child," I growl menacingly.

He holds up his hands and walks over to Connor. They both look at me like I'm a zoo animal. I lunge at them like the feral dog I am. "What? Do you want a piece of me too? Have I been a big *joke* to all of you? All these years? Wind Ty up. Put him on stage. Use his songs. Rip his soul out. Pat him on the head. Fucking repeat. It's all fine, right? We've made our money, right? You're all rich now, right? Well fuck this. I fucking *quit*. There is no more LTZ. It's fucking *over*. If I never see any of you again it will be too *fucking* soon."

I storm out of the dressing room to see the foundation artists standing around with their mouths wide open. It's clear as day. My band is finished. My foundation is over. Endorsements gone. Marriage...shit. I've blown it all up. I guess it was inevitable. I ruined my life.

The fatal decision to slice open an envelope has destroyed my entire life. "There won't be a show tonight, kids," I say as I head for the exit. Only to be met by five police officers who throw me against the wall, pull my arms behind my back and lead me outside.

In the distance, Zoey appears like an angel. Except dressed in all black. Cupping our son in her belly. Her wild, blonde hair flowing behind her as she rushes toward me. "Ty. Baby?" I stop because I know it's probably the last time I'm going to see her. I manage to keep eye contact as I'm pushed into the cop car. All I know in this moment is that she deserves more than I can give her. So does my son. I've got to break this fucked-up cycle once and for all. I'm the common fucking denominator. Which means I can't be part of their lives. I turn so I can't see her anymore. It hurts too fucking much.

The car drives away, and I don't look back.

I can't.

Not after what I just did.

I've sealed my fate.

Chapter Twenty-Five

WHEN I WAKE UP, I'm in a hospital room hooked up to a bunch of monitors. Panic hits me. Immediately, I reach down and cradle my bump. Mom rushes over to me from the window. "Zoey. You're awake. Don't worry. You're fine. The baby's fine."

Thank God.

I squeeze my eyes shut. Tears stream out. I vaguely remember riding in the ambulance screaming for Ty. Worried about my baby. Then I remember what I saw at The Mission. I look up at my mom. She smooths my hair back. "Well, it seems like there's a bit of a shitshow going on, my darling girl."

Dad comes in with two coffees. "Oh, good. You're awake. How are you feeling?"

"Um, pretty scared." I look at him incredulously. "What the hell is happening? How are you so calm?"

Mom sits next to me. "First, you're fine. You fainted. Dr. Sabel is on the way here to run some tests. The ER doctor has you hooked up to some fluids to get you hydrated. They're monitoring your blood pressure. It's come all the way back down to normal, so all looks good."

"Okay." My voice is barely a whisper. I'm so relieved.

Mom takes my hand. "As for the rest, we're not exactly sure of the details. Here's what I know: Ty attacked Carter. Zane attacked Ty. Ty was arrested. Zane and Fiona are in ICU with Carter. He had a heart attack. Lianne is on her way. Connor and Ronni are outside in the waiting room with Alex and Jace."

"Ohmygod." I clutch my bump because Rufus starts kicking. Hard. "He's kicking. It's the first time I've felt more than a flutter."

Mom places her palm next to mine. "Oh, Zoey. How wonderful."

And that's when my waterworks really start. I can't help it. My hormones don't allow me to stay Fonzie, as my dad says. "What is going on with Ty? I need him, Mom. He's who I need right now."

"He's in county jail. He'll be arraigned in an hour or so. Carter and Zane aren't pressing charges, so he'll likely pay a fine and be released." Dad sits down on the other side of me. "I took care of it. I called in a favor with a law school buddy at the prosecutor's office."

"What a mess." I wipe tears from my eyes with my thumb. "I'm sorry, Dad. There's a lot going on that I haven't been able to talk to you guys about. Ty's under a lot of stress."

"Hey, can I come in? The nurse told me you're awake." Alex stands at the doorway.

I nod and wave her in. My folks depart to give us some privacy. She sits by my side and clutches my hand. We shed a few tears. "I don't know what's going on, Alex. Your phone went dead and the next thing I saw was Ty getting arrested. What did he do?"

"I didn't see it. According to Jace, Ty, Carter, and Zane went to the dressing room to talk about something. They were in there a long time. We all heard the yelling. Apparently, Ty exploded and beat the ever-loving shit out of Carter. He was actually unconscious. Zane beat the shit out of Ty to get him off Carter. Jace and Connor kicked the door in and stopped the madness. Zane screamed horrible stuff at Ty on his way out the door. Ty said really hurtful stuff to Jace and Connor." Alex winces. "He quit the band and told them to fuck off. Luckily, no one was there so it hasn't hit the news. But it will, Z. You need to be prepared. "

"None of that matters, Alex." I shake my head. "The only thing that's important to me is Ty's well-being. He was so happy this morning. So excited to play. Something must have happened to set him off."

Alex gulps. Closes her eyes. Shakes her head. Then slowly pulls a piece of paper out of her purse. "I'm pretty sure this has something to do with it. When the police were talking to the guys, Ronni and I tried to clean up the dressing room to help Fee out. It's completely destroyed. As you can imagine, Fiona is devastated. On so many levels. Anyway, I found this. I read it, Z. But, I haven't showed it to anyone, including Jace. And I won't. It's none of our business, but I knew I had to keep it safe. Here."

She hands me the paper.

"What is it?" I take it from her and immediately realize that its Ty's paternity results. Why did he open it without me? I scan it and see Carter's name. What the fuck? Then it all hits me. "Oh. My. God."

"Help me up, Alex." As my BFF assists me out of bed, I clutch her hands. "What is going on right now? Please tell me the truth."

"Connor and Jace are all incredibly pissed. Fiona too. I haven't talked to Zane. Or Ronni. I'm not going to lie, this might have been the last straw. Ty was completely belligerent. Out of control. Understandably, I suppose. But Zoey? Whatever all of this is about? Ty can't continue to make the band absorb the brunt of his issues. I know he had a bad childhood. But what he did is not okay. It just isn't. Carter could *die*." She shakes her head. "I'm really not sure where LTZ goes from here."

"You don't know the whole story, Alex. Trust me. Don't say something you can't take back. I promise you, there is more to this than any of you know." She may be my best friend, but I will not allow anyone to say a bad word about my husband to me. He's my priority. Always.

"I love you, Z." Alex grips my hand and exhales a huge whoosh of air. "It's just... Fuck. You're right. I don't want to *ever* say anything to you I can't take back. Here's the deal. We all have our own lives. Our own struggles. Our own obstacles to overcome. All of those guys have bent over backward for Ty. For years. They have protected him. They have loved him. They have defended him. Ty lives in his own world and doesn't often see what he has in front of him. All of those guys are gems. Actual gems. Over many years, I saw how Ty behaved firsthand. None of them deserved what he put them through then. They definitely didn't deserve what just happened today."

The bottom of my stomach drops out. Do the guys really think so little of Ty?

"Okay. I've heard enough. I'm not going to discuss this with you, Alex. With all due respect, if the guys really have a problem with Ty, then the guys need to have that discussion. Not you and me. I love you. You're like my sister. But, Ty's my husband. He's my only concern right now because he needs me. If that puts me on the other side of the LTZ fence that seems to have been built?

Fine." I look around the room for my purse just as Dr. Sabel comes in.

Alex heads for the door. "I love you, Z. I hope this all blows over. I really do. Jace and I are heading to my mom's to pick up Lena. Ronni and Connor just left. Zane and Lianne are in the ICU with Carter. Fiona's back at the restaurant trying to recover from the disaster. Text me when you're in a better place. No matter what happens, you're my best friend. I'm always here for you."

As I'm enduring Dr. Sabel's exam, I think about Alex and the rest of the LTZ women. I love them. We all have such a great time together. What if Ty is an outcast with his band? Then I'll likely have to make a choice. I cradle little Rufus before I put my shirt back on. Think about my life. About my husband.

There is no choice. None at all. I'm team Ty and Rufus. Above all else.

When Dr. Sabel gives me the all clear, a nurse wheels me out with my parents beside me. Omar waits for me at the entrance. I get up but rather than get in the car, I have a different plan. "Mom, Dad. Could you please go pick up Ty from the precinct when he's released? I'll meet you back at the house. Omar? Please wait for me. I'll be twenty minutes, tops."

I find my way to the ICU, where Lianne is sitting in the waiting room engrossed in her phone. I've never seen her look bad. Even in the hospital she's gorgeous in some sort of flowy cream-and-white pantsuit. Her red hair is up in an intricate knot. She doesn't notice when I sit across from her until I say her name.

"Oh, hi, Zoey." Lianne sounds tired. "How are you feeling?"

"I got the all clear. How are you?"

She manages a watery smile. "It's not been my favorite day."

"Yeah." I show her the paper. "You obviously heard the shocking news."

A single tear trickles down her cheek. "Just when I think he can't hurt me any worse..."

"It did happen before you were with him, right?" I reach across the aisle for her hand. She gives it to me. "Ty was born before Zane."

"I know." She shrugs.

"It still hurts." I sigh.

"So much." She weeps silently. "We were only officially together for a few weeks before I got pregnant with Zane. But we'd slept together before that. He was the hottest guy in town. I thought I was the shit. God, I had this idea we'd be Seattle's 'it' couple. I guess I should have known he was fucking other women. Hell, he fucked other women when we were still together. It's one of the reasons I left him. But getting some underage street girl pregnant? I just can't fathom."

I squeeze her hand. "Lianne, he's a completely different person now and has been for so many years. Do you love him?"

She looks up at me. Tears stream down her face. "I'm pathetic. I've never loved anyone else in my life."

"I think you and I are a lot alike, Lianne." I smile because I want her and Carter to find their way. Despite this. "And I think Carter and Ty are a lot alike."

At that moment, Zane comes out of the room and sees us together. He looks exhausted. His usually animated voice is flat. "Hey, Zoey."

"Zane. I'm sorry about Carter. How is he?"

"Sore. Sad. Shell-shocked." He sits next to Lianne and covers his face with his hands. "What the fuck is happening right now? I can't comprehend that Carter is Ty's father. That Ty is *actually* my *brother*."

Lianne cuddles her son. Kisses his head. The love between them is palpable. "Were you able to talk to him about it?"

"Not really." He hangs his head. "It's not the right time. He needs to get his strength back."

I have to know what went down. "Zane, do you mind telling me what happened?"

"Well, it happened so fast. When we first started talking, Ty showed us a picture of Jada with Ty as a baby. Carter actually recognized her as a girl who came around The Junkyard." Zane scrubs his hands over his chin. "Zoey, Carter truly has no memory of sleeping with Jada. He's just as blindsided as Ty."

"For the record? I had no idea Ty brought that envelope with him. I thought we'd open it together. There's a lot of, well, shit we've been dealing with." Without giving away details that would betray Ty's trust, I proceed to explain our meeting with Alicia Spock. What we learned about Jada's family. About Jada, herself. When I finish, Zane and Lianne look at each other. Clearly realizing that we are all finding ourselves in the same position.

"Zoey, in all honesty, I don't think I can take much more today. I need to get to Fee. And Mia. I think all of this is going to take a little time." Zane pinches the bridge of his nose. "Carter needs to heal. Physically. Mentally. He loves Ty, he'll want him in his life. I do too, it's just? A lot. Can we take a rest until we know where Ty's head is at? Is that okay?"

Lianne grabs my hand. "I promise, I'll keep you up to date." She holds her phone out to me. "Program your number in here."

So I do.

When I step outside the double doors to ICU, I take a few deep breaths. Center myself. I check my phone. Nothing. I find my way back to where Omar is waiting to take me home. During the ride, I shoot separate texts to Fiona and Ronni letting them know I love them and will be in contact soon. I'm not about to apologize on Ty's behalf because, well, I still haven't talked to him. I'm really not sure if he has anything to be sorry for.

Dad finally texts me that Ty is due to be released within the hour. When I call Lisa, she answers on the first ring. "Zoey. I saw a news report. How can I help?"

"We need you." I recap the events of the day. Again. I'm also careful to let her know I haven't spoken with Ty yet, but he'll be home soon and I don't know what I'll be dealing with.

"Zoey, the first advice I can give you is to do your very best to be consistent and predictable. Clearly this entire chain of events from yesterday triggered him. It's important for you to know your boundaries. You, alone, cannot make this better. You can validate Ty and his feelings, but you can't fix this."

"I may not be able to fix the situation, but Ty is my husband. I'm carrying his son. I love him. He's the most important person to me. So, I will do whatever it takes to help him. Or, get him help," I say with conviction. "I know if Ty's father was anyone but Carter, he wouldn't have reacted like that. He was completely prepared to see the name of a man he didn't know."

"That might be true, but again, focus on yourself first. Then Ty." Lisa's caring voice grounds me. Gives me hope. "It's important for the next few days to model for Ty that self-care is okay. He's most likely remorseful. Depressed. Stay the course and practice what we've been working on. Reflect back what you hear him say when he speaks. Listen without trying to solve the problem. Once he feels heard, then you can ask if he wants to work on solutions together."

I take a deep breath. "Are we going to be okay? I'm scared that all of the progress we've made has been destroyed in an instant. Ty lashed out. There's no question. He laid hands on Carter, and Carter's not doing very well. He'll survive, but according to Zane, he was just as blindsided as Ty was."

"If you can remember one thing, try not to take anything that Ty says personally. Don't worry about the repercussions with his band or Carter just yet. They don't know about his CPTSD. They do not have the tools you have. Or Ty has."

I pause for a moment. Take in what she's saying. Comprehending that we truly have a long road ahead of us.

Lisa interrupts my thoughts. "Zoey, when Ty gets home, he may shut you out completely. Are you prepared for that?"

The thought of Ty freezing me out hasn't ever crossed my mind. It scares me to death. "I'm not. Today was supposed to be the opposite of what happened. Celebratory. Fun. Lighthearted. Instead, well, I'm facing the fact that we're back to square one."

Lisa taps her pen on her wrist and looks up. "Well, this was a terrible day. But tomorrow is a new start. Keep the faith. I've seen tremendous progress over the past few weeks, Zoey. This might be a setback, but the two of you have a lot to look forward to. Hopefully, without the weight of the past bearing down on you so oppressively."

"I hadn't thought about it in that way. I really appreciate you, Lisa." I feel little Rufus twisting and kicking. I rub my belly. She's right. Ty and I have so much goodness in our lives, something very peaceful takes root inside me. "I really feel hopeful we can get through this. That all of us can get through this."

Lisa smiles and nods enthusiastically. "One of my favorite research studies on CPTSD indicates the best medicine can be found within the healing power of relationships. Our brain has incredible power to create new neural connections throughout our lifetime. What this means, Zoey, is you and Ty have the ability to form a secure attachment that will override everything else. Over time, these types of incidents will happen less and less. Maybe not at all. And if they do? You have the tools to get through."

"It feels like a lot is riding on me, Lisa."

"I understand. Let me say this, while I'm confident we will find a treatment plan to get your family through this, I want to remind you about the inpatient CPTSD facility I recommended. The timing isn't ideal because of the baby. But, given the circumstances? Maybe the timing is actually perfect. He could be home before your son is born."

"Maybe." I sigh. "Would you be available to do a session with us? Even tonight if I can convince him?"

"Of course. We will find a time. Tonight. Tomorrow. Text me. I'll be here."

After we hang up, I head into the living room. It's nearly dawn, but I turn on the electric fire. Go back to the kitchen and put on a kettle to make us some herbal tea. I get the text from my dad letting me know they're almost home. So, I sit at the counter and wait.

My husband needs me. More than ever.

And nothing is going to stop me from making sure he's okay.

Nothing.

Chapter Twenty-Six

NOTHING ABOUT THE PAST twelve hours makes sense.

Other than what I've been told, I have virtually no clear memory of what happened after I found out Carter Pope was my father yesterday. I don't remember what was said. I don't remember being in a fight, although it's clear I was in a bad one. I mean, why else would I be in fucking jail? I'm sore as fuck. My nose is broken. My face is fucked.

Oh, but I know that I royally fucked up. The way everyone is treating me? Not super hard to figure out.

It's just that everything's cloudy. A ménage of images in my head that have no rhyme nor reason.

Like whatever Mike Pearson's yammering on about. He hasn't stopped talking since he and Sergey picked me up from jail. I honestly couldn't tell you a thing he's said. Until now.

"Zoey's fine. She was at the hospital but is home now. She's very anxious to see you." At the mention of Zoey's name, I immediately tune in to my father-in-law.

"What did you say?" My voice is hoarse. Sore.

Mike squints at me from over his glasses. "Are you using drugs, Ty?"

"What? No."

"I've been talking to you since I picked you up. Could you do me the courtesy of paying attention? After you beat the shit out of Carter, it wasn't easy to get you out of jail, son." His voice reminds me of how he talked to me in New York. When he refused to let me see his daughter in the hospital after her accident. How shitty I felt when he diminished my role in Zoey's life.

"You have no idea what—" I look out the window. I'm not picking a fight with Zoey's dad. "Never mind."

"Enlighten me."

The last thing I'm going to do is give him ammunition against me. Given his assumption that I'm on drugs, I'm pretty sure Zoey hasn't told him about my CPTSD. I glance back over at him. "I appreciate that you pulled in a favor, Mike. I do. I've got a lot of shit to deal with. Could you please tell me what happened to my wife since I haven't been able to talk to her in twelve hours?"

"She fainted when she saw you in the back of the police vehicle. They took her to the same hospital as Carter. Her mother was with her the entire time, and both she and the baby are just fine."

"Thank God." I nod. Let out a huge breath. I gaze over at him. "Thank you. Truly."

Mike taps his finger to his lip. "Carter Pope is your father. That had to come as a shock."

"How do *you* know that?" Instantly my body is on high alert again.

"It's all in the police report. They interviewed Zane. Jace. Connor. The kids from your foundation." Mike pats my knee. "Carter had a heart attack, Ty."

It's all too much. I palm my face. "Is he alive?"

"Yes. And he's stable."

My mind is once again a whirlwind. It's too much. Unpacking all of this shit. Overwhelming.

The security gate opens and we pull into the driveway where Mike's car is parked. We pull in next to it. "I'm exhausted, Mike. Can we discuss everything with you and Olivia after I've had some sleep? I don't have anything left right now."

"Of course. Remember what I told you at your wedding. All I'll ever ask of you is to treat my daughter well." He opens the door. Before he gets out he turns back to me. "And, you are my son. A part of my family now. Remember that. Olivia and I love you. I'm sorry that you're going through such a tough time. We're both here for you if you need us."

Before I can process what he's said and get out of the car, he's already driving off.

Sergey opens my door and I follow him inside. When he sees Zoey sitting at the counter, he waves to her and retreats to his quarters. All I can do is stand in the doorway and take in the beautiful vision of my pregnant wife. She holds out a cup to me, which compels me to move toward her. Instead of handing me the tea, she pulls me into her arms. Kisses my whole face.

"Ty, I love you so much," she whispers in my ear and places my hand on her belly. "We're both here for you."

"Can we not talk tonight?" I say against her hair. "I need a shower. I need you. I need to sleep."

"Yes."

I help her off the barstool. She takes my hand and leads me to the shower. Turns on all of the jets. Strips me naked. Takes off her clothes too. We step into the glorious warm spray. Zoey tenderly washes every inch of my body. I sit on the wide bench so she can shampoo and condition my hair. Every touch soothes me. Makes me believe that things are going to be okay with us.

Even though I know they're not.

So, I'll take this. One last time. Before I release her like she did for me all those years ago.

I cup her breasts. Memorize her nipples, so dark and sensitive. I suck them between my lips. One after the other. Smooth my hands over her protruding belly. One hand slips between her legs. I push my fingers inside her. Rub my thumb over her clit, supporting her with my other hand against her lower back.

"Make love to me, baby." Zoey takes hold of my cock firmly. Pumps me with her small hand exactly the way I showed her in her bedroom so many years ago. "I need you."

I turn her so she's facing the mirror. She watches me skim my hands over her body from behind. Kiss the small of her back as I carefully pull her onto my lap. Once her legs are resting over mine, I nibble on her neck. Her shoulders. Her earlobes. My hands caress our baby and move lower to her pussy.

She writhes against my erection while I strum her to orgasm. Her back arches when she shudders through it. Her arms reach around and encircle my neck. Her lips graze my cheek and chin before her mouth meets mine, our kisses deep. Like we will never get enough of each other, which is true.

At least for me.

As much as I'd love to slip my cock inside her, we can't do that here. Too dangerous for my son. I guide her to standing and step around her to grab a towel. I dry her off and then myself. "Let's go to bed, butterfly." I nuzzle her neck and take her hand.

There's something different about the way Zoey looks at me as I lead her to the bedroom. Like she can see through me into my soul. Into every part of my being.

Oh, she doesn't say anything, she just looks at me. Her eyes shining with such pure love it takes me aback.

I lay her down on the bed. Place the backs of her thighs over my shoulders and kneel on the floor. I feast on my wife. Savor every bit of her pussy. Flick my tongue over her clit until she cries out with another release. Only then do I crawl up into bed with her. We lie side by side, facing each other. She grips my face with her hands. Presses her forehead to mine. I pull her leg up over mine and enter her shallowly. Just enough to feel her wet heat.

"You're my soul, Ty." Zoey says against my lips. "I'm yours. Just feel us."

Our arms are wrapped around each other. We're pressed together in every way possible. I'm inside her a little, but we're barely moving. Just staring into each other's eyes. All of the madness disappears and I'm right back where I was yesterday morning before all hell broke loose. I'm in love with my wife and we're having a baby. My future is in front of me. The past is in the past.

As if she's reading my mind, Zoey squeezes around the tip of my cock. Holds it.

Her eyes flutter closed and I feel a whoosh of energy pass between us. Unlike anything I've ever experienced.

In this moment, our bodies are merged but our connection transcends sex. Or orgasms. Or pleasure. Every ounce of poison living inside my brain dissipates into the ether. And is replaced with a pure, white light. Filling my heart. Filling my soul. Filling every molecule in my body.

In this moment I realize, I have something so very rare. I *know* what true love is. I *am* capable of true love. Zoey *is* my true love.

In this moment, we are endless.

Chapter Twenty-Seven

Three Months Later

OMAR PARKS THE CAR and helps me out. Nervously, I get my bearings and waddle up the walkway. My belly is so huge now, I can't see my feet. Or my ankles, for that matter. They're so swollen it's uncomfortable to walk right now, but I've waited patiently to be here. My discomfort is secondary on this monumental day.

The heat wave of late October means I'm sweating by the time I reach the heavy wood door. I raise my hand to knock, but Carter opens the door before I have the chance. When he gets a glimpse of my huge self, his eyes bug out comically. "Look at you." His smile is wide. "He's grown a lot in two weeks."

"Wanna feel?" I take Carter's hand and place it where my son kicks me. He's an active little guy, nearly ready to make his debut. It's still funny to me to watch the wavy motions of my belly when he moves around in there. What's not so funny? I have to pee every ten minutes. I excuse myself.

When I return, Carter pulls me into his arms. "Thank you for everything, Zoey."

"You've done a lot of work Carter." I hug him tightly. "Are you ready? I don't want to be late."

He helps me down the steps to the car. When we're safely in the back seat, Omar heads toward King County International Airport. I pull up my tracker and am happy to see we're in good shape time-wise. We park next to the little terminal. Rather than get out, we decide to wait in the cool air-conditioned Land Rover until Ty's private jet touches down.

Exactly twenty minutes later, Carter and I watch Ty descend the steps onto the tarmac. His long, dark hair flows behind him. He's wearing a white t-shirt. Threadbare jeans. Black Doc Martens. When he sees us, his eyes fix on my huge belly. He looks up at me in surprise, drops his bag and runs toward me.

"Oh, butterfly. He's gotten even bigger." He places his hands on either side of my enormous bump. "I love you. I love both of you so much."

We kiss like we haven't seen each other in months, when really it's only been a week since Dr. Sabel made Omar drive me home. Just in case. I'm due any day now. Ty and I made the decision for him to finish up his program in Arizona. It was a slight risk that I'd go into labor, but it was the right thing to do for our little family.

Carter beams at his son. Waiting patiently with open arms. Ty looks over at him shyly. He's still getting used to Carter's enthusiastic acceptance of being his biological father. Ty walks into his arms and they embrace. "Carter. Thanks for coming."

Zane? He's trying. But it's still weird. He's struggling with all of it. He'll get there. I hope.

"I wouldn't have missed your homecoming." Carter throws an arm around Ty's neck. Ty takes my hand. We pile back into the Range Rover after Omar retrieves Ty's luggage and throws it in the back.

Ty clutches my hand tightly. "I'm nervous."

"You'll be fine." Carter turns around from the front seat. "Believe me, after all of my fuck-ups, yours is a piece of cake. It all just takes time."

I lean my head on Ty's shoulder, listening to Carter's sage words. Funny how times have changed. I wind my fingers through my husband's and we rest them on his thigh. He kisses my head. I look up at him. He mouths, "I love you." I mouth it back. His sweet kiss follows. I relax against him and the motion of the car lulls me to sleep. Ty gently squeezes my shoulder to wake me up when we get to our destination.

Carter leads the way up the walk to Zane's house, where the entire band is waiting, along with their significant others. Ty hasn't spoken to anyone since the "incident" as he and I call it, but I have. I can't say all of the guys have come around completely. Then again, Ty hasn't told his story yet.

We shall see.

We can only hope today will be the start of LTZ's healing.

If it isn't? Both Ty and I are prepared. And patient. He's been at the treatment facility for three long months. I joined him after the first week. There was no way I'd have let him go through everything on his own. Lisa was with us every step of the way. Carter even joined us for a couple of weeks. He's started therapy for his own similar issues.

No matter what happens, Ty has done a lot of hard work. We now have a solid foundation to move forward in whichever way our lives take us.

Together. With our son when he arrives.

Fiona opens the door. I haven't seen or heard from her in months, but I give her grace. Ty's breakdown caused a lot of damage to something that was important to her. She's recovered. *Gus* is keeping her really busy, or so I've been told. "Hey, Fee," Carter embraces her warmly before heading inside.

She looks at Ty and me warily, we all say awkward hellos before following Carter inside. I suck in a breath when I see Zane sitting with Lianne. Alex and Jace are on the couch. Connor is looking out the window at the city. Ronni looks up from her phone. Ty grips my hand and helps me sit in one of the oversized armchairs. He takes the seat next to me.

Carter stands behind Ty and places his hands on Ty's shoulders. "Guys, I appreciate you all coming here today. Ty and I have a few things to say. I sincerely hope that it will be our first step to healing."

When Connor moves from the window to sit next to Ronni, everyone looks at my husband. I reach over and squeeze his hand. I say quietly, "We're all family, Ty. No matter what, it's all going to be okay." He nods and then faces his audience.

"I don't know how much all of you know, but it's no secret I've been in Arizona at a clinic that specializes in mental illness," Ty addresses the group. "Specifically, I was diagnosed with CPTSD a few years ago, and I kept it from everyone. Including Zoey. I thought it would be easier if you all thought I was an addict."

Alex's jaw drops open. Jace and Connor exchange a glance. Fiona strokes Zane's hair when he squeezes his eyes shut in obvious distress. Carter sits on the arm of Ty's chair. "I've been with Ty at the treatment facility. It turns out that I also have CPTSD, which led to my addiction issues."

"What does CPTSD mean?" Ronni directs her question to Ty.

"It's a trauma and stress-related disorder, which is similar to PTSD that developed because I was exposed to repeated trauma throughout my childhood. I'll be honest, Ronni. I was ashamed when I received my diagnosis. That's why I kept it from all of you and why I'm here to ask for forgiveness. Regardless of what you might think, I love each and every one of you in this room. I haven't done well in expressing it. I hope that's behind me. I don't want to hide anymore."

Ty leans forward and catches each and everyone's eye in the room in the magnetic way he addresses a crowd when he's on stage. "I know all of you have some idea of how I grew up. My mom was an addict. But, there was a lot more that I never told anyone. The truth is, from the time I was a young child my mother beat me. Tortured me mentally. Allowed others to abuse me. Because of my CPTSD, I've lived in a constant state of fear. My entire life I've felt like an outsider. I didn't understand how I fit into the world. Or how to trust those closest to me. I'm proud to say I'm a survivor. But I am living with mental illness. And I always will."

Everyone begins murmuring and whispering. Alex and Ronni burst into tears. Jace, Zane, and Connor look shell-shocked. Lianne already knew, so she comforts Fiona.

I want Ty to get what he needs to say out before he loses everyone's attention, so I step in. "Everyone, please. Let Ty finish. This is important for his healing process. It's a big deal for him to be open and trusting with all of you."

"Thank you, babe." Ty gives me a grateful smile. "My mom died, as you know, right before Zoey and I got married. It wasn't long after I told her about my abuse. Then my diagnosis. By this time, she was pregnant so we started working with my therapist. I was doing really well. Then a lawyer contacted me about my grandparents' estate. A couple days before the...incident, I found out I'd inherited a shit ton of money. And, access to my paternity results. Never in a million, trillion years would I have thought Carter was my dad. When I opened the envelope and saw his name? I blacked out. All of my trauma caught up to me and I lashed out. For the record, I'm incredibly grateful that the man I've always considered to be my father is *actually* my bio dad."

Carter shakes his head. "For the record, I was shocked too. I'm not proud that I don't remember sleeping with

Tyson's mother. But I've always thought of Ty as my son, so really the only thing that's changed is the fact our blood matches."

Zane's expression is unreadable. I can't imagine how it feels to come to terms with the fact the man you considered your brother is *actually* your brother. I hope he and Fee will open their hearts to us again. Ty misses them. So do I.

Ty takes a deep breath. "I'll shut up now, but before I do. I'm sorry. I said horrible things to all of you. Things I truly didn't mean. I can't expect any of you to understand. This information is probably, well... It's a lot. I just need you all to know while I'm never going to be cured, I've done everything in my power to learn how to manage my CPTSD. I understand if you don't want anything to do with me. If the band is truly broken up. I hope that isn't the case, because I was so fucking excited to start things up again. No matter what happens, all of you are my family. I hope you'll find it in your heart to forgive me. To learn more. To talk to me. I'm an open book. I'm not hiding anymore. And I'm not going to let what happened fucking define me anymore."

Ronni gets up and kneels by Ty. Takes his hands. Looks deeply in his eyes. Hers are full of tears. "I *understand*, Ty. I'm sorry you felt so alone for so long. You're a good man, sweetheart. You deserve happiness. I'm here for you. Connor too." He nods but doesn't say anything.

Jace comforts Alex, who is now bawling hysterically. I get up to go to her, but Jace holds up his hand. "Not right now, Zoey. We have our own things going on, and she can't handle this."

"Alex?" My mouth falls open. "What?"

She shakes her head. "Give me a day or two, Z."

"Guys, we've gotta head out." Jace wraps his arm protectively around Alex. "I'm glad you're dealing with your shit, Ty. As Alex said, give us a day or two to process."

As they get up to leave, Ty hands Jace a printout about CPTSD we had made prior to the meeting. "Just in case you want to know more."

The entire room begins chattering and talking. Whispering. Looking. Then looking away. It's not cohesive. It's messy. Just like real life. Well, I guess this is our real life.

I hoist myself up from my chair and clap my hands to get everyone's attention. "You guys, if I could just say one thing I'd appreciate it."

The room goes quiet. Ty takes my hand and squeezes. "If any of you are like me, you're probably feeling a lot of different things. I handed Alex and Jace something we put together that will give you the basics. Rather than leave here today and speculate, I think it will explain a lot."

"I'm so tired of family drama," Fiona mutters. "I've had enough to last ten lifetimes. I'm sorry, Zoey, it's just the way I feel."

"It's okay," I assure her. "I just want you all to know that what happened to Ty wasn't his fault. He's the bravest man I know. Not only is he embracing his diagnosis, he's determined to do more to reduce the stigma around mental illness. Through the foundation. Through everything he does going forward. At the very least, we wanted to tell you what is going on. You all deserve to know the truth. Neither of us wants any child to go through what happened to Ty."

Ty and I exchange a look. It's time for us to go. Nothing more will be accomplished today. We say quick goodbyes. Instead of walking the four blocks, Omar drives us. When we get safely inside, Ty wraps his arm around me and Baby Rufus, who actually has a real name now. We just haven't been able to stop calling him by his nickname. "You did so good, babe."

"It's funny how telling the truth isn't as hard as lying and hiding shit." Ty kisses my cheek.

I waddle to the couch and plop down while Ty and Omar unload the car. Sergey is due back from vacation in a couple of weeks, but we're keeping both men on staff. Security for our growing family is our top priority. Especially after next week.

It will all be out in the open. Ty's survival story will be on the cover of *Celebrity Pulse* magazine. A deep dive on everything he went through and how far he's come. One thing my husband is adamant about, is education. He feels if he can help one child escape the type of environment he was subjected to, it will be worth exposing his most painful memories.

"Would you like a foot massage?" Ty sits next to me and pulls my feet into his lap.

"If I wasn't married to you already, I'd lock your shit down right now. Ahhh," I sigh and relax against the cushion when Ty jams his thumb into my arch.

Ty works on my feet for a while before leaning over and kissing me. "I love you more now than I've ever loved you, Z. I still can't help but believe that me seeing you from the stage that night was divine intervention."

I run my fingers through his hair. Stare into his eyes. Ty's becoming a lot more woo-woo as he's healing, which is awesome. I always felt we were meant to be. He and I are so much older now. We've been through so much together. And apart.

It's *so* much better together.

"I feel the same way, babe. I've realized a true happily ever after is being able to come through a shitstorm together and make it to the other side." I sigh contentedly.

No one but us knows that when Ty first flew to Arizona on his own, he left his journal behind with a goodbye note much like the one I left him when I was eighteen. The same Carter bullshit about how if you love someone you need to set them free. Little did he know, when he agreed to the three-month program, I'd already finalized my own plans to move to Arizona temporarily. To be by his side. To keep my promise to never leave him. A promise that I will keep until the day I die.

I place my hands over his. We intertwine our fingers and rest them on my belly. Sure enough, the kicks start. Ty laughs heartily. "It's so cool to see your belly move. It's almost time, you know. To meet him."

"Have you given any more thought to meeting Jemma or any of your mother's family?" I settle back against him.

"No. I'm not ready for that. I want it to be me, you, and Rufus. Carter and your folks. And then I need work things out with my LTZ family. Even if we never make music again. I'd be sad, but maybe someday they'll forgive me. I'm patient. For now, it seems like the guys are pretty occupied with other stuff. Maybe they've moved on."

"Well, in fairness, we'll have our hands full too. Any day now."

"It's all going to be okay, Z." Ty tips my lips up for a kiss. "I have faith the rest will fall into place."

I have faith too.

But also more than that.

I have proof. Proof that true love conquers all.

I'm looking into his eyes right now.

Epilogue

I CAN'T STOP SMILING. I gaze down at my beautiful wife. Her eyes flutter a bit as she sleeps. Her arm is flung over her head on top of wild blonde hair, which is piled in some sort of messy knot. I can't help it, I bend down and kiss her lips. Slip her a little tongue for good measure. She moans, then stirs and blinks awake.

"Ohmygod, you creeper." She yawns. Smiles. Stretches her arms above her head.

I hand our son to her. "Yep. I am. In my defense, he's ready for breakfast, and you're the only source."

Oliver Pope Rainier was born eight weeks ago. Seven pounds nine ounces. A thatch of dark hair. Like everything she does, Zoey was a rock star. She gave birth to him naturally, I'm still not sure how. I was there every step of the way and wow, I had no idea about childbirth. Watching our son come into the world was so much more intense than I imagined. The minute I saw him? The purest love.

There's *nothing* I won't do for him.

So yeah, Zoey and I are both completely obsessed with him. We've been nesting, the three of us. No visitors. With our parents being the exceptions. Oliver's little personality is starting to come out now. He's so chill. A Zen baby. Sleeps well. Eats well. Pees and poops like a champ. Smiles like a madman.

I'm here for everything, I can't imagine missing a second.

Being a dad is the best.

Zoey pulls her tank down over her breast and helps him latch on to her nipple. I crawl back into bed and sit behind her. This way, she can relax against my chest while he feeds and I can wrap my arms around the two of them. His little hand curls around her finger as he gets his first drink. God. It's the best watching them together. I kiss the top of her head. "I love morning time, butterfly."

"You say that every day." Zoey looks up at me. Nuzzles my neck. We sneak a few kisses while Oliver suckles away.

When Ollie is done with breakfast, Zoey hands him to me and takes a long shower. I burp him, change him, and rock him back to sleep. He's draped across my bare chest wearing only a diaper when Zoey returns to the bedroom holding up her phone. "Caterers will be here at noon."

"I could have cooked." I shift slightly so she can join me back in bed.

She slips under my arm and lies against my chest. Her face even with Ollie's. "But then we wouldn't have this extra hour to snuggle."

"Or, we could put him down for a bit..." I smile when she looks up at me and nods enthusiastically.

I lean over to place our sleeping son in his bassinet. When I turn back around, Zoey's stripped off her bathrobe and wears nothing but a cheeky grin. "Are you sure? I'm not on birth control, babe. We could have Irish twins if we're not careful."

"If we have ten Ollies, I'll be a happy man." I yank off my boxer briefs and capture my wife's lips. We've only had sex once since our son was born. We had no alone time during the three months we were in Arizona. I'm all pent-up, that's for sure.

But I elect to go slow, Zoey's body's been through a lot, after all. Taking a few minutes to make out with my wife is a luxury. We slowly explore each other, suckling each other's tongues. Nibbling. Tasting.

I turn Zoey so her back is toward me and massage her shoulders. Kiss down her back. Lick her spine. Slip my hand around to cup her breast and slide it down to her stomach. She flinches a bit and moves my hand down toward her pussy.

"Hey, babe. What's wrong?" I kiss my way up to her neck and cup her face so she'll look at me.

She shuts her eyes, almost embarrassed. "I'm still so poochy."

Ah, that's not going to do. She's my beautiful butterfly. I wrap my arms around her and look down at her body from over her shoulder. My dark hair mixes with hers over her neck. Her belly is gorgeous. Slightly plump with a few streaky marks, evidence that she carried our son and kept him healthy throughout all of our madness.

I run my hand across her stomach tenderly. "You are beautiful. I love all of you. Remember what I said the first time we were ever naked together?"

"Never hide?" She giggles.

"Exactly. Come here." I kiss her with everything I have. I don't care if she's thin or fat or just a little poochy, I love her as she is. Because she's perfect. I nibble her ear and cup her breasts. A little milk leaks out and I lick it. Lave her nipples and suck a bit. To show her that even though her boobs are primarily for feeding our son right now, I'm still obsessed with them in that way.

As evidenced by my dick, which is as hard as a steel pole against her thigh. She grips me and strokes. Slowly. Maddeningly. I have a little leak of my own, which she uses to lubricate my tip. "God, I've missed fucking you."

"We can't get too crazy with boy-o right next to us." I practically pant when she picks up the pace. I dip my fingers into her pussy to find her dripping wet, as expected. "I am going to taste you, though."

"Oooh. Let me do you too."

Obligingly, I flip around so my cock is even with her mouth and I dive right into her sweet heat. Plunge a couple of fingers in and out of her. My head about flies off my shoulders when she sucks me nearly all the way down her throat. Yeah, we worked through all of that in therapy. Now, I truly enjoy blow jobs.

I know I've got to work fast, or I'm going to lose it. I suck her clit hard and wiggle my tongue. Within seconds, she comes so hard she cries out. Too loud.

Comically, we both flop over to look at Oliver, who remains blissfully ignorant that his parents are going at it next to him. When we're both convinced he's still sleeping, I pull her on top of me. Slip inside. Wrap my arms around her lower back. Her eyes roll back when I hit her spot.

"Fuuuuck. Ty," Zoey moans as I rock her against me. Quietly, we move together. She bites her lip and her eyes squinch shut when I get her there again. Her mouth opens in utter ecstasy, but she manages to be quiet when she gushes her release. When her pussy clenches around my cock, I blow. Try desperately not to yell with joy.

God, I love fucking my wife. I'm not sure when we're going to porn-star fuck again, but anytime I'm inside her, it's a goddamn miracle.

"Jesus, I've missed this." Zoey lies back against the pillows, panting.

I stroke her hair. "Well, I see no reason why we can't do that again later."

Her phone buzzes on the nightstand. "Shit, Ty. We need to get up and get ready. Caterers are arriving in an hour. Mom and Dad are going to be here in thirty."

"Let's go then." I set up the baby monitor and we quickly shower, or re-shower in Zoey's case.

We both manage to get dressed. Zoey in a button-down blouse with leggings. Me in a black Henley and blue jeans. Oliver is awake and cooing, fascinated with his tiny fingers, just as the doorbell rings. I head out to let her parents in while Zoey dresses our boy.

The entire kitchen is bustling when Zoey comes out with Oliver dressed in a tiny pair of jeans and a black t-shirt to match me. Olivia immediately sweeps her namesake into her arms.

The rest of the afternoon is a blur of decorators. Food preparation. Organized chaos. Zoey is a little tense, but

I'm feeling as Zen as Oliver right now. Now that I've shared all of my secrets, I'm free. Not cured. But healing, and that's pretty awesome.

A few minutes before all the preparations are complete, the doorbell rings. Sergey leads Carter and Lianne into the living room. She's stunning in a floaty pink dress. He's in a black suit. "It's not a dress-up occasion, Carter."

"Ah, well. That's okay." He winks at Lianne. She blushes. I notice they're holding hands.

When they spot Zoey and Oliver, I'm long forgotten. But, just in time as Connor and Ronni come in with their one-year-old twins. Connor sets up a playpen and puts the kids into it. "You'll thank me later, so you will." His smile lights up the room.

Ronni hugs me. "You look great, Ty. I'm so excited to help out with the foundation."

"Thank you, Ronni." Zoey embraces her. "We can't wait to include mental health awareness and implement technology education."

True to our plans, Zoey and I are using the money I inherited from the Rogers Family Trust to expand my foundation to include a special program for kids who suffer childhood trauma. Not only give them music and arts education, which literally saved my life. But also computer programming skills. And access to mental health resources. I really want to help people break their cycles, because I know I'm one of the lucky ones. Not everyone has a Zoey in their life. Or an Oliver to motivate them.

Or an LTZ to give them purpose.

"We're here, motherfuckers." Zane bops in with Fiona and Mia close behind him. Mia immediately runs to Carter, who's holding Ollie. She's obsessed with her cousin. It's still so weird for both Zane and I that we're actual half-brothers. I can't say we've worked it all out yet, but we're trying. We've even started writing songs again.

The caterers start passing out hors d'oeuvres and drinks. Even though I could technically have some wine, I still refrain. My meds are at a great level. I'm not going to fuck around. Doesn't mean my non-sober guests can't have a glass though.

Zoey pops into the bedroom to feed and change our son. When she's gone, Alex and Jace arrive with Helena, who clings to Alex's neck. "She's not feeling good, could I lay her down for a bit?" Alex asks.

"Of course, take her into our room, Zoey's back there with Ollie." I wave her back. When she closes the door behind her, I turn to Jace. "I miss you, man. I hope you and I can spend some time together, just us."

"Yeah. That would be good." He looks exhausted. Black circles under his eyes. His hair is really long, slightly unkempt. "I'm sorry we've been a little, well... I won't get into it tonight."

Carter clinks a spoon on his glass. "Before we sit down to dinner, I just have something I want to say—"

"Wait, Carter." I stop him. "Zoey and Alex are in the back with the kids."

"No, we're here." Zoey comes out leading Alex by one hand, the baby monitor in the other. Both of them sporting red-rimmed eyes. Zoey shoots me a look that tells me to bite my tongue. "Go ahead."

Carter looks down lovingly at Lianne, who sits on the ottoman next to where he's standing in front of the fireplace. "Exactly two years ago, Ty stood here and proposed to Zoey in front of all of us but you, my love."

"Best decision ever." I hug Zoey tightly to me when Alex disengages from her to sit on Jace's knee. "I can't tell you how much it means to me that you're all here with us this Christmas Eve. You're all my family, and I love you."

"Well don't steal my thunder, son." Carter puts his hand on his hip. "I've got a little proposal to get through."

Everyone in the room gasps. Joy permeates the air. Lianne looks shocked as hell.

"Lianne, you are the only woman I have ever loved. The only woman for me. You've been there for me throughout all of the hell I put you and Zane through. You've been my best friend and only lover for many years now. Life is short, babe. I've lived too long without you being officially my girl, will you marry me? Finally?" Carter sinks to one knee and holds out a gorgeous diamond ring.

Lianne looks utterly shell-shocked. As does Zane. And Fiona. I feel a bit bad that I was the son who helped Carter get ready for this proposal and not Zane, but Lianne isn't my mother. So, it wouldn't have been a surprise otherwise. Besides, all I want is for my loved ones to be, well, loved. Having love in your life is life changing, I'm living proof.

"Yes, Carter." Lianne bursts into tears. "You are the only man I've ever loved. I've cursed you for it, for sure. But it's the truth."

In a repeat of two years ago, everyone crowds around Carter and Lianne, hugging them and wishing them well. Checking out the ring.

And, just like two years ago, both Jace and Alex look miserable. Christmas Eve is not their holiday, apparently. "What's up with Alex?" I say to Zoey, who clutches my hand.

"Not here," she whispers in my ear. "I can't let what she told me ruin this beautiful moment."

I hug Zoey tightly to me. Decide to distract her with a kiss. "I love you, butterfly. I can't believe this is our life. My entire family is here, and I've never felt..."

I can't finish, I'm too choked up.

"I know." She gestures around. "We've gone through hell and back to get here, but it's all been worth it."

"And everyone will find their way, just like we did." I wrap my arms around her. I can't help but smile, because Zoey and I will be here for them, every step of the way.

"We've been trying to save her life, Jace. All I can tell you is they're still working on her now." ...Jace & Alex's Encore is next in Limitless Encore.

Want more Kaylene sign up for her mailing list.

Behind the Scenes

ENDLESS: ENCORE EDITION

Whew!

YOU MADE IT THROUGH Ty and Zoey's journey. I hope it broke your heart and pieced it back together again. At the end of every book I love to give you some insight into why I wrote it. This one is going to be a bit long, so bear with me.

Here goes:

When I first released ENDLESS, I felt such an incredible sense of accomplishment. My first full-length novel. *Wow.* The realization of a creative dream. When it was received so well by <u>you</u>—my awesome readers—my heart was full. With each new release LIMIT-

LESS, FEARLESS and TIMELESS – more and more of you were drawn into the world. And when you finished Zane and Fiona's story, many of you thought that the LTZ series was finished.

But I always had a plan. A bigger plan. A plan to delve deeper into these couples. Why? Whenever I finish a great romance book, I'm always sad. Obviously, the HEA is a given in the romance genre – but what really is an HEA? *An engagement? A wedding? A baby?*

Sure, all of these things are happy. Happy events. But is it really a HEA?

As anyone who has been in a long-term relationship knows, HEA means a lot of things. It's all of the love, and sexy times. It's the goofy fun times. The vacations. The get togethers with friends and family. The pets. The kids. The long drives. Day-to-day life even.

But when I look back at my own relationship? Knowing my husband and I are still deeply in love not only after all of the fun times – but after going through some excruciatingly tough times – death, illness, work/life balance, being business partners, family dynamics etc, etc?

I know the truth: Once you are committed, getting through tough times together is the true definition of an HEA.

Which brings me to Ty and Zoey in ENDLESS: EN-CORE.

A lot of readers viewed Zoey and Ty as a couple who were a little immature. This was by design. They were immature. Mainly because they fell in love so young and so intensely on a deep, guttural level. In many ways they were frozen in time and when they got back together, their "love" brains were stuck at 18 and 21.

So now they are engaged and having the time of their life together. But it doesn't mean that Ty's past has gone away. In the first book and throughout the first part of the series, I deliberately kept Ty's upbringing vague enough so that I could really explore what makes him tick. I dropped hints. His personality is consistent.

During my meticulous research on the topic of CPTSD, it made me think about so many of the kids I knew growing up. Some of the musicians I worked with. Heck, friends and family who I'm close with. We really do not know what people have been through in their lives and why they behave the way they do.

Zoey is drawn to Ty for his sweet and loving nature. Ty is drawn to Zoey because she's the first person who ever truly loved him. They are complete soulmates. It doesn't mean that Ty is able to come to terms with his diagnosis. Or his past. Or the fact that he will ALWAYS fear that the person who is supposed to be closest to him might hurt him. Or leave him.

Zoey knows something is wrong, but it takes her some time from seeking advice into becoming the strong partner to Ty that he needs—and deserves. She also learns how to set her own boundaries, and make sure she's putting the oxygen mask on herself as they hurtle through some very, very tough challenges.

In the end, it is super important to me to do my part in destigmatizing mental illness. The reality is we are surrounded by people who suffer from anxiety to PTSD to bipolar disorder and everything in between. They are our significant others, our parents, our friends, our siblings, our co-workers, or even ourselves.

In other words, I hope that you see Ty and Zoey as I do. A strong couple who are facing life together in *sickness and in health*. Who are committed to doing everything in their power to support each other and fight for their

HEA. In the end, they evolve into mature, considerate partners. A couple who have what it takes to keep their love alive forever. Through all of life's challenges.

They show us that true love is *endless*.

Don't worry, we still have three more **ENCORES**, and I promise Ty and Zoey will pop up in the other worlds I have planned for years to come so you can check in with them from time to time.

Thank you for reading,

Acknowledgments

THIS BOOK WAS AN absolute labor of love, and I couldn't have done it without the help and support of the following awesome rock stars:

Cover Artist/Graphic Designer/Finder of Hotties: Regina Wamba

Editor: Grace Bradley

Formatting: Willow Yanarella

PR: Dani Sanchez, Wildfire Marketing

Literary Agent: Stephanie Phillips, SBR Media

Website Maven: Sherri Kiarsis, Ruby Moon Designs

My Right Hand: Willow Yanarella

My VIPs/Readers/Alpha and Beta Readers Sheila, Kris, Laura, Amy, Tracy, Beth, Anna!

OMG! To the ARC readers, bloggers, bookstagrammers & my Street Team – I can't do this without you.

Thank you thank you thank you for helping spread the word—I'm overwhelmed by your love, support, kindness, etc. Thank you for making my dream come true!

Dedication

THIS IS DEDICATED TO everyone in my life who has suffered from or dealt with the stigma of mental illness. You are not alone. There is always hope.

Love,

About the Author

KAYLENE WINTER IS AN best-selling author of steamy, contemporary romance.

Each character-driven novel is filled with snappy dialogue, pop-culture references and enough steam to make you fan yourself. Kaylene weaves authenticity, emotion and angst into a turbulent rollercoaster ride of love, passion and soul-searing romance always ending with a delicious HEA.

Kaylene lives in Seattle with her amazing Irish husband and gorgeous Siberian Husky. She loves creating art of all kinds.

Other Titles